WHEN YOU READ THIS I'LL BE GONE

Also by Anne Moose:

Arkansas Summer
House of Fragile Dreams

WHEN YOU READ THIS I'LL BE GONE

ANNE MOOSE

MISSION VIEJO, CA

For Katy, Beth, and Sue. And for all the Londons.

♥

CHAPTER ONE

Dear Misha and Sam,

I know there's nothing I can ever say or do to make up for the hurt I've caused you, but this book will at least explain what happened and why I did what I did. I don't expect forgiveness, but I do want you to know the truth.

It's ironic that, with this book, I may finally achieve the success as an author I've always wanted. There was actually a bidding war for this one, believe it or not. My agent assures me it's bound to do extremely well, and we've already sold the movie rights. I've made arrangements for both of you to receive equal shares of almost all the money it makes, including a sizable advance. My lawyer will explain everything to you in detail. Of course, no sum of money or book can ever restore what you've lost, but I hope that after you read this, you'll understand why I had to write it. As far as your father is concerned, I've tried to be as kind to him as possible. It's not my intention to cast embarrassment, or shame, or blame on anyone. I simply want to tell the truth. But I'm sorry if parts of it hurt him, and you. If I could go back in time and change history, I'd do it, but there's no going back. All I can do is pray that, in time, you'll forgive me.

All my love,
Mom

ଔ

It's funny, looking back on all that happened, to realize how much hinged on tiny details. If I hadn't hit a slowdown outside of Ogden. If, upon arriving at the hotel, my cabin had been ready. If I hadn't gone out onto the porch after arriving in my room. If just the smallest thing had changed on one single day, things might have played out differently with the man who tipped all the dominoes. Of course, there's no denying that I tipped them, too. But it's painful to contemplate how easily fate might have turned if only things hadn't lined up exactly as they did.

On the day everything started, I'd driven from my first stop in Salt Lake City to a hotel in the Gallatin Valley, near Bozeman, where I was slated to sit on an author's panel at a writer's conference the next day. I'd chosen not to fly because I love a long drive through beautiful scenery. My husband hates spending long days in a car, so since he wasn't with me, I decided to take advantage of the opportunity to drive and do things *I* like to do, like pull over to take pictures, or listen to a book or music of *my* choosing. I'd heard good things about the Gallatin Valley, so I booked myself into a hotel "resort" with charming little cabins overlooking the Gallatin River.

The hotel turned out to be everything I'd hoped it would be. The lobby, the restaurant overlooking the river, the large bar and sitting area, one whole side of which was floor-to-ceiling windows—it was all picture perfect, lushly furnished with leather furniture, wildlife-themed artwork, and the kind of rich, rustic decor that you find in all the most upscale mountain lodges.

When I checked in, my cabin was still being cleaned, so I waited in a comfortable leather chair by a window with a view of the river and a wide green lawn, enjoying a complementary glass of wine. It was then that I first noticed the man who would become central in this story.

Handsome and tall, with the kind of self-confidant bearing that makes you take notice, his presence was hard to ignore. He had just checked in and stepped over for a few moments to gaze at the river. As he was departing, he looked at me and smiled. I smiled back and raised my glass to the view in what felt like a mutual acknowledgment of the glorious scene outside the window. Maybe that was the detail that sealed my doom, but I'll never know for sure.

ↀ

When I finally arrived at my cabin, I was thrilled to find a room as beautifully appointed as the lodge. There was a big four-poster log bed, a comfortable sitting area with a leather sofa and matching chair, a working stone fireplace, and a porch right out over the lawn, where three Adirondack chairs by the side of the river beckoned—although the wind was up and it was starting to get chilly.

I unpacked my suitcase, and it occurred to me that I might need a reservation for dinner. Hoping I hadn't waited too long, I called the front desk and managed to get a reservation for seven-thirty.

With almost two hours to wait, I took a bath, changed my clothes, then put on a sweater and jeans and went out onto the porch to watch the river and think about the Bozeman conference. But it was hard to concentrate on anything but the rush of the river, the freshness of the air, and the sparkles on the water reflecting the sun, which hadn't yet started its descent. I pulled my knees up to my chest and, with a deep feeling of warmth that was partly the result of the cabernet I'd consumed earlier, I felt better than I had in months.

Around seven, the man I'd seen in the lobby made his second appearance. This time, he crossed the lawn to the left of my cabin and made his way down to one of the Adirondacks. He settled into one, then didn't move for several minutes, seemingly transfixed by the tumbling water.

For some reason, I couldn't take my eyes off him. I don't know how to explain it. I'm not inclined to have a wandering eye, nor was I thinking about him in any particular way. But I was definitely watching him as he sat there by the river, not moving a muscle.

Soon, almost as if he could feel my eyes on him, he turned around and looked straight at me. An instant later, he stood up, raised a friendly hand, and headed my way.

"Can you believe this place?" he asked when he was almost at my doorstep.

I noticed, when he smiled, that he had perfect white teeth. He also had wavy salt and pepper hair that reminded me of Paul Newman. Truthfully, he was nearly as handsome as Paul Newman. But, in any case, here he was at the threshold of my porch, as affable and appealing as a golden retriever. He had changed into a flannel shirt and cargo pants and now looked like the kind of sporty guy who'd probably come to Montana for the fly-fishing or whitewater rafting. If there were such a thing as an Outdoor GQ, he'd have been a good candidate for the cover.

"Where've you come from?" he asked genially. "I'm here from Seattle."

"California," I said.

"This your first time in Montana?"

"No, I've been here before, although not to this specific area. I've been to Yellowstone and Glacier."

"What brings you here this time?"

"I'm attending a conference in Bozeman tomorrow."

I looked out over the lawn to the river, then to the mountains rising immediately behind. "It's so beautiful here. I'm glad I decided not to stay in town."

"It's beautiful, all right," he said. "I'm here for three days. How about you?"

"Just two."

"I'm Tom, by the way," he said, stepping up onto the porch and extending his hand.

I took his hand and squeezed it. "Valerie. Nice to meet you."

"Are you here alone?" he asked, raising his chin to my cabin, "or is there a Mr. Valerie hiding in there somewhere?"

"There is a Mr. Valerie, but he's not here with me."

He smiled. "Do you think he'd mind too much if I asked you what you were doing for dinner? I have a seven-thirty reservation, and I'd love to have some company if you're interested. I promise my intentions are strictly honorable."

"I have a reservation at the same time, and I'd be happy to join you," I said. "Thanks."

He looked at his watch. "Tell you what. I'm going to run back to my cabin and take care of a couple of things.

I'll meet you at the restaurant at seven-thirty. Sound good?"

"Sounds great," I said.

With a light wind picking up, he strode off, and I stepped inside to get ready, not giving his invitation a second thought beyond being pleased I wouldn't have to eat alone.

CHAPTER TWO

DINNER WAS DELIGHTFUL, ALTHOUGH the restaurant was the type that delivers works of art consisting of ninety percent swirly patterns on a plate and ten percent actual edible food. I ordered lamb, and the meat that arrived in a tiny chop was not much larger than a postage stamp. For forty-six dollars, I'd hoped for at least a dollop of potatoes or rice and maybe a Brussels sprout or two. But no, the meat stood lonely atop flat curlicues of some type of pulverized vegetable.

Eyeing the plate, I joked that I should have ordered the twenty-two-dollar garden salad. Tom's steak was somewhat heartier, but not by much. Fortunately, when I inquired about bread, the waiter brought us a small loaf of sourdough, which we gratefully buttered and consumed.

Notwithstanding the scarcity of food, we had a pleasant meal, making up for our meager entrees by drinking most of a bottle of wine.

"Tell me about this conference you're attending?" Tom asked early on.

"It's a writer's conference," I said. "Nothing major. Just a small event associated with Montana State. I'm going to be part of a panel discussion."

"So, you're a writer," he said, sounding intrigued.

"Don't be too impressed," I said. "Not a very successful one."

"You're being modest," he said, smiling.

"Not really," I said.

I waited a couple of beats, thinking he might inquire about my writing. When he didn't, I said, "So, what about you? What kind of work do you do?"

"I'm a building consultant," he said. "And geologist. I do ground surveys and geological reports for large construction projects. I live in Seattle, but I travel all over the world for my work."

He paused and seemed to study my face. "I was just in Alaska, and in a couple of weeks, I'll be in Peru. It's one of the great parts of my job."

"What an interesting life you must have with all that travel," I said.

"I like it," he said. "Although for everything I've gained on the adventure side, I've lost something on the family side, I'm afraid. But I'm not really complaining. I love my work."

I glanced at his naked ring finger. "You've never been married?"

"Once," he said, his expression turning solemn.

He looked down at his plate as if thinking, or maybe remembering, then raised his eyes and went on. "It's not every woman who can deal with all my traveling. I suppose I'm selfish."

He stopped for a moment and cut his meat. "I *do* have lady friends. Some accuse me of having a woman in every port, but it's not true."

"Do you have any kids?"

He placed his fork on the table, took a drink of wine, then reached into his back pocket and pulled out his wallet. A moment later, he handed me a laminated photo. "That was my daughter's high school graduation picture."

"She's pretty," I said. And she was.

I studied the photo for a moment, then handed it back. "So you just have the one?"

He nodded, then slid the picture into his wallet before putting it back in his pocket.

"What about you?" he said. "I gather you're married. How's that going?"

I reflexively scoffed at the question. I didn't mean to, but while packing for my trip, I'd found part of a condom wrapper in my husband's luggage, so he wasn't high on my list at the moment.

"I shouldn't have reacted that way," I said, noticing Tom's interest seemed piqued. "I've just never been asked about my marriage quite like that before."

He remained silent, his expression seeming to say, *Keep going; I'm interested.*

When I didn't, he said, "I'm sorry, it's none of my business."

"It's fine," I said. "And my marriage is fine. Really."

"Like I said, it's none of my business."

"No marriage is perfect," I added after a moment.

He raised his eyebrows.

"You know what I mean."

Tom's face relaxed into a smirk. "I'm sorry. I shouldn't be giving you a hard time. I just find marriage really interesting. I'm not sure I know any couples who are genuinely happily married. And I know a lot of people."

"Seriously?"

"Do you know many?"

I gave the question some thought. "I can think of some happy marriages. My parents had a good marriage, and I know some reasonably happy couples."

"Really? Because most of the people I know are either divorced or staying together for the kids. Or money."

"I don't know," I said. "I hear you about the kids thing. I'm not sure I'd still be married if I didn't have any. I have two. A boy and a girl. They're both in their twenties now."

Tom looked surprised. "You don't look old enough to have kids in their twenties, and I'm not handing you a line."

"Well, they're *just* in their twenties," I said, blushing. "And I started young. Too young. But, anyway, I've always figured it was a good thing—kids keeping you together."

"I suppose," he said. "And I'm sorry if I've raised too personal a subject. I'm just always curious about other people's lives. Maybe because mine's so unusual."

I smiled. "You're okay. And I know what you mean about marriage. It's definitely hard, but no marriage will ever be perfect. You just have to keep working at it."

I was saying this despite the fact that I'd been thinking about divorcing, if not killing, my husband Steven for about the last thirty-six hours.

I picked up my wine glass. "Tell me about Alaska and Peru. Your life sounds fascinating."

I looked at him expectantly, hoping he'd go for the change of subject.

Fortunately, he did.

By the time dessert arrived, I was pretty well captivated, especially by stories he told me of a small village in Ghana where, after completing a contract, he'd spent more than a month helping with a water project that provided clean drinking water to over three hundred people.

At one point, he took out his phone and pulled up photographs he'd taken of the children in the village. That was a turning point. That's when I started to see the man sitting across from me with very different eyes. The look on his face as he described how the children would follow him around the village, the glowing smiles of those children—it all made a big impression on me.

Later, we talked about loving Italy, and that led to a discussion about art, and then literature. He topped it all off with a somewhat terrifying lecture on the perils posed by Mount Rainier, which, to my surprise, is an active volcano.

By the time the bill arrived and he'd won a brief tussle over the check, I was thoroughly enamored, but I had no weird or inappropriate thoughts about him. Nor did he push for anything after he walked me back to my cabin and said goodnight. I never even considered that things would go further. I was simply pleased to have spent a lovely evening with a fascinating man who, in the course of a dinner, made me feel better about myself than I had in years.

CHAPTER THREE

THE NEXT MORNING, I woke up early and took advantage of the breakfast buffet at the lodge. Outside the window next to my table, green grass glistened, and the mountains behind the river were shrouded in wispy vapor. A light rain the night before had snow-dusted the peaks, which were intermittently visible as clouds progressed across the dreamy landscape.

As I sipped black coffee and indulged in scandalous portions of bacon, scrambled eggs, and sourdough bread, my mind was primarily on Bozeman. My only real thoughts of Tom were to be happy for his absence, preferring solitude as I mentally prepared for the conference and soaked up the natural tableau.

I was signing my bill before returning to my cabin when a white-tailed deer and spotted fawn appeared suddenly on the lawn, stopping to graze down close to the river. As I sat watching, Tom came up behind me and placed his hand on my shoulder.

Startled, I let out a gasp.

"I'm sorry. I didn't mean to scare you," he said.

"No problem," I laughed. "I just didn't see you come in."

He raised his eyes to the scene outside. "That's quite a view out there this morning. I guess you've probably gotten some glimpses of the snow up there in the clouds. And it looks like you have company." He nodded out the window at the deer.

"Aren't they beautiful? They just showed up a minute ago." I pushed my chair out and stood up. "I wish I could ask you to join me, but I have to go get ready to drive to my conference. You can have my table, though. It's the best seat in the house."

"Indeed it is," he said, pulling out the chair to my left.

He smiled and sat down, placing his mug of coffee on the table. "Drive carefully, and good luck on your panel."

"Thanks," I said, then I hurried back to my cabin, pleased with my timing and wondering how he planned to spend the day.

ʃ

The conference in Bozeman was in a large tree-shrouded brick building in a pretty section of the MSU campus. I easily found the room where my discussion was scheduled, and I arrived in plenty of time to introduce myself to the three other members of the panel. The room was actually a small auditorium, and I was happy with the way it was filling up.

I hadn't known what to expect, but by the looks of things, it was shaping up to be well attended. I was suddenly glad and not embarrassed that I'd brought almost half a box of my latest novel, which I'd dropped off at the "book sale" room when I first arrived.

At one o'clock sharp, the moderator began the discussion, starting with a brief bio of each member of the panel. By comparison, my credentials were meager, but I smiled and attempted to exude confidence. With years of successful teaching experience, I told myself that what I lacked in a prestigious position and awards, I'd make up for at the microphone.

My faith in myself was borne out. I did fine. And I realized each time I spoke how much I missed teaching and deep-down regretted taking a sabbatical (strictly speaking, a leave of absence). Had I any hope of receiving tenure, I'd never have done it, but as a mere lecturer, with few of the benefits that accrued to full or even assistant professors—and almost no time for my own writing—I'd decided to temporarily jump off the train, with assurances from the university that they were fine with it.

I was in the middle of speaking about the importance of authentic dialog in historical writing when I noticed Tom sitting in the back row of the auditorium. For a moment, I faltered, but I quickly regained my bearing and managed to finish my point without any trouble. But, going forward, I was self-conscious, not understanding how he'd managed to find me or why he'd come.

By midway through the session, I was firmly back on track and mainly felt flattered by his presence. I met eyes with him once, and we shared a nod, but before the discussion ended, he stood up and left. I had expected him to hang around for the meet and greet that followed, but he didn't. He listened for thirty or forty minutes, then vanished.

ᘓ

I spent the rest of the day attending other sessions at the conference and signing books at a table I shared with the other writers on my panel. Later, three of us went out for dinner, which was both pleasant and inspiring. At eight-thirty, when I finally arrived back at the hotel, I was surprised to find Tom sitting on my porch bundled up in a heavy coat, holding a glass of wine. The bottle and another glass sat on the table next to him.

"I hope you don't mind," he said when I opened the sliding glass door upon seeing him. "The view is much nicer on this side of the property. My cabin's on the other side of the lodge, and you can't see the river from my porch."

He picked up the bottle and nodded at the empty glass. "I figure I owe you an apology for showing up like that. You probably think I'm a stalker."

"It did seem a little weird," I said. "How did you even find me?"

"I had to drive to Bozeman to pick up a couple of things at a sporting goods store, and when I saw that I was near the university, I googled your conference on a whim and realized I was only a block away."

He shrugged his shoulders. "I figured, what the hell. I had an hour to kill before meeting up with a fly-fishing guide, and since I was right there. But I'm sorry if I made you uncomfortable."

"I had you pegged as a fly fisherman," I said, happily accepting his explanation and apology. "But it's a little too *fresh* out there for me. I'll have a glass of wine, but come inside out of the cold. Maybe you can even help me get this fireplace going."

Tom took charge of lighting the fire. As it began to warm the cabin and we got settled with our wine—me on the couch and Tom in a chair—it did dawn on me that I'd been hasty asking him inside. In fact, I said something, just to break the ice and make it clear that my intentions were not in too cozy a direction.

"Please don't misinterpret my inviting you in," I said. "I'm just not crazy about the freezing cold."

He smiled. "Don't worry. I know you're a nice married lady. I hope you won't misinterpret my showing up on your doorstep."

He nodded out the window at the river. "I guess, besides wanting to apologize for today, it's a little hard being alone in this kind of setting. I have a natural tendency to want to share a place like this with someone. But if having me here makes you uncomfortable, I can leave. This *is* an awfully romantic setting." He raised his eyebrows comically.

I raised mine back. "No kidding. But I'm good now that we've talked about it. Just don't tell my husband."

I laughed nervously, and the crackling fire and flickering light suddenly seemed so romantic it was ludicrous.

"What's funny?" Tom asked.

"Nothing. It's just the situation."

Embarrassed, I blushed and changed the subject. "So tell me about the fishing."

"It was loads of fun," he said. "Although, sadly, the trout were elusive."

He poured more wine into his glass, then topped mine off as well. "I've done plenty of fishing. Mostly deep-sea fishing. This is the first time I've donned waders and fished with a fly reel. It's harder than it looks."

He grinned. "As they say, all I caught was a cold. But I'm determined to catch a fish, so I'm going out again tomorrow. I may regret it, but I signed up for early morning when I'm assured the trout are hungriest."

Soon the conversation turned to my writing, my books, and teaching. Hearing me speak had sparked his interest, it seemed, and he asked me a lot of questions. It's not often I talk about myself, and I'll admit, I enjoyed the attention. He seemed genuinely interested in what I had to say, and it was the first time in years I'd had such an intimate exchange with a man whom I found attractive. And I was finding him extremely attractive.

Before I knew it, I was having thoughts that were *not* the thoughts of a nice married lady. They were lusty and graphic, and I actually started to feel scared by the sheer power of the physical reaction I was having. Parts of me that hadn't been awakened in years were suddenly coming alive. When I'd invited Tom to come in from the cold, I'd had no expectation of reacting to the situation this way. In truth, I had probably never reacted to a situation this powerfully. It was terrifying, but also thrilling.

"So how do you like being a big-shot university professor?" Tom asked at one point.

"Unfortunately, I'm a lecturer, not a professor," I said, trying to tamp down my extra-curricular thoughts. "But I do love teaching and being in academics. Grading papers is brutal, though."

I made a face. "You wouldn't believe how much time and energy it takes to mark up English papers. Finally, last term, when I couldn't take it anymore, I put in for a year's leave of absence to work on a new novel."

Our eyes were locked in the firelight, and I smiled. "To be honest, the book's stalled out, and I miss the teaching, but I don't miss the rest of it. Not at all."

Tom was staring at me with a strange look on his face, and I wondered if he was also feeling the wine and setting and anything *resembling* the arousal I was now feeling full on, and, if so, what I should do about it. My rational brain told me it was time to stand up and shoo him out the door. Another part of me was calculating a host of "What ifs," the most prominent being, *What if, just this once, I do something crazy and reckless? No one would ever know, so what would be the harm?*

I was also thinking about the condom wrapper in Steven's luggage.

Tom continued to look at me, and I continued to calculate, and soon a long silence hung between us, seemingly dripping with meaning.

"You're looking at me funny," I said finally, doing a little fishing myself.

Before he answered, I decided I'd go with whatever came back. If he indicated he was thinking like I was, I'd be in. If not, I'd shepherd him out the door and undoubtedly be happy in the morning that I did.

I held my breath, and my pulse quickened.

"What if I told you I was having a fantasy about you right now," he said. "Would that upset you?"

At first, I didn't speak. I was frozen in fear, but my body was reacting in the extreme. I knew it was wrong—that I'd probably regret it—but I finally answered.

"I know I shouldn't," I said, "and I can't believe I'm saying this, but if we can agree it'll be a one-time thing, I'm willing to go with the fantasy."

"Agreed," he said. Then he placed his wine glass on the coffee table and moved over to the couch, never taking his eyes off me for a moment.

What came next was a delicious blur of deep, hungry kisses, flickering body parts, sweat, passion, and a level of pleasure and adventure beyond anything I'd experienced in years. It feels wrong to describe it this way, but I'm trying to be as honest as I can without being crude or graphic. To put it simply, the reality that unfolded in that fire-lit cabin was beyond any fantasy I was capable of conjuring. If I'd had any doubts that Tom had been around the world, they died on the high-thread-count sheets of that king-sized log bed.

When I finally slept, it was like the sleep of the dead. I don't remember cracking an eye until it was almost ten-thirty the next morning—which, I realized with alarm, was almost check-out time. Tom was nowhere to be found.

CHAPTER FOUR

LOOKING AT THE CLOCK, I was too worried about the time to contemplate the various implications of what I'd done. I had a splitting headache and needed a shower, so I put everything else out of my mind and headed for the bathroom, desperately needing a cup of coffee and hoping I wouldn't be charged extra for checking out late.

Soon I was standing under a stream of hot water, my panic over the time giving way to panic about the night before. Memories began to flood my consciousness, causing a mixture of regret, arousal, and, frankly, shock. I had never imagined I was the kind of person who'd even be tempted to do the kinds of things I'd jumped into so easily, and yet here I was, showering off the residue of lovemaking with a virtual stranger.

Although I knew I needed to get myself packed up and out, I let myself linger in the shower, reliving scenes that seemed to have happened to someone else—including one that had occurred in the exact spot I was standing. In the light of day, and even with my pounding head reminding me I'd had too much to drink, I couldn't reconcile the person I'd thought I was with the woman I'd been with Tom. I considered the condom wrapper in Steven's luggage and suspicions I'd had about him for years, and I wondered if I'd done this as payback or if, deep down, I was no different than he was. It also occurred to me in a self-serving moment that maybe I was simply human. (Could I chalk up my transgression as a not-that-surprising moment of weakness and shrug it off that easily?)

Feeling sore in multiple places, I shook my head under the hard spray of water and looked down at my body, wondering if I had any visible marks. Seeing nothing, I put my face in my hands.

There was no denying it. Given the chance for what seemed like a safe adventure on the wild side, I'd taken it, and now, like it or not, I was left with what felt like a whole new picture of myself to reckon with. I wasn't sure how it might impact me long term, but I didn't have time at the moment to think about it, so I turned off the water, dried myself, dressed quickly, then packed my bag and loaded up my car. By the time I arrived at the lodge to check out—my hair barely combed and apologizing for being late—it was eleven-thirty. I managed to get a coffee, but I missed out on the breakfast buffet.

ℛ

Now in the car with a long day of driving ahead of me, I had nothing but time to consider what I'd done and who I'd done it with. Despite my not-inconsiderable feelings of guilt and remorse, I did find myself thinking about Tom with lusty admiration. If I were going to transgress, at least I'd done it with someone interesting and intelligent. Under other circumstances, I could see falling for him full bore. But these were not other circumstances, and despite my issues with Steven, my commitment to my marriage and feelings of regret strongly eclipsed everything else. In short, as lust and glossy recollections of Tom faded in the rearview, my eyes became more and more focused on the road in front of me.

As I left Idaho and entered Utah, I was laser-focused on arriving home and working things out, if for no other reason than for my kids, who, despite being in their twenties, would be crushed by a divorce. Steven was far from a perfect husband, but I had no appetite for all the problems associated with a breakup—the issues around holidays, money, the house... No, I was intent on keeping my family intact, and I had *no* desire or expectation of anything ongoing with Tom. We had done almost no talking once things became physical, but the one thing we had talked about and agreed upon was this: Our "affair" would be a one-time thing. We would make and share a memory of a time and place that was perfect, but only for a night.

I was having this exact thought when my phone buzzed to indicate an incoming text. Feeling more and more anxious about my marriage, I wanted to see if it was Steven, so at the next exit, I turned off, stopped at the stop sign, then fiddled with my phone to read the text.

It was a good thing I'd stopped because what I found might have caused me to run off the road. Tom, it seemed, was ignoring our agreement that neither of us would contact the other. In Middle-of-Nowhere, Utah, I was suddenly staring at a photo of myself fast asleep—totally naked—on the high-thread-count sheets of that king-sized log bed.

With my head spinning and heart racing out of control, I proceeded through the stop sign, then took a right and pulled over onto a dirt shoulder. Not believing what I was seeing, I felt like I'd been plunged into a completely differ-ent reality, and I had *no* idea what to do.

I tried to calm down and think, but no amount of deep breathing would slow my racing heart or quell the fear that suddenly gripped me. I knew in my bones, and in my sick, roiling stomach, that this could be serious.

℅

It was a good while before I could think straight. I'd al-ways had a nervous constitution, jumping and startling at the smallest things. Now, my hair-trigger nervous system made me wonder how I'd ever be able to return home and behave normally.

I looked at my phone. How had Tom gotten my number? I hadn't given it to him. With my heart speeding up again, I realized he must have gone through my phone while I was sleeping, which meant he might have all kinds of information about me. The scenarios I began conjuring were terrifying, starting with the possibility he might have Steven's phone number. *How many times had I told myself to password-protect my phone?* I wondered bitterly.

"Calm down," I commanded myself out loud. My au-thor's imagination was running wild.

I tried to think optimistically. *Maybe it wasn't as bad as it seemed. Maybe he was just trying to be playful.*

I considered texting him back, nicely insisting he stick to our agreement and delete the text and photo. I had my doubts about the wisdom of engaging with him, but I final-ly collected myself and wrote this message: "Not funny. Please delete, and good luck with the trout. I'm heading home and will delete on my side, too. Please, no more contact. Thanks!"

After I sent it, I deleted the text thread, then stared at my phone for several minutes, barely breathing. To my relief, my phone stayed silent. Maybe I would get lucky and it would end there.

I was just psyching myself up to get moving again when my phone rang, sending my adrenaline back through the roof. It was Steven. He had to know I was driving and might not answer, so I let it ring, wondering if he'd leave a message. He did, and after I listened to it, I cried like a baby.

This was his message: *"Hi, Valerie. I know you're pissed and probably don't want to talk to me, but I want you to know how sorry I am about everything. You know how I can get when we fight. But I swear you're wrong about what you found. I think I have an explanation, but I'll save it for when you get home. Drive safe, and I hope your conference went well. I love you. Please call me when you get a chance."*

Ϩ

By the time I finally got back on the highway, it was almost three o'clock. I hadn't received any more texts from Tom, and Steven had not called back either. I thought about calling Steven myself, but I was spending the night in Salt Lake and wanted to get there before dark, so I figured it was best to focus on driving. I desperately wanted to hear Steven's voice and tell him that I wasn't mad anymore, but I knew it would be better to wait. It sounds terrible, but I figured the longer I made him wait, the more anxious he'd be to patch things up, and I needed him to want to patch things up.

Two hours passed, and I still had nothing more from Tom, which gave me hope that maybe he wasn't crazy after all. I'd been forcing myself not to think about him, but now that I was starting to relax, I began sifting through all the moments we'd spent together—both the G-rated and X-rated—and I could think of no serious red flags. It's true it was strange when he showed up at the conference, but apart from that, he'd seemed not only completely normal but exceptional in almost every way.

Slowly, I began to convince myself that the text was an anomaly. As I passed a sign indicating I was sixty-five miles from Salt Lake, I managed an actual smile, and my body began to loosen up. I even started to appreciate the blue sky and magnificent clouds, which, under normal circumstances, would have been the main focus of my attention. I still experienced a wave of nausea each time my mind lit on the photo, but I was starting to believe I'd be fine. And I *promised* myself that if somehow, some way, catastrophe really were averted, I would never *ever* do anything crazy or stupid again—for as long as I lived, so help me God.

CHAPTER FIVE

I HAD JUST CHECKED into my Salt Lake hotel and was thinking about going to the restaurant for dinner when I got my second text from Tom. Thankfully, this one had no photo, but it still scared me to death. He sent just three words: *Thinking of you.*

I considered calling and begging him to stop, but I was afraid to. I understood now that he could be unstable, so I figured engaging with him might make things worse. I vowed to change my phone number as soon as I got home. In the meantime, I'd delete the text and pray he'd eventually leave me alone.

Moments after deleting the text, I grabbed a book from my suitcase and went downstairs for dinner, trying as hard as I could to put him out of my mind. To say the least, it was a tall order. I tried to read but found myself reading the same paragraph over and over, unable to absorb even the simplest sentence. I finally gave up and focused on my phone.

Because of my rush to get checked out of the hotel, I hadn't opened my email all day, nor had I looked at my pictures from the conference. *The conference.* It seemed like another lifetime ago.

I decided to open my pictures first, and what I discovered made my stomach heave.

Tom had taken pictures of me with MY PHONE. And by the looks of it, he'd taken quite a few.

Before finding the nerve to swipe through them, I had a thought that stopped me cold. *My email.*

I'd seen my texts, and they'd seemed fine, apart from the messages I'd received from Tom. But when he was messing with my phone, he'd also had access to my email. Trying not to panic, I opened my Gmail.

My worst fears were confirmed in an instant.

To my horror, my Inbox was filled with responses to messages sent from my phone, each with the same Subject line. Stacked one on top of another, they looked like this:

Re: What do you think?

Re: What do you think?

Re: What do you think?

Re: What do you think?

I opened one up, then—feeling an urgent wave of nausea—threw my phone in my purse, pushed away from the table, and sprinted across the restaurant for the bathroom. Thankfully, the door to the single-person ladies' room was not locked. Barely making it to the toilet, I dropped my purse on the floor, leaned over the bowl, and violently expelled the contents of my stomach.

Afterwards, in a state of terror and disbelief, I rinsed my mouth and stared at my face in the mirror. Inhaling deeply, I battled hysteria. I needed to control myself so I could think, but it was impossible to stifle my fear. I trembled and gulped air.

Three sharp knocks on the bathroom door made me jump. "Just a minute," I called.

I doused my face with cold water, trying to quell my panic, but when I raised my eyes to the mirror, all I could see was the beginning of the end of my life. I could feel it in my bones. Life, as I had known it, was over. All for a single fire-lit romp in an overpriced hotel.

೦೩

Back upstairs, I knew I needed to review both my email and my photos, but I sat terrified on the side of the bed. When I finally mustered the courage to look, I pulled back the spread, then propped two pillows against the headboard and switched on the lamp. The phone rang, sending my already hammering heart into overdrive.

Steven.

Too stricken to answer, I let it ring, hoping he'd leave me a voicemail so I could find out if he knew anything. In the meantime, I'd pull up my email and see if his name was among the replies. I hadn't seen it earlier, but new messages were probably flooding in.

Thankfully, I found nothing there from him. I also noted with a tsunami of relief that my children were absent from the list, which turned out to include members of my writers' group, my agent, and my best friend, Carol. Of course, this didn't mean they hadn't received an email, only that they hadn't replied.

I needed to check my Sent messages, but my adrenaline skyrocketed at the mere thought. I squeezed my eyes closed and tried to suppress a rising panic. Deciding to put it off, I opened the reply from Sonia, my agent. Her message was short: "Valerie! Are you OK? What the hell is this???"

Horrified, I now looked more closely at what Tom had sent. There was no text, just a single picture like the one I'd gotten, but with part of a hairy leg in the foreground like some deranged parody of *The Graduate*. I might have been grateful it was only his leg, but I quickly realized this was only the first email. With things getting worse by the second, anything seemed possible.

My phone rang again. Seeing Carol's name, I immediately picked up.

"Valerie!" she cried. "What the hell is going on? What was that email?"

"*Carol*," I gushed, "you just wouldn't believe what's happening. I did something really stupid, and now I have no idea what to do. Steven just called, and I can't even think straight."

I went on to explain everything as quickly as I could, then told her I needed to hang up to see if Steven had left a message.

"Have you thought about calling the police?" Carol asked before we hung up. "This guy seems like he could be dangerous."

"I haven't had time to think about anything," I said. "This is all just hitting me now..."

I gulped air, struggling to hold myself together. "I know I did something terrible. But I swear to God, he didn't seem crazy at all. He was intelligent and charming as hell."

I visualized him talking about children in Ghana—going on about the geology of Mount Rainier. "None of this computes. It's like something out of a horror movie."

"Go ahead and listen to Steven's message," Carol told me. "But what should I say if I hear anything from anyone? Do you even know who all has seen the picture?"

I closed my eyes and shook my head in despair, knowing I needed to check my Sent messages, but dreading what I would find. "I don't know yet," I said.

I choked back tears and found it almost impossible to think clearly with so much fear and uncertainty buzzing inside of me. Then I had an idea. "What if we tell people my email's been hacked and the picture is a fake? Do you think anyone will believe it?"

I knew it was a stretch, but it was all I could think of, and I couldn't imagine anyone believing *I'd* send a picture like that.

"It's worth a try," she said. "If that's what you want, I'll go with that. But are you going to be okay? I'm worried about you."

"I'm all right," I assured her, although I was a million miles from all right.

After we hung up, I checked my voicemail. Steven *had* left a message. This one was similar to the last, with no hint he was aware of anything besides the fight we'd had before I left. In his mind, he was still the one in the dog house.

I wanted to call him, but I had no idea what to say, and I doubted I was capable of sounding natural. I knew the only sensible thing to do, under the circumstances, was to come clean and pray he'd forgive me. Considering what I was sure he'd been up to, it seemed only fair. But I had a hard time picturing things going that way. We'd been together for more than two decades, and I knew the more likely scenario was that he'd become enraged and stop listening the instant I told him what I'd done. I loved him—at least, some of the time—but listening was not his strong suit, nor was he known for his even temper.

Much as I hated to admit it, I'd married an arrogant, self-centered man who was the diametric opposite of my father. But now, after what I'd done, what was I? I shook my head and couldn't believe I'd ruined my life so blithely.

When I finally found the courage to look at my Sent messages, my nerves went into a tailspin. I didn't count how many emails Tom had sent, nor did I open any of them. But the list went on and on, continuing well past what I could see without scrolling, and each had a photo attachment.

Knowing I needed to scroll, I braced myself and slowly moved down the list, praying that, by some miracle, Steven and my kids wouldn't be there. Eventually, close to the bottom, there they were, among the first that went out. Not able to bring myself to open the messages, I closed my email and curled into the fetal position.

I remained in a near catatonic state for probably close to an hour. The phone finally brought me back. Seeing it was Steven again, I abruptly picked it up. I was so out of it by then, I didn't think about the consequences or have any idea what I might say. I knew only that there was no avoiding a worst-case scenario, so I answered with a leaden "Hi, Steven," knowing full well that, in seconds, fury might strike me with a thunderous roar.

My worst fears were realized, and I experienced the onslaught with a strange sense of unreality. As I listened to Steven's disembodied rage, it felt like it was happening in some other universe that had no connection to me—*me*, the perfect student; *me*, the straight-laced, ultra-conscientious academic; *me*, the play-it-safe perfectionist who never colored outside the lines. And yet it *was* happening to me. I was sitting in a hotel room, and everything I'd worked hard for my entire life was disintegrating into a violent torrent of shit issuing like a hurricane from my phone.

"How could you have done this to me and the kids?" Steven was shouting.

"You disgust me!" he was shouting.

"I thought I could fucking trust you!" he was shouting.

"You've destroyed our family!" he was shouting.

"I've been getting phone calls!" he was shouting.

"I feel sick!" he was shouting.

I tried a couple of times to break into his tirade. With an apology. With an expression of deepest, sincerest remorse. With an explanation. But he wouldn't let me speak. Like virtually every argument we'd ever had, he was a steamroller barreling down a one-way street, incapable of hearing any side but his own.

Hurling hatred and hellfire, Steven's outrage was all-consuming. Our marriage was over, and the blame was all mine. There would be no acknowledgment of condom wrappers, or late meetings, or instances of infidelity that

I'd turned a blind eye to for years. Nor would his chronic overspending, excessive drinking, or selfishness be of any relevance. No. All of it was violently swept off the table by a one-night affair. And what could possibly compare to the email that went out to practically everyone we knew? The answer was *NOTHING*, in italics and all caps.

"We're fucking done!" Steven eventually yelled to put a period at the end of a long ugly sentence. Afterwards, he lowered his voice and struck the final blow. "When you come home, I don't want you to speak to me. Just get some things together and go. I don't even want to look at you."

Then he hung up, leaving me to the agony of imagining the fallout that was inevitable with my children.

CHAPTER SIX

FOR THE NEXT HOUR, I thought about death. Ending my life in a warm bath seemed so much easier than facing my new horrific reality. I doubt I would have done such a thing to my kids, but to this day, I'm not entirely sure I'd be alive if my thoughts hadn't been interrupted by a phone call from Misha. When I saw her name, I recognized it as a lifeline, but I also understood she had the power to push me closer to the cliff, so picking up my phone felt like pulling the trigger in a game of Russian Roulette.

"Misha," I said, putting the phone to my ear.

"*Mom!*" came rushing back. "Are you all right? What was that email? And whose leg was that? What's going on? When I saw that picture, I thought you might be dead!"

The thought of her and Sam studying that picture sickened me, and I became paralyzed with guilt and shame.

"Are you there?" Misha cried, panic in her voice.

"I'm here," I said, but my throat was so constricted I couldn't say more, although I knew I was frightening Misha, who was repeating, "*Mom?*"

"I'm sorry," I said when I was finally able to muster a voice.

"What happened to you?" she asked, clearly in a state of confusion. "Were you kidnapped, or roofied or something? I can't make any sense of this photo you sent. I spoke to Sam—he's the one who told me to check my email—and he's really freaked out. He says Dad's freaked out, too. What the hell is this?"

Her question about being "roofied" gave me an idea, and suddenly I was buoyed up by hope. It was like a cartoon light bulb had switched on over my head and I could see a way out of the darkness.

I came back with a lie, and as I was telling it, I couldn't believe I hadn't thought of it before. It made so much more sense than the hacked email idea. I made a mental note to call Carol the instant I got off the phone with Misha.

"I was drugged," I said, almost giddy with the possibility of getting my life back. "I was in a hotel near Bozeman for the writer's conference, and a man I met must have put something in my drink. He and I were talking while I was having a glass of wine in the hotel bar, and the next thing I remember, I woke up naked in my hotel room. Now I'm hearing about all these emails he sent out using my phone."

"*Oh my God, Mom.* Have you told the police? I hope you've called the police."

I instantly understood the full weight of my lie, and I was uncertain what to say. "I haven't," I said. "I know I need to. I've just been so upset and confused. But I will. In the meantime, I'm worried about Sam and your father. And, Misha, he sent pictures to practically everyone I know. It's just unreal."

"But why would he do that?" Misha asked. Her tone became tentative. "He did rape you, right? Or did he just take pictures? Mom, I'm sorry I'm asking—you must feel terrible. I'm just so confused."

"I'm confused, too," I said. "I don't remember anything. But can we maybe talk about it another time? Right now, I'm having a hard time even thinking about it. It would be more helpful at the moment if you'd call Sam and tell him what I told you. And your father, too. Dad called earlier, but all he did was yell at me, and he wouldn't let me explain what happened. You know how he is. He just screamed at me and told me to come home and pack my things."

"Are you kidding me?" Misha cried.

"I wish I were," I said.

"I'm calling him as soon as we hang up. I can't believe he did that to you," she said. "But, Mom, I'm worried about you. Do you want me to come to where you are? Where are you, by the way? Are you still in Bozeman?"

"I'm in Salt Lake. But don't worry about me. I just need a little time to pull myself together, and I need to straighten out the email thing. I don't know what people must be thinking. It's like a nightmare. I hope everyone will understand..."

"Of course, they'll understand," Misha said. "But I can't believe what you told me about Dad. That makes me *sick.*"

"I'm not too happy with him. But I want you to know how much I appreciate *you*, Misha. I love you so much."

"I love you too, Mom. I'm so sorry this happened to you."

"Don't worry about me. I'll be all right. We'll talk more later, okay?"

"Okay, Mom. I love you so much."

"I love you, too..."

A moment later, we said goodbye, and I cried for a solid ten minutes. I *hated* lying to Misha, but, at the same time, I was overcome with relief that I might have found a way to pull my life back from the abyss.

When I was spent and calm enough to talk, I called Carol and pitched the *"I was roofied"* alternative to the hacking story.

"It does seem more plausible," she said, "but how do we explain him sending out the emails? Does that make any sense?"

"It does if he wanted to humiliate me," I said, thinking of the explanation on the spot.

"But wouldn't it also implicate him in a crime?"

I thought about it for a moment, then said, "Let's just go with it for now and worry about coming up with an answer to that later. Hopefully, once we give people a story that seems reasonable, they'll accept it without asking a lot of questions. In fact, let's tell everyone that I don't want to talk about it. That should work, right? Don't you think it's understandable I wouldn't want to talk about it?"

"I guess so. But I'm still worried about this guy. What's his name?"

"Tom. Or, at least, that's what he told me."

"Have you heard anything more from him?"

"No," I said.

"Well, be careful. If he's capable of doing what he's done so far, Lord only knows what else he might do."

"I'll be careful," I said. "But, look, I'm going to write an email about the roofie thing and send it out to everyone. If you hear from anyone, that's the story I want to go with. Okay?"

"Whatever you want," she said. "I just hope you know what you're doing."

☙

I spent the next few minutes crafting an email that I immediately sent to everyone who'd received the picture. The list was long, and some of the recipients were so painful to contemplate that I had to force myself to put them out of my head. The absolute worst were "Group" addresses I'd used to send emails to students in my classes. It would be a miracle if my photo had not, by now, been forwarded to every student on campus. And who knew what might be "trending" on social media platforms? Thinking about it made me want to curl up and die. Here's what I wrote:

Dear friend or colleague,

I know you must be shocked and confused by what you received from my email account early this morning. I'm as shocked as anyone because I have *no* recollection of the circumstances surrounding it, nor do I understand why it was sent. I only know that last night I was drugged to unconsciousness. The man responsible then used my phone to take and send pictures to a large number of people in my Contacts list. I'm sure you can understand how upsetting this is for me. I beg you to please delete the email and not share it with anyone. (The emails in my Sent folder are available as evidence for the police, so your copy isn't needed.) If you haven't opened the email, I implore you to delete it unopened. I'm certain you can sympathize with the pain and humiliation this situation is causing me.

Also, please don't be offended if you write or call me and I don't respond. At the moment, I'm not up to talking or answering emails. But don't worry about my well-being. I'm upset, but I'll recover. I just need some time.

With gratitude for your cooperation and understanding,

Valerie

Wanting to get the letter to people as quickly as possible, I proofread it once, then began sending it to everyone on the list, trying not to dwell on the names or the staggering number of emails he'd sent. I didn't count, but there had to be a least fifty—including the group addresses, which added probably fifty or sixty more. And he'd managed to include some of the worst people I could think of, including my mother-in-law, the chairman of my department, the Chancellor—the editor of the NYT Book Review! It was unbelievable.

When I was finally finished, I checked my Inbox and could see that, in addition to there being quite a few more replies to the original email, I was already getting replies to the one I'd just sent. I didn't have the stomach to read any of them. Instead, I turned off my phone, rolled over onto the bed, and resumed the fetal position. I tried to sleep, but no matter how hard I tried, I couldn't stop spinning all the horrifying realities I'd have to face. Above it all loomed questions with answers I couldn't fathom: How could I have been so wrong about Tom? And why—*why* was he doing this to me?

CHAPTER SEVEN

I MAY HAVE MANAGED to get some sleep, but if so, it wasn't much. When the sun rose the next morning, I was awake to witness its ascent as dusty light began filtering in through the east-facing window of my hotel room. Pulling the covers over my head, I squeezed my eyes shut, longing for oblivion. *If only I could have just a little peace before facing the day.* But sleep continued to elude me. There would be no peace.

At eight o'clock, I stumbled out of bed and made the terrible weak coffee that seemed obligatory in all American hotels. I ran a bath and stewed for about an hour. I was so tired and emotionally ragged by then that I finally approximated the oblivion I was looking for, partly because my head now ached so badly it drowned out my thoughts. Insensibility via pain was better than nothing, so I embraced the mixture of thudding misery and hot water as I nursed my cup of dishwater coffee.

When I eventually got myself dressed and ready to check out, I still hadn't found the courage to turn on my phone, but it occurred to me that I needed to at least call Misha and let her know I was alive, so I sat down on the side of the bed and tried to mentally prepare myself to re-connect to the world. *This new terrifying world that I'd some-*

how have to navigate. I picked up my phone and stared at it, telling myself that whatever it held, it could wait.

I made a deal with myself: I would call Misha—or, better yet, text her—then get in the car and drive. That was it. That was all I could handle. I would not check my emails or read my texts or answer any calls.

I pressed the power button on my phone and held it down. Moments later, it sprang to life, and I went directly to my text messages, intending to send a note to Misha. Multiple unopened messages tempted me, but one stood out among the rest. It was from Tom.

Closing my eyes and shaking my head, I renewed my vow to shut everything out and head for home. I wrote these words to Misha: "Hitting the road now. Will not be answering calls or texts in the car. Please let Sam and your father know. And don't worry about me. I'll call you when I get home. Love you."

After sending the message, I stared at the text from Tom and held my breath. Then, against my better judgment, but knowing it would gnaw at me if I didn't, I opened it and read these words: "I know what you've been telling people. Too bad no one believes you."

In a fit of fear and shame, I threw my phone on the bed, then stared at it in misery, understanding that whatever was going on with this man, it wouldn't be solved by a simple story. And how did he know about my lie? Was he guessing, or had he somehow seen the email I sent out?

Impulsively, I picked up my phone and dialed his number, desperate to understand what he had against me. I understood now that wishing him away was not an option. He wasn't going away. But he didn't answer. His phone just rang and rang, culminating in a robotic message stating that the recipient's voice mailbox was not set up.

∞

When I was finally back in my car and heading for home, I tried as hard as I could to blank my mind—to achieve some kind of numbness. But it didn't happen. With hundreds of miles in front of me and an increasing number in my wake, I spun everything again and again, remembering every moment with Tom and imagining all the worst possible consequences of what he'd done. *What I'd done.* I hashed and rehashed and eventually realized that for all the shame and embarrassment that was surely in my future, my crime was not that earth-shaking. If you believed the statistics, the sin I'd committed was as common as a cold. I wasn't proud of my behavior, but neither had I murdered anyone. But, of course, I always came back to the pictures, which might have been breaking the internet for all I knew. And now there was my lie to worry about. I didn't know how to face any of it, or if I could ever recover from a humiliation of such magnitude.

I was in the middle of this thought when I looked in my rearview mirror and noticed a black SUV on my bumper. I looked again, and, to my horror, the driver looked like Tom. With my heart in my throat, I pressed the accelerator, now staring straight at the road ahead, afraid to re-check the mirror.

A minute or so later, I finally found the courage to take another look. The car was still there. With nothing but monotonous desert and dry, craggy mountains on both sides of us, we were essentially in the middle of nowhere, with few other cars or even trucks on the road. *Why*, I asked myself, *when it would be so easy to pass, would someone tailgate me?* It had to be Tom.

I stared hard into the rearview, but now, seeing little more than a shadow, I couldn't be certain it was him. I prayed my imagination was getting the better of me—that the driver was just one of those jerks who enjoys intimidating people out of the left lane.

With my speedometer now registering ninety-two miles an hour, I turned on my blinker, moved to the right, and took my foot off the gas. As I began to slow down, I looked to the left, hoping to see the SUV whiz by and leave me in his dust. But as I slowed, so did the SUV, until we were cruising side-by-side. I glanced over, then locked eyes with a sneering man I'd never seen before. With his passenger-side window rolled down, he yelled, *"Fuck you!"* Then he flipped me the finger and stepped on the accelerator, revealing a back window and fender covered with ultra-right-wing, pro-gun bumper stickers.

Now I understood his animosity. He was reacting to the stickers on my bumper: *Another Mother for Sensible Gun Laws* and *Arms Are For Hugging*.

As he disappeared into the distance, I was relieved but still unnerved, so I slowed down some more, then pulled off onto a wide shoulder and stopped, wanting to calm down. With my breathing starting to normalize, I stared at my phone, wondering what it held. I'd turned off the sound and vibrate functions and could see nothing but my GPS, so I had no idea who might have been trying to reach me or what new horrors might have occurred since I'd last checked my messages. Affixed to the dashboard, it seemed to be daring me to look.

Longing for moral support, I was tempted to call Misha, or maybe Carol, but I decided against calling anyone. I needed to drive, not get myself more stirred up. I thought bitterly about Steven and wondered if he'd tried to call. I shook my head and battled a deluge of grief and tears in an abrupt upswell of emotion. If I'd come to understand anything over the last few days, it was that my marriage was over and had been for years. I just hadn't wanted to face it. I closed my eyes tight and tried to stave off a full-blown panic attack. How was I going to return home and face anything or anyone?

Moments later, resisting the urge to reach for my phone, I blew my nose, placed the car in drive, and turned back onto a road with not a single other vehicle in sight. In a landscape as bleak and desolate as my thoughts, I'd never felt more alone.

CHAPTER EIGHT

BY THE TIME I was starting to be inundated with signs for Las Vegas, my fear of returning home had snowballed into such a monster that I couldn't cope with the prospect of another long stretch on the road, then having to face Steven. I decided to stop in Vegas for the night and take advantage of one of its famous hotel deals. I thanked God I was on leave and didn't have to be anywhere. If I wanted to take another day to get home, there was no reason I couldn't.

The instant I made up my mind to stop, the load weighing me down lessened. Just a little, but enough to where I could breathe. As I passed signs for the MGM Grand and Caesars Palace, the refuge of a Vegas hotel room became more and more appealing. I stepped on the gas, shaking my head at my cowardice but relieved by the prospect of hiding out. I exhaled hard and glanced at myself in the mirror. "What have you done to your life?" I said out loud. "How can this be happening?"

ଓ

An hour later, I was in the bustling lobby of the Las Vegas Hilton. I booked myself for only one night but was assured by a snappily-dressed young man with a goatee that if I wanted to, I could add additional days by calling the front desk before ten the next morning.

Once I had my key, I tuned out all the gambling hub-bub and headed for my room on the sixteenth floor, think-ing, along the way, that I'd spotted Tom no less than three times. I shook my head at myself, thinking ruefully that I'd have to check under the bed as soon as I got to the room.

I'd stopped at a grocery and bought wine, crackers and cheese, some fruit, and a number of other assorted items, so I had enough food to hole up for several days if I want-ed to—although the second I entered the room, I began fantasizing about room service. I wanted a steak, or at least a hamburger. And French fries. An entire day of non-stop worry with almost nothing to eat had rendered me both famished and more than a little desperate for a drink.

I opened the bottle of wine (full disclosure, I bought two) and immediately began perusing a menu I found on the desk next to the TV. Deciding to forgo the tempting but significantly more expensive steak for a cheeseburger and fries, I called in the order, then planted myself on the bed with the wine and my phone, which I'd powered off before leaving the car. *I'll turn it on after I eat*, I told myself, staring at it with dread.

By the time the food arrived, I'd polished off half the bottle and was well on my way to being drunk. I hated myself for drinking, but my anxiety was so immense, I needed to dull my senses. When I'd finished the burger and fries, I was completely sated, with both food and wine. That, combined with my overall exhaustion, made it tempting to simply go to sleep and deal with my phone in the morning, but I knew I needed to at least call Misha. I wasn't so far gone that I'd put her through any more wor-ry, so I bit the bullet and turned on my phone.

As I feared, I'd gotten a slew of calls, several from Misha but also from Steven, Sam, Carol, and a host of other friends and colleagues who were all probably worried and wondering what the hell was going on with me. Some had left voice messages, but I ignored them and dialed Misha. She picked up after the first ring.

"*Mom!*" she cried, her obvious fear making me instantly sorry I hadn't called her sooner. "*Where are you? I've been calling you all day!*"

"I'm sorry," I said. "I did tell you I wouldn't be answering calls."

"Couldn't you have at least called me from a gas station or something?" she whined. "I've been worried about you."

"You're right. I'm sorry," I said.

"Where are you? Are you home?"

"I stopped in Vegas. I'm too tired to drive all the way home, so I got a room and have decided to take an extra day. I didn't get *any* sleep last night. I'm hoping I can get some tonight so I'll be safe for the drive tomorrow." I paused, picturing her sweet face. "I'm sorry I worried you. I know I should have called sooner. I've just been trying to focus on the road and not think about anything else. I'm sure you can understand. I'm feeling terrible."

"Of course I understand," Misha said. "You did say you wouldn't be answering your phone. I just figured you'd check your voicemails when you stopped for gas or whatever."

"I'm sorry," I said. "I should have called you sooner. Did you talk to Sam?"

"Yes, and he's worried about you, too. We all are."

"What about your father? Did you call him after we talked?"

"Yeah," she said, and I could tell by the way she said it she was unhappy with him. "He was super defensive. He claims you should have told him you were drugged, but I think he feels bad about the way he acted. He didn't come right out and say it, but I think he's sorry. Has he called you?"

"Yes, but I haven't listened to his messages yet. I called you first."

My heart started to race just thinking about talking to Steven. "I honestly don't want to talk to him," I said. I shook my head and took a gulp of wine. "I hate saying negative things about him, but he was so terrible to me. He can be so..." I struggled to find the words. "You know..."

"I know," she said, "but you really should call him. Sam, too."

"You're right," I agreed. "And I'm sorry for putting you in the middle of things. It's just so hard to talk about."

"I know. I love you, Mom."

"I love you, too, sweetie," I said. "Do you think you can do me a favor?"

"Anything."

"Can you call Sam and your father one more time for me and tell them I'm safe, taking an extra day, and need to sleep? I don't feel like talking anymore tonight. I'll call them tomorrow. *I promise.* But can you do that for me? Tell them I'm fine but just can't talk now?"

"Don't you think you should at least talk to Dad?" she said. "I know he was an asshole, but I think you should give him a chance to apologize. I'm sure he's sorry."

I wasn't so sure. I was also uncomfortable about the roofie story and wanted to put off talking to him as long as I could. "I'll think about it," I said. "But call him and tell him that if I don't talk to him tonight, I'll call him tomorrow before I start driving."

"O-kay," she said tentatively, her tone registering disapproval. But even as she was saying it, I knew I wouldn't call him. I also knew I probably wouldn't be driving in the morning. I needed to deal with the contents of my phone. But what I needed more than anything at the moment was sleep. Everything else would have to wait.

The instant I hung up with Misha, I powered off my phone, rolled over, and blinked out.

ಳ

The next morning, I called the front desk and booked my room for another day. I didn't necessarily plan to spend another night, but neither was I in a hurry to leave. Certainly not by ten o'clock. It was already eight-thirty. I'd slept for almost ten solid hours. I stared at my phone on the bed. With a sick feeling in my stomach, I picked it up and held down the power button. Almost the instant it sprang to life, Misha called.

"*Mom,*" she said with urgency. "Have you seen the news about the fire?"

"No. What's going on?"

"That big frat house up the street from the modern art gallery burned down last night. At least two people were taken to the hospital, and someone else is missing and might be dead."

"Oh no," I said. "I wonder if any of my students are members of that fraternity."

"Sam has friends in that house," Misha said. "He's over there now and says it's total chaos. The whole place went up in flames. The footage they've been showing on the news is unbelievable. You know the one I'm talking about, right? That huge brown shingle with the big porch out front?"

"Of course. Do you think Sam's still over there? I need to call him."

"I just talked to him a minute ago, so he's probably still there.

"I'll call him after we hang up," I said, quietly relieved to have a reason other than my own situation to speak to him.

After promising Misha I'd let her know when I arrived home, I dialed Sam, part of me hoping he wouldn't answer, and part of me anxious to get it over with. My heart pounded as I listened to the phone ring. When he finally picked up, there was so much noise in the background, I knew he'd have a hard time hearing me.

"Sam," I said, "I just talked to Misha, and she told me about the fire."

"Mom," he said, sounding frantic. "*Where are you?* I've been calling and calling. Why haven't you been answering your phone? Don't you know how worried we all are? Where are you? Are you home?"

"I'm fine," I said, then I broke down, relieved to hear concern in his voice, not disgust or blame.

"Mom. Don't cry, Mom..." Sam said.

I walked to the bathroom to get some tissues and blew my nose. "I'm sorry," I said. "I'm just so embarrassed and humiliated."

"Don't be. Nobody blames you for anything. I saw the letter you sent out. People will understand. Have you seen a doctor yet or talked to the police?"

"No, I'll talk to you about that later. For now, I'm just trying to deal with the trauma and embarrassment. I can't even tell you what it feels like..."

"Are you home now?"

"Not yet. I'm in a hotel and probably won't be leaving for a while. But what's the story with the fire?"

"I don't know, but it's pretty terrible. At least a couple of guys are in the hospital, and one's still missing. You should see the place. It's nothing but smoldering cinders. It's that house that almost got kicked off campus last semester."

Suddenly there was a lot of noise on the line, and I could hear someone talking on what sounded like a loud speaker. "What's going on?" I asked. "Can you hear me?"

"I can hear you, but just barely," he said. "Hold on a second."

I waited. After a few moments, he was back. "Looks like the missing guy's been found. He's not hurt or anything. But when are you getting home? Have you talked to Dad yet?"

"Not yet. I'll call him soon."

"Well, call me when you get home. Do you know when it might be?"

"I don't know, but it'll be late if it's tonight. Let's maybe talk tomorrow. But don't worry about me. I'll be all right. I just need a little time."

"I love you, Mom. And please try not to worry about what people think. All anyone cares about is you're okay. If anyone thinks anything else, fuck 'em."

"You're the best. Thank you."

"Drive safe," Sam said.

"I will. I love you so much," I whispered. Then I hung up and cried—out of relief, and because I loved my kids so damn much.

☙

Talking to Steven a short time later was a different story. If he was remorseful about how he'd talked to me during our last "conversation," he had an odd way of showing it. He didn't roar at me this time, but neither was he warm, and he never apologized or demonstrated any concern for my well-being, although he did mention he'd talked to Misha and been told about the roofie. With respect to that bit of information, he berated me for not telling him myself. When I responded that he hadn't given me a chance, he denied it, which is what I expected.

"When are you getting home?" he demanded finally. "I've been getting calls and don't know what to tell anyone."

"Why don't you tell people I've been through a trauma and need some space for a while," I said.

"I'm just going to stop answering the phone. I'll leave it to you to describe the trauma. I want to stay out of it."

His tone was so cold I almost hung up on him. "I'm moved by your compassion," I said.

"What do you want from me?" he yelled. "You don't think this is hard on me, too—having the whole world see nude photos of my wife with some goon in a hotel room? Do you have any idea how humiliating this is for me? Have you even thought about me for one second?"

"Have you thought about me?" I shot back.

"This is so typical," he said. "It's always poor you, and I'm the bad guy."

"It's typical, all right."

"Just come home," he said. "I'm tired of dealing with this on my own."

Without saying another word, I hung up. And I didn't feel guilty anymore about lying, because it made no difference. Even believing I'd been drugged and raped, Steven could think only of himself.

Disgusted, I fell back on the bed, then realized in a flash of insight that as terrible as Tom was, I was even angrier at Steven. I knew—finally—that my marriage was over. And it was long overdue.

CHAPTER NINE

AFTER THE CALL FROM Steven, my problems compounded because now I had to add a divorce to the pile of shit I needed to deal with. For years I'd been trying to avoid the inevitable hassles of ending our marriage, but it seemed I couldn't avoid them any longer. Things had just gone too far. I looked at the clock. *Nine-thirty.* Moments later, I heard three knocks on the door, then, "Room service." My breakfast had arrived.

Soon I was sitting at the table eating eggs and toast, no longer able to avoid my phone. I decided to look at my email first, hoping to find some compassionate messages that would make it easier to face the pictures. I did find a host of warm messages, thank God. Most were just a few words, with assurances that they'd deleted the original email. Some were longer and more involved, but I just skimmed them, being mostly interested in trying to feel better. And it helped. With my lie about the roofie, I'd managed to create a narrative in which I was sympathetic, so people were kind, but nothing vanquished my shame and embarrassment.

Those terrible photos. I imagined the memes, the cruel comments, the jokes, and all the people who might, at any given moment, be laughing at me, or disgusted by me, or imagining me in the crudest possible way. It was too much. Especially when I thought about my kids.

After skimming through most of the emails (noting, with alarm, that the number I received was relatively small compared to the number Tom had sent), I finally found the stomach to open my Photos app, and I was shocked by the sheer volume of pictures he'd taken, although most were virtually identical. To my great relief, none were crude or more revealing than the few I'd already seen. I was naked and uncovered, but my position on my side was reasonably modest—although one of my breasts was visible, and my face was recognizable. My dark wavy hair was splayed across the pillow so perfectly, it looked contrived. I wondered if he'd arranged it, and the scene that popped into my head was like something from a movie about a psycho. And that's who he was—he had to be. *A psycho.* A psycho who'd presented as one of the most attractive, interesting men I'd ever met. It was hard to compute.

I'm embarrassed to admit it, but as I swiped slowly through the photos, the fact that they were flattering was not exactly a comfort, but it was a relief. (Nude photos were bad. Ugly nude photos would have been worse.) Only a few showed any part of Tom, and mercifully, it was only ever his leg.

When I finally came to the last picture, my heart jumped into my throat. *There was a video.*

Me in the shower.

In a full-on panic and barely breathing, I played it, hating myself because I knew what I'd find. The shower door was frosted glass, so my body was blurred, but my voice was clear, and my words were not those of someone who'd been drugged or molested.

"Care to jump in and join me?" I called cheerily over the din of running water. *"I'll wash your back or anything else you can think of that might enjoy a little soap."*

"Fuck!" I screamed, not caring who heard me. I threw my head back and cursed again, this time lower, with tears flooding my eyes. My heart pounded in my chest, and I couldn't think straight, but one thing was abundantly clear: If Tom released this video, I'd be exposed as both an adulterer *and* a liar. And I'd be crucified for the lying. In the age of *"Me too,"* when women's stories of sexual abuse were finally being heard—and, more importantly, *believed*—this particular crime would be considered unforgivable.

What had I done?

I answered my own question. *I'd ruined my life.* With one careless decision, I'd destroyed my reputation, my family, and virtually everything I'd ever worked for.

"Fuck!" I repeated, this time in a whimper.

With my heart still hammering, I forced myself to examine my Sent messages, praying that none contained a video attachment. I'd assumed that only photos were sent out, but now I wasn't sure. I scrolled slowly down the list to the end, eyeing each listed email in detail. To my great relief, none appeared to have an attached video. Then I had a thought. *Had he sent the video and photos to himself?* If so, he'd probably have deleted the email to avoid me seeing his address.

I opened my Trash folder to see what was there, but it was empty. I knew I hadn't emptied the folder myself, so I was certain he'd done it, which more or less confirmed, in my mind, that he'd sent himself an email. *And what else might he have sent, then deleted?*

I contemplated YouTube, so-called "revenge sites," and all the other websites to which a video or photos could be uploaded, and my imagination went spinning. Eventually, I became so unraveled that I threw down my phone, fell back on the bed, and sobbed.

CHAPTER TEN

BY NOON, I WAS cried out and numb, with absolutely no desire to leave the hotel or deal with any of the various nightmares that awaited. Shortly after I discovered the video, my phone began buzzing, so I'd turned it off, not wanting to talk to my agent, Misha, Carol, or any of the other people who were suddenly anxious to reach me. The only person I really wanted to speak to was Tom. *Why?* I wanted to ask him. *Why did he want to hurt me?* I might have been tempted to call him, but I'd deleted his texts, which was undoubtedly a blessing. I'd only have made things worse.

Wondering what I should do—if I should quit hiding out and head for home—I had a thought that made me stare at my phone with a renewed sense of dread. I flipped to the Google search field, held my breath, then searched for my name.

I don't know what I expected to find, but I was relieved not to find it. If nudie photos of me were now circling the globe, it wasn't immediately apparent. All that came up were the normal book-related sites that I made a habit of checking and links to my LinkedIn, Facebook, and Instagram profiles. Out of habit, I opened the link to my latest novel on Amazon to check the reviews.

When my book appeared, I noticed that the number of customer reviews had ticked up to over two hundred. A moment later, I was shocked by the review at the top of the page. Showing yesterday's date, it had a single star and was titled, "This book is terrible, and the author is a fraud." The review then proceeded to trash my writing, the plot, my characters, and the overall concept of the story. It also implied I was a plagiarist. The final sentence of the last scathing paragraph read, "Giving this book even one star is generous. If I were the author's teacher, I'd give her an F and kick her out of school." The name associated with the review was *Truth*, but I suspected it was Tom. In fact, I knew it was, and I couldn't help wondering what other sick surprises he had in store for me. Things kept getting worse and worse.

Hours later, as I was packing up, I tried to mentally prepare myself for both the long drive home and the fall-out waiting for me when I got there. I'd listened to all my voicemails and read the texts and emails from everyone who mattered, and responded to everyone with a variation of the same simple message: *Thank you for your concern. I'm fine and heading home. We'll talk when I get back.*

I considered calling or writing Steven but decided, in the end, to simply send him a short text letting him know I'd be arriving home that night. He didn't answer back, and I wasn't surprised. He was dreading my homecoming as much as I was.

I knew, deep down, that whatever happened with Steven would be for the best. I just hoped we wouldn't have to suffer too much before coming out the other side. I was resigned and braced for the breakup of my marriage. It was everything else I was most worried about. What would be the consequences with my kids? My career? My friendships? And what other nasty surprises might I expect from Tom? It all felt like some gigantic rock cliff looming over my head, ready to come crashing down.

The drive was long, and I did much of it in a daze. When I finally turned into our driveway, it was dark, and I was exhausted. Lights on both floors were an indicator Steven was home. I stared at the living room window, knowing he was probably in his chair, fully aware I was outside and afraid to come in. I wondered if I could get away with heading straight upstairs, putting off the inevitable showdown until I'd had some sleep. I doubted it.

All the way home, I'd imagined different ways things could go, and all of them were bad. I'd learned early on—although too late—that it was impossible to talk to Steven about our marriage. The instant he felt criticized, he went full nuclear. No exceptions. There could never be any working things out or trying to understand one another's point of view. With Steven, it was *keep it to yourself or suffer the consequences*—the consequences normally being cruelty, a knock-down drag-out, days, if not weeks, of barely speaking to one another, and then, finally, a mutual but silent agreement to forget it and move forward.

But with each incident, we chipped away parts of our relationship that could never be recovered. Above all, we chipped away at our love and respect for one another. Now, sitting in the driveway awaiting my fate, I knew there was little, if anything, left to chip away. We'd crumbled into a pile of nothing.

☙

I'd been sitting in the driveway for probably fifteen minutes before I finally found the courage to get out of the car. With my purse over my shoulder and luggage still in the trunk, I walked up our front steps and tested the door. It was locked, so I fumbled with my keys, then unlocked the door and stepped inside. Moments later, having decided to forego the stairs and get whatever was going to happen over with, I was standing in front of Steven, who was exactly where I expected him to be, watching a rerun of *Law and Order*.

He picked up the remote and muted it. "So you're finally home," he said, a blank expression on his face.

I'd always considered him handsome, but unshaven, and looking uncharacteristically gaunt in the uneven light, he appeared kind of pathetic, and older than his forty-five years. He was wearing a white t-shirt and gray sweatpants, and the remnants of a frozen dinner were next to him on the lamp table, which also held a bottle of Jack Daniels, an empty glass, and an ashtray containing a stubbed-out cigar.

"What now?" he said, seeming half-drunk and barely moving a muscle. "Are you expecting sympathy? A welcome home?"

"I don't expect anything good," I said. "So how about we skip the fight and cut straight to the silent treatment? What would be the point of all the rest of it? We both know where this is going, and it doesn't matter if I was drugged and raped, or if I did what you've been doing for years. You and I both know that either way, our marriage is over."

"This is not about me!" he roared, suddenly animating out of his stupor. "Don't you dare make this about me. This is about the shame you have brought to this family. To all of us."

He leaned forward in his chair, then stood up in what seemed like a deliberate move of intimidation. "Have you considered the embarrassment—the *agony*—you've caused your children? *Have you?* Do you know how many people have seen that fucking picture? Are laughing at you? Laughing at *us*? And do you think *anyone* for even one fucking second buys that ridiculous story about being drugged?"

He picked up the glass ashtray and hurled it against the bricks beside the fireplace, causing it to shatter in all directions. "You are a disgrace!"

I froze, and I knew there was nothing I could say that would penetrate his anger. I also knew that if I *had* been raped, this scene would be playing out just as it was. I almost wished I had, because I'd at least have had the satisfaction of righteously yelling back. But I wasn't interested in pushing a lie. I just wanted out.

I turned around and headed for the hallway, intending to go upstairs and set myself up in the guest room.

"Where the fuck do you think you're going?" Steven called after me. "Do you think we're done here?"

I did an about-face and went back to the living room. "What more do you want from me, Steven? It doesn't matter what I say, or what happened, or what people are saying, or any of it. There's nothing I can do to change history. I'm sorry you're embarrassed. I'm sorry the kids are embarrassed. I've talked to both of them, and I'll continue talking to them, and they'll be fine. We'll all survive."

He started hurling something back, but I shut him down. "You and I both know that if you weren't out there having sex with God knows who, this never would have happened. You're a fucking hypocrite!"

His face was turning red, and I could see he was becoming dangerously enraged, but I kept going. "As soon as I can, I'm filing for divorce. Then you can fuck whoever you want, and no one will care."

He plopped back down in his chair and filled his empty glass. "You make me sick," he said. "You create this ridiculous spectacle, then have the nerve to make it about me. To blame *me*—like I'm responsible for you letting some nutcase take pictures of you and send them to everyone we know." He contorted his face. "You disgust me."

Resisting the urge to cry, and with my legs feeling like rubber, I turned around and headed back to the hallway. "You disgust me too, Steven."

"Don't you even think about trying to take this house!" he screamed after me. "I paid for this fucking house!"

I went outside to retrieve my suitcase and another small bag from my car, then returned and headed upstairs with Steven still yelling.

"Why are you coming back? Go stay at a hotel. Maybe you'll get lucky again!"

I could tell by the sound of his voice he was starting to get seriously drunk.

Knowing better than to engage with him any further, I ignored him and continued up the stairs and entered our guest room, closing and locking the door behind me. I sat down on the bed to think. After only a few moments, I decided I *should* go to a hotel. With him drinking like he was, things could get a lot worse.

Now Steven was hollering even louder. "Don't you dare think you can fucking waltz in here and pretend nothing has happened. You have shamed and disgraced this family! And if you think you're going to get some fancy lawyer and take this house and everything I've worked so hard for all these years, you'd better think again!"

As he was bellowing, I was compiling a mental list of things I needed to take with me to a hotel. The clothes in my suitcase weren't sufficient.

I got up, opened the door as quietly as I could, then carried my luggage to our bedroom so I could get into my closet.

The moment I entered our room, I thought about the gun Steven kept in his bedside table. We'd had more than one fight about that stupid gun, which he kept loaded "in case of a home invasion." I detested guns, and I knew damn well it was more a safety issue for us than it was for a burglar. Now the threat seemed very real, so I decided—just to be on the safe side—to take the gun and hide it.

Steven was now yelling that I was a selfish cunt who never considered anyone but myself (he knew I detested the C-word). He was sounding more and more unhinged, so before moving the gun, I pulled my phone from my purse and turned on the Record function. Then I crept into the hall and placed it inside a vase on top of a narrow table near the stairs, where it would pick up his ranting.

It wasn't the first time I'd done this. I'd played him recordings of himself in the past, hoping he'd be embarrassed by his behavior. It had never resulted in an apology—he'd only ever raged that I'd betrayed him by recording him without his consent. But I'd seen shame written on his face, even if he wouldn't acknowledge it.

After depositing my phone, I returned to our room and stared at the gun in the open drawer. Steven was still screaming and sounding more and more drunk.

"You fucking bitch! Do you think you can go off and behave like a whore and then come back and turn my kids against me? You're a fucking joke, and now the whole world can see what a goddamn pitiful joke you are!"

Trembling, I picked up the gun and was surprised by how heavy it was, and how terrible it felt in my hand. Just the look of it made me feel sick.

I was staring at the gun, wondering where to put it, when Steven suddenly stormed into the room, scaring me so badly I jumped and almost dropped it.

"What are you doing with that?"

His face was a shocking red, and veins bulged like snakes on both sides of his neck. *"You have no right to touch that!"*

"I was going to hide it because you're scaring me!" I said. "I told you I didn't want this in our house, and this is exactly why."

Tears began streaming down my face, and my legs were close to buckling.

"Give me the gun," he said, emphasizing each word.

"I can't," I said. "Not when you're like this. You're not thinking clearly. Let me just put it back in the drawer. I'm sorry I took it out. *Please.* Just let me put it back."

"Give it to me *right now*!" he yelled, and this time the look in his eyes was so chilling I nearly lost control of my bladder.

"Please, Steven," I said in the gentlest voice I could manage. "Go back downstairs. I'll put the gun in the drawer and then leave and go to a hotel."

"Shut the fuck up and give me the gun," he said.

With icy cold eyes and his right hand outstretched, he started to move in my direction, like he was going to grab the gun. Instinctively, I raised it and pointed it at him.

"Stay away from me," I said, my arms now shaking as badly as my legs. "I mean it." I pointed with the gun toward the wall to his left. "Move over there so I can get out. Then I'll leave. I promise."

He started toward me again, so I pointed the gun back in his direction, feeling, as I was doing it, like I was having an out-of-body experience—like I was watching myself from above. It all seemed so surreal.

Steven laughed mockingly, then stumbled and righted himself. I'd never seen him this drunk or been more terrified. This was totally uncharted territory.

With my eyes now so full of tears I could barely see, I held the gun with both hands, feeling its weight and the gravity of the situation like a suffocating nightmare.

"Can we please just stop this?" I begged in a whisper. My throat was so clenched with terror that it was hard to talk. It was hard even to breathe. "Let me put the gun back in the drawer."

I still had the gun pointed at him, but it was so heavy I struggled to hold it steady. Taking a deep breath for courage, I slowly lowered it and began to lean towards the bedside table. "I'm putting it back," I said, keeping my eyes glued to Steven. "Then I'm...."

Before I could get another word out, he lunged at me and grabbed the gun with both hands. Because he was drunk, he tripped and fell, causing the gun to go off in an explosion so deafening I was initially stunned.

When I regained my senses, my first thought was to wonder, with horror, if he'd been shot. Shaking uncontrollably, and with my head and ears feeling the splitting effects of the gunshot, I forced myself to look. I didn't see any blood, but lying in an awkward heap with both arms hidden underneath his body, Steven wasn't moving. The gun was out of sight—either still in his hands or under the bed.

Panicked, I knelt down and reached for his neck to see if I could find a pulse. Just as I managed, with great relief, to discover he was alive, I noticed blood beginning to flow from beneath him.

Hearing something behind me, I turned around and was shocked to see Tom standing in the doorway.

"I heard a shot," he announced, as though his appearance inside my house were the most natural thing in the world.

"I need to call 911," I mumbled, struggling to process this new development. Things had gone so nonlinear by then, it felt like reality itself was unraveling. But one thought stood out in the fog, and that was that Steven needed an ambulance.

He let out a low moan. Now more blood was appearing from beneath him.

"It was an accident," I said, looking back at Tom. "I was going to hide the gun, and he tried to take it from me." I felt like I had cotton inside my aching head and could barely hear myself. "*I need to call 911.*"

"Where's your phone?" he said, his voice strangely calm.

I struggled to understand the situation. *What the hell was Tom doing inside my house?* Between adrenaline, fear, the impact of the gun on my ears, and now Tom materializing out of the ether, I felt like I was on drugs. Straining to think, I remembered hiding my phone. It was probably still recording.

"We have a landline in the guest room," I said, nodding toward the room next door. I stood up, hoping my legs would hold me. "We have to go call."

"Get some things together," Tom said. "Clothes and whatever toiletries you might need. *Fast.* I'm taking you. When you're ready, I'll call 911. Where's your cell phone? Where's your purse?"

"What do you mean *you're taking me?*" I said. "What are you talking about?"

"Where is your purse?" Tom said again, ignoring my question.

I looked down at Steven—who wasn't moving or making any more noise. "This is your fault!" I screamed at Tom. "You did this! Why are you doing all this to me? Look what you've done!"

"Your purse!" Tom demanded.

Trembling and confused, I nodded across the room to where it sat on the floor next to a chair. Tom went and picked it up, then dumped its contents onto the bed.

"It's not here," he said. "Where's your phone?"

"I don't know, I must have left it in my car," I said, hoping he'd let it go. "But we have a phone in the other room. We have to call right now!"

He spotted my luggage near the closet door. "I'm going to grab your bags. We'll call, and then we're leaving."

He pulled a gun from under his shirt and pointed to the items he'd dumped onto the bed. "Take any of that you want, then I'll call. What's your house number?"

I stared at the gun in his hand, then down at Steven, who might have been dead at that point for all I knew. Blood was now pooling near his upper torso.

"Why are you doing this? Where are you taking me?" I said as I shoved things back into my purse.

I wish I'd had the presence of mind to scream—a neighbor might have heard me—but I was in such a state of panic I couldn't think straight.

Tom demanded my house number again. I gave it to him, and a moment later, he pulled a roll of duct tape from his pocket and proceeded to tape my mouth and wrists. Then he gripped me by the arm and pushed me into the guest room, where he picked up the phone.

The last thing I remember before he led me out of the house was the sound of Tom talking in a strange voice to the 911 operator.

Things just kept getting crazier and crazier.

CHAPTER ELEVEN

"IF YOU TRY ANYTHING stupid, I swear I'll go after your daughter," Tom whispered as he opened the car door and pushed me inside. The threat stunned me. Things had gone so far off the rails by then, I believed anything was possible. So right there, I decided to cooperate—at least for the moment. I had *no* idea what he wanted with me or what to expect, but I did know that whatever it was, I couldn't let it extend to my kids.

After closing the door behind me, he took my bags, including my purse, and threw them into the back seat. I silently prayed he wouldn't give any thought to the whereabouts of my phone. I'd told him it was in my car and worried he might check. He didn't, thank God. Instead, he rushed around and got into the car, started it, and pulled away from the curb.

I didn't hear any sirens or see any indication that anyone was racing to Steven's rescue. I wondered if an ambulance was really on its way. Tom had left the door to our house ajar so they'd know to come in when no one answered, but would they come before Steven bled to death? Or even come at all?

I began making frantic noises, hoping Tom would pull the tape off my mouth. He initially ignored me but finally reached over and yanked it off.

"I don't think they're coming," I gulped, ignoring the pain. "We can't go off and leave him to die!"

"They're coming," Tom said. "It's only been two minutes. They're on their way."

"You can't be sure," I said.

"I'm sure. They're coming."

"Can we pull over and see?" I begged. "Please?"

He turned and looked me in the eye, then shocked me by pulling over. "They're coming."

We waited with the car idling and neither of us speaking. I wanted to ask him why he was torturing me and where we were going, but I didn't want him to change his mind, so I kept my mouth shut.

After a minute, we heard sirens, then saw flashing lights racing in our direction from several streets up. Before they got close, Tom pulled out and turned down a side street.

"What if that wasn't for him?" I said, terrified we might be leaving Steven to die.

"It was for him," Tom snapped. "Now stop talking."

"They'll think I shot him and fled the scene!"

"Be quiet or the tape goes back on."

"Why are you doing this to me?" I murmured as the gravity of my situation began to sink in.

Tom didn't answer the question. He just scowled and said, "Last chance." Then he looked back at the street and sped up.

CB

We were on the freeway heading east when we exchanged our next words. I'd tried a couple of times earlier to get him to talk to me, but each time he'd ordered me to keep quiet.

It was strange looking at him during that time—the time he refused to talk. I could see a push-pull of some kind going on inside of him. He was conflicted. There was no doubt. Whatever this was that was going on, it wasn't easy for him. It was evident in the set of his jaw, in the way he tightened and loosened his grip on the steering wheel, even in his scent. He was as afraid as I was. I also detected a sadness that I remembered seeing briefly when we'd been together in the Gallatin Valley.

Thinking about the night we'd spent together was difficult. I hadn't wanted to think about it, but now, as I tried to divine what possible reason he might have for all the senseless things he was doing, I searched my memory for some clue that might answer the question. When I finally allowed myself to relive the moments we'd spent together—both in the restaurant and in my cabin—all I could remember was intelligence, empathy, passion, and a hint of sadness, which, at the time, I chalked up to loneliness, or possibly a loss of some sort.

Was the sadness I detected an indicator of some deep mental illness he was adept at hiding? I had no idea. I just hoped and prayed that if a push-pull really were going on, his good side would win out. I was sure there was good in him. I'd seen it. Now, sitting terrified next to him with my wrists taped together, I resolved to appeal to that part of him. I didn't know what else to do.

Tom initiated our ice-breaking conversation, if you could call it that. I'd been seeing for the last ten or fifteen miles that he was starting to relax. He wasn't gripping the steering wheel as tightly, and his breathing had normalized. It was as if heading east into the mountains was having a calming effect on him. I'd calmed down some, too—at least my heart had stopped racing. With my adrenaline no longer surging, I was able to think more clearly, and what I was mostly thinking about was Steven. What if they hadn't found him in time and he'd died? I was also sick with worry about my children. Would they think I'd shot their father and then run off? I prayed the police would find my phone and listen to the recording. But by the time they found it, anything might have happened, and my kids would be going crazy.

"I know you think I'm a lunatic," Tom said as I was having this thought. He didn't look at me. He kept his eyes on the road, which was so dark, it felt like we were flying through space. "I haven't always been this way. Life has done this to me."

He initially left it there, and I remained still, hoping he'd go on. I figured if he opened up, I might be able to talk my way out of whatever this was. After a minute, he finally continued, almost as if he were talking to himself.

"It's interesting to discover what you're capable of doing when you don't give a shit about your own life anymore. When you have nothing left to lose and have gone, mentally, totally numb."

He stopped again, and again I waited.

"I've studied history my whole life," he said, "and I've often wondered how men can do such terrible things to one another. It's been a great mystery to me. But now I understand. *There's a line.*" He raised his right index finger from the steering wheel like he was emphasizing the point.

"Of course, there can be many reasons for crossing it—or rather, many things that can push one over it. But once you cross over, previously unthinkable things become shockingly easy."

His words sent a chill down my spine, renewing my terror. It seemed clear in that moment that he planned to kill me.

He glanced over, almost casually, like we were two friends on a carpool ride to work. "I don't know if I can explain it—you know, how it feels on the other side. But I've crossed over. I'm not proud of it; it's just where I am. But I want you to know that I have no desire or intention to hurt you. I never wanted to hurt anyone. But, like I said, here I am, and there's no going back."

I wondered what had *pushed him over the line*, but I was afraid of setting him off, so I didn't ask. Instead, I took a breath for courage, then said, "What is it you want from me? Why are you punishing me? I did tell you I was married. Is this some kind of..."

"That's not it," he snapped. He shook his head, and his expression darkened. "You'll find out soon enough."

I tried to think of something strategic to say, but I drew a blank. And he was right; I did think he was a lunatic, and I didn't believe for a second that he wasn't going to hurt me.

I watched him, and I could see the push-pull thing again. I was dying to know what he was thinking, but I kept quiet, believing it best to let whatever was happening inside of him dissipate before engaging with him any further. We drove for a long time without talking, hearing only the hum of the car engine and tires on the pavement as we headed deeper into the mountains. I slipped in and out of what felt like an altered state. I was dead tired and discovered I could stare at the road and become mesmerized into a place of relative calm. I oscillated between the refuge of that almost hypnotized state and a state of panic, in which my mind rocketed from one alarming thought to another.

I saw horrifying possibilities at virtually every point on the compass, so I tried to stay in the altered condition. Tried not to wonder where we were headed or what would happen to me once we got there. Tried not to think about Steven, or my kids, or any of the countless ways in which my life had been blown to smithereens over the course of just days. I'd have to face it soon enough. Or maybe not. Maybe, despite what Tom said, I was heading for a quick death. In any case, for the present, I did my best to blur it all out. When I did have anything resembling a clear thought, I made a commitment to myself to do whatever it took to survive—if only for the sake of my kids.

CHAPTER TWELVE

I SOMEHOW MANAGED TO sleep. When I woke up, I was surprised to find us bumping through pitch black over a narrow dirt road. Soon it got even narrower, and we eventually turned and stopped in front of a small log cabin that appeared out of nowhere at a dead end. It must have been the rough road that woke me because Tom hadn't spoken.

I looked over at him, and he nodded toward the cabin. "We're here."

Apart from a general understanding that we were somewhere in the Southern Sierra Nevadas, I had no idea where "here" was, nor did I know if it would be a one-night stop, a long-term prison, or the place I'd die.

Wherever we were, it was remote. It was too dark to know for sure, but it didn't appear as though there were any other structures nearby. We were surrounded on all sides by thick woods and dense low brush, and the road we'd come in on was seriously rugged.

I mentally berated myself for falling asleep. Having been unconscious during the last part of our journey, I had no idea if we were two miles or twenty miles from the nearest house or town. My instinct told me we were far from even the nearest paved road, but I couldn't be sure. I shook my head with regret. I should have stayed awake memorizing every twist and turn, but it was too late now.

Tom opened the door on his side of the car and got out. A moment later, he opened my door and used a pocket knife to cut the tape from my wrists. "Time to move," he said.

I hesitated.

"Come on, move," he said, this time more forcefully.

I got out and stood by the SUV in a state of subdued terror. Tom went around to the back, lifted the door, and pulled out a box. Then he handed it to me and gestured to the cabin.

"Go on over. I'm going to let you in. When you get inside, start unpacking. There's a big cupboard on the left side of the kitchen. Put everything in there." The box was filled with bags of rice, bread, peanut butter, and a variety of canned goods.

Struggling with the heavy load, I followed him to the cabin. Glancing back at the car, I could see it was stuffed with all kinds of food and supplies, including paper goods, gallon bottles of water, and at least one bag of fresh fruit and vegetables.

After Tom opened the door, he nudged me inside and switched on a light to reveal an interior that was surprisingly nice. I hadn't expected anything in particular, but if I had, I'd never have predicted what I was suddenly seeing. The cabin was not large, but it was well and comfortably furnished. With a stone fireplace and leather sofa, it was bizarrely reminiscent of my room at the Gallatin Valley hotel. I wondered if he'd brought me here in some sick effort to recreate our *"origin story."* The thought made me want to turn and run.

As if reading my mind, Tom said, "Take off your shoes."

"What do you mean? Why?"

"You know why," he said. "Take 'em off. And hurry up. I have a lot to unload."

Reluctantly, I handed them over.

"Now, go ahead and start unpacking," Tom said, urging me toward the kitchen. "I'll be right back."

Too nervous to do anything but obey, I stepped into a kitchen that was astonishingly modern and clean. I placed the box on a small wooden table surrounded by four matching chairs. The cabin itself was old, but as I looked around, I could see it had every convenience, including a microwave, electric stove, large refrigerator, and even what appeared to be a trash compactor. We might have been remote, but this was no rustic, bare-bones cabin. It was comfortable and well equipped, and Tom was now filling it with food, including meat that he began placing into the freezer part of the refrigerator.

"Come on, step it up," he said, noticing I was just standing by the table, not moving. He pointed to a floor-to-ceiling cupboard. "All the dry goods and canned stuff goes in there." His tone was almost genial.

I'd been trying not to think about what would happen once we arrived at our destination. Now, his change in demeanor seemed to suggest he expected us to resume where we'd left off in Bozeman. I wondered what kind of terrible scene would play out before the night was through.

I took some deep breaths and tried to choke back my fear. I needed to clear my head so I could think.

I pulled a bag of rice and a can of black beans from the box and began filling the cupboard. "Is this your place?"

"No questions tonight," he said. "Let's just put everything away so we can get some sleep. We'll have plenty of time to talk in the morning."

I liked the sound of "sleep" but wondered what he was thinking and what would happen in the morning. I was literally afraid to guess.

γ

When Tom had brought everything inside and it was all put away, he pointed to a set of wooden stairs. "There's a bed up there in the loft," he said. "That's where you'll sleep. I'll sleep down here on the couch."

The relief I felt at that moment is hard to overstate.

He nodded at a door to the right of the living room. "Bathroom's over there. Go ahead and brush your teeth or whatever. You should find everything you need—toothbrush, toothpaste, soap. Your bags are in there, too. Change into something to sleep in. And don't take too long. We need to get some rest."

When I'd brushed my teeth and changed into sweatpants and a t-shirt, Tom followed me up to the loft, which contained a double bed and lamp table on top of a large braided rug. I dreaded what might happen next. Tom had said he wanted to sleep, so why was he following me up the stairs?

"Get in," he said, nodding to the bed.

My heart pounding, I got in. I hated being so compliant, but I saw no other choice. Tom was well over six feet tall and outweighed me by probably sixty pounds.

As I lay down, he opened a small backpack over his shoulder and pulled out a pair of handcuffs connected by a long stainless-steel chain.

"Sorry to have to do this," he said, "but I need to make sure you don't try to leave. And, just so you know, as soon as I go back down, your shoes and my car key are going into a safe under the stairs. Eventually, these measures may not be necessary, but, for now, this is how it has to be."

He placed one of the handcuffs around my right wrist and the other around a heavy slat in the iron headboard of the bed. Then, almost like a father tucking in a child, he pulled a feather duvet over me and said goodnight. I was relieved that, for the moment, he was leaving me alone, but I noted his use of "eventually." He was thinking long-term.

After he went back down, I heard him washing up in the bathroom and moving around between the kitchen and living room. A few minutes later, he turned off the light and settled on the couch to sleep. I didn't hear him pull out a sofa bed, so I assumed he was curled up in a sleeping bag, which, given his size, couldn't have been comfortable. But, soon, I heard him begin to snore.

It was a long time before I was able to sleep. I had so many fears—not just for myself, but for my family. I lay awake for hours imagining all kinds of horrific scenarios. But, surprisingly, once I finally nodded off, I slept for the rest of the night, only waking when it was morning and I smelled coffee and heard water running in the bathroom.

When I first woke up, I experienced a brief disorientation, confused about where I was. Seconds later, reality hit me like a freight train. Today was the first day of...what? I didn't want to think about it. I wanted it all to be a bad dream.

Not anxious to face whatever lay in store, I stayed quiet, trying to reason out what to do. The only thing I could think of was to look for any opportunity to escape, or maybe try to talk Tom out of whatever this was. As to what it was, I couldn't help remembering Ted Bundy, who reportedly presented as both charming and sane. Was Tom like that? A serial killer? Would he keep me as a sex slave and then kill me? I worked myself into a panic of fear and dread, but the need to empty my bladder eventually forced me to call and ask to be freed of the handcuff.

Moments after I called, Tom appeared, but before he removed the cuff, he cautioned me with what sounded like a prepared speech.

"I'm going to take that off," he said, "and you'll be free to go down and do whatever you need to do to clean up. Then we can have some coffee, eat breakfast, and have a talk."

He pulled the key to the handcuff from his front pants pocket. "I know you're scared and probably have all kinds of ideas about what's going on here. But I'm not going to do anything terrible to you, so just get that out of your head."

"You're not going to do anything terrible to me?" I shouted, anger overtaking my fear. "Even if you let me go this second, you've completely destroyed my life!"

He looked me straight in the eye. "I understand what you're saying, but this here—now—*this* is not what you're thinking. So don't do anything rash or foolish. Give me a chance to talk to you. Can you do that?"

I glared at him and held up my wrist so he could unlock the cuff. I won't say I wasn't curious about what he planned to tell me, but one thing was clear: Despite what he might think about himself or want me to believe, a man with anything but sick intentions did not take a woman to a cabin in the middle of nowhere and chain her to a bed.

He removed the handcuff and stood over me for a few moments and just stared. When he finally turned to go back down the stairs, I threw a question after him. "Have you checked the news to see if there's anything about my husband?"

"There's no way to check the news from here," he said. "This place has no internet. But he's fine. If he'd been hit that bad, there would have been a lot more blood."

I started to counter that I wasn't so sure, but he shut me down.

"Put it out of your head," he ordered like a commanding officer. "We have other things to think about. For now, the outside world doesn't exist. It's just you and me."

CHAPTER THIRTEEN

WHILE I WAS IN the bathroom getting dressed and washing up, Tom cooked breakfast. I inspected the window as a possible means of escape, but it was the split type that only opens halfway from the top down. I peered out to see if I could spot any other cabins, but all I could see were dense woods.

It was cold, and I would have liked a hot shower, but there was no lock on the door, so I opted for what my daughter called a "sink shower," then brushed my teeth and ran a wide-toothed comb through my hair. By the time I got out, Tom had produced two plates of grilled ham, scrambled eggs, and toast. I was starving, so I immediately sat down and started eating. Moments later, Tom presented me with a cup of coffee.

"Do you take milk?" he asked. His voice was casual, like I was a customer and he was a friendly waiter.

"Black's fine," I mumbled, shoveling a large forkfull of eggs into my mouth. I hadn't eaten anything in almost twenty hours and was already wondering if there were more eggs. Tom sat down to my right and started eating himself, creating a scene that was surreal. To look at us from the outside, you'd think we were a couple on vacation, not a kidnapper and captive.

When I'd cleaned my plate, I sat back in my chair and looked at Tom expectantly. He took a last bite of ham, stood up, and took our plates to the sink.

"So, okay," I said after taking a breath for courage. "Are you going to tell me what all this is about?" Fear hit me like a hot wave, and I tried to steady my face as I awaited his response.

He turned around, pulled his wallet from his back pocket, and came back and stood next to me. Wearing a blue and green flannel shirt and cargo pants—and with just a hint of a beard—he reminded me, once again, of a guy you'd see on the cover of Field and Stream. He didn't look the part of a maniac.

He opened his wallet, pulled out the photo he'd shown me in Montana, and tossed it onto the table.

"That's your daughter. I saw this when we had dinner together," I said.

"You don't recognize her," he said. It was a statement, not a question, and he delivered it with smoldering anger.

"You obviously think I should, but I don't. Was she one of my students? Because I've had *thousands*, and most of my classes are in huge lecture halls. There's no way I'd recognize every student who'd ever sat in one of my classes."

He seemed to be processing this information, and there was pain in his eyes.

"Was she maybe a friend of one of my kids?"

"*Stop!*" Tom barked. "This isn't a guessing game. Her name was London."

Suddenly I had the smallest inkling of a memory. Not of the girl, but the name, because it was unusual. I also picked up on his use of the past tense. She was dead. I must have had some connection to her, but, for the moment, her name ringing a bell was all I had. I decided to keep the recollection to myself.

"I don't recognize her," I said. "But I get it that something terrible happened to her. I'm sorry."

I looked into his eyes with genuine sympathy, because now I understood that whatever was going on was connected to a magnitude of pain and grief that, even as a mother, I had a hard time imagining. "Can you tell me what happened?" I asked gingerly.

Fearing he would explode, I held my breath. I could see by the color darkening his face that he was struggling with strong feelings, but whether he was battling his temper or holding back tears, I couldn't say. I only knew he was in the grip of powerful emotions.

After a prolonged silence, he appeared to quell whatever storm was raging inside him. He was studying me like a puzzle.

I let out my breath.

He looked down at the picture, then seemed to become lost in thought. Again, I could see he was trying to tamp down feelings too big to hide.

After what seemed like a long time, he raised his head and looked me straight in the eye. "There's a lot to tell," he said. "I'm going to tell you, and then you're going to tell the world."

I was stunned. *"I'm going to tell the world?"*

In a spontaneous expression of relief and hope, I collapsed into tears. Despite his assurances, I'd been sure he was going to kill me—or, at the very least, hold me captive and torture me. Now, suddenly, I had an inkling there might be some other less terrible possibility. Bottled-up terror burst out of me in half-stifled sobs.

"I have to give you credit for giving me the idea," Tom said, ignoring my outburst. "Or not you, I guess, but the older lady sitting next to you at the writer's conference."

I couldn't have been more confused. *"What are you talking about?"*

"It was when you were discussing how hard it is for writers to find publishers these days. She commented that it's easy for famous people to get book deals."

I vaguely remembered the remark but was still bewildered. "I don't follow what you're saying. What's this big idea she gave you?"

"I'm going to make you famous."

∛

"You're going to make me famous," I repeated, the words not yet sinking in.

"Count on it," Tom said. "By the end of this week, you'll be one of the biggest stories in the country. It has all the elements—sex, violence, mystery. Everyone will know your name and be wondering what happened to you."

He paused with a look of satisfaction. "We don't know what your husband's condition is, or what the thinking is about your disappearance, but it doesn't matter. What matters is *you're gone,* and the mystery of your whereabouts will grow bigger every day."

"Everyone will think horrible things about me, including my kids!" I shouted. "You think that's the kind of famous I want?"

"It doesn't matter what you want. The only thing that matters is you'll be big news, and when you finally reappear, every publisher under the sun will want your story."

I shook my head in stupefied silence, understanding the logic of what he was saying, but not seeing what was in it for him. I didn't have to wonder long.

"You don't know it yet," he said, "but London is the heart of your story—is the *point* of your story. And you're going to write it right here." He nodded at the table, and the look on his face was dead serious.

What he was suggesting was ridiculous. I wasn't going to write a book with a gun to my head—chained up every night and my kids frantic with worry and thinking the worst of me. There was no way I would do it, or could do it even if I wanted to.

"And what about you?" I said. "I don't see how any of this happens without you going to prison—or worse if the police find us."

"You just let me worry about that. All you need to worry about is the writing." He reached down and picked up the photograph. "I'm going to give you a story that'll break your heart."

"I'm sorry about your daughter, but I can't possibly do what you're asking. Not here, at least. Let me go home. I'll write it from there. I promise."

"You'll do it here."

"Or what? You'll kill me? I don't think you're capable of that."

"*Believe it!*" he shot back. "I'm a fucking ghost with absolutely nothing left to lose. I'm capable of anything."

He looked at me with eyes like steel. "You *will* do as I say. And I know once you start thinking about it, you'll realize you have a lot to gain. It might be hard on you at first, but in the end, you'll get what you want. You'll be the belle of the fucking ball."

"I don't want to be the belle of the fucking ball! I'm thinking of my children!"

"I'm thinking of *my* child!" Tom bellowed. *My only child!*"

With his words scorching the air between us, he glared at me with a look so intense, I wondered if he really were capable of hurting me.

"Listen to me," he said in a low growl. "I'm not making a request. You'll do what I tell you, and I don't care who suffers for it."

With eyes blazing, he stomped into the living room, then out the front door of the cabin, leaving me trembling, confused, and more than a little frightened.

CHAPTER FOURTEEN

"THERE'S SOMETHING I DON'T understand," I said when Tom eventually rejoined me in the kitchen. "You said you got this idea from the panel discussion in Bozeman. If that's true, what were you doing there in the first place? I've been thinking about how we met and all the different weird elements, and I don't understand how everything fits together. It doesn't make any sense."

"It's not relevant," was his curt response.

He held a cardboard box he'd pulled from a narrow closet near the bathroom door. He set it on the table, reached in, and pulled out a small framed photograph, which he placed on the table in front of me. "*This* is all that's relevant."

The photo was London, only in this one, she was maybe five or six years old. She was dressed as a doctor, with a white coat, stethoscope, and toy doctor's bag gripped in her hand. Grinning in front of a twin bed lined with stuffed animals, she couldn't have looked sweeter.

I stared at the picture, then looked up at Tom, and I understood the pain in his eyes because I understood the fierce love inspired by that kind of innocence—by the miracle of one's own perfect child.

After holding my gaze for a moment, he moved the box to the floor, then stood the picture upright on the table where we could both see it. "We're going to get started. The sooner we do, the sooner you can get out of here."

He pulled a yellow pad and pencil from the box on the floor. "Take notes," he said, placing the items in front of me. The expression on his face was so sad that, despite everything, I felt for him.

I picked up the pencil.

He looked at the picture for several seconds, then back at me. "She spent almost three years in and out of the hospital before this was taken. She was diagnosed with childhood leukemia when she was four. *Acute lymphoblastic leukemia*, to be exact."

He slanted his gaze downward, then tightened his lips and paused to collect himself before continuing.

"It felt like thirty years to us—my wife and me. It was an endless, gut-wrenching fucking nightmare, with I don't know how many hospital stays, chemotherapy, blood transfusions, bone marrow transplants, opportunistic infections she picked up because the chemo wiped out her immune system—fucking pneumonia..."

He stopped and took a breath. "She teetered at the precipice of death *for years*, and all the time, we were terrified that after everything we put her through, she'd die anyway. But she didn't die. Despite everything she went through—all the probing and prodding and sickness and surgeries, all the times she was too weak to raise her head, the times she spent Christmas in a hospital bed and missed out on birthday parties, and playing outdoors, and practically everything else that makes a normal childhood special and magical. Despite *all of it,* she was courageous and good-natured. And she was *so* much stronger than I was, or my wife was. She helped *us* through it. *Can you imagine that?* There were times we didn't know if she'd live or die, and she helped *us* get through it."

He stood up, went to the sink, and blew his nose. After a few moments of regrouping, he returned and sat back down.

"She was incredible," he continued, his voice weighted with anguish. "And she adored the doctors and nurses who took care of her. To her—to all of us, really—they were like angels. And they saved her. They did it, and gave all of us back our lives.

"When she finally let herself believe she had a future—and, *believe me,* even at four, she understood she might not—she started talking about how when she grew up, she was going be a doctor. She wanted to cure little boys and girls just like they had cured her."

He nodded at the picture. "I remember that like it was yesterday. It was the first Christmas she spent at home in two years. She got that little coat and doctor kit from the doctors and nurses at the hospital."

He picked up the picture and studied it, then passed it to me. "That's my little girl. That's London. She grew up to be a healthy young college student with her whole life ahead of her. And her essence never changed. That sweet little girl you see there, she never changed."

I stared at the photo in my hands.

"Then you and your fucking university killed her," he said.

Feeling like I'd been punched in the gut, I looked up to see Tom glaring at me as though I, personally, had killed his daughter.

"What do you mean the university and I killed her? What are you talking about?"

He leaned over, pulled a small cloth-bound book from the box, then sat up and dropped it on the table. "This is her diary. This will tell you, in her own words, what she experienced as a freshman at your illustrious university."

With my face turning hot, I stared at the book in front of me.

"Go ahead and pick it up," Tom said. "Her writing is meticulous. You won't have any trouble reading it. There are more you can read later, but you need to see this one first."

I reached for the diary—its fabric cover a design of purple violets—then opened it and thumbed through the middle. Tom hadn't exaggerated. The pages were filled with tiny, perfectly rendered printed letters. It was the most immaculate handwriting I'd ever seen.

"She's been keeping a diary for as long as I can remember," Tom said. "I never read any of them until after she died. Reading them now feels like a betrayal. I have a stack of these about three feet high. Most of them I haven't read."

He gestured to the book in my hand. "That one I *have.* That's the most recent." His lips trembled, and his eyes were wet. "That tells the story. And you're in there."

With a sick feeling in my stomach, I glanced down at the small book and wondered what on earth I would find. I flipped to a place near the end, but Tom stopped me.

"No," he said, pulling the diary from my hand. "Not that way. Start from the beginning. And start *right now*."

He stood up, pulled out my chair, and ushered me to the living room sofa.

I sat down, and he handed me the diary. "Read," he said. "Tomorrow, you start writing."

β

I did start at the beginning, and it was immediately apparent that London had started a brand-new diary for her brand-new life as a college freshman. The first page was a vivid description of the exciting day that virtually everyone who's gone away to college has experienced. The day she moved all her things into her dorm room and finally embarked on the academic journey she'd been dreaming of for years. Unfortunately, that first thrilling day she spent fixing up her half of the room and meeting her roommate was followed by others in which the reality of life on campus did not measure up to the dream. In the end, disappointment met catastrophe, and what had felt like a broken promise turned into a full-blown horror story.

By the time the sun set on the excruciating afternoon I spent reading London's diary, I understood why Tom believed that both the university and I had played a role in London's death. We were far from the guiltiest parties, but the story that unfolded in London's own hand had so many elements that were familiar, it was hard to argue we were completely innocent.

CHAPTER FIFTEEN

TOM HAD WATCHED ME read, circling the dim interior of the cabin like a shark. When I finally set the diary down and rubbed my eyes, he stopped in his tracks.

I knew he was waiting for me to say something, but I had no words. I tried to conjure something—some response that would describe the depth of my feelings about what I'd just read—but nothing came, so I just sat mute. With him staring at me in silence, I stifled the urge to cry.

"I don't know what to say," I said finally. "I can't even imagine..."

I leaned back and stared at the small book, and while it filled me with grief and horror, it also raised questions I was afraid to ask. Like what had happened to her after her last entry?

I raised my eyes to Tom. "Have you shown this to the police?"

"The police are *useless*. So is the fucking university."

"What about the press? Have you talked to any journalists?"

"I'm talking to *you*," he spat. "*You're* going to write this story, and it's not going to be some fucking article in a newspaper that'll be forgotten in a week. I want a book."

Feeling the heat of Tom's gaze, I had to stop myself from shaking my head. "What I just read is horrific," I said. "I don't know what to say. But what you're asking..."

"You'll do it," he commanded.

He walked to the fireplace and began pulling logs and kindling from a large basket on the hearth, reminding me eerily of the first time I'd watched him build a fire.

"Take the rest of the day to think about it," he said. "Tomorrow, you start writing."

For the next few hours, I stared into the fire, my head swirling with horrible images from the diary and worries about Steven and my kids. For the first time ever, I was grateful my parents were no longer alive, and that I was an only child. It was terrible imagining what was being said about me in the news. On top of everything, I was afraid a SWAT team might burst through the door any minute and start shooting.

By the time Tom and I sat down to eat a simple dinner, I was in a pretty confused and fragile state.

"I hope you were getting your head straight in there," Tom said, nodding to the living room. "I know you can do this. You just need to set your mind to it."

His tone was almost light, sounding more like the Tom I'd met in Montana. It was hard not to think of him this way—as two completely separate people. I didn't want to summon "The Bad Tom," so I was hesitant to answer.

I stared at my plate and tried to tamp down my fear.

"You need to pull yourself together," Tom said. "The sooner you do, the sooner we can get out of here."

I forced myself to sit up straight and look him in the eye. "I don't know how you expect me to do what you're asking. I'll have to fictionalize almost all of it. I'll have to make up the dialog—most of the characters..."

"There's *a lot* you won't have to make up," Tom said, his temper flaring. "It's all there. You can invent the dialog. Use your imagination. But use it to tell the fucking truth. Isn't that what writers do?"

"Look, I understand you're in pain, but..."

"*No buts!*" he shouted. "*And no excuses.* You're writing this book."

I sat shaking my head.

"You want to get out of here?" he said.

"What do you think?"

"Then cooperate."

"Can we at least check the news?" I practically yelled.

"Not yet," he said. "For now, we need to lay low."

I thought about my phone and wondered if the police had found it and listened to the recording.

"You know they'll probably kill you if the police find us. Is that what you want? Is that what you think London would want?"

"*Fuck you,*" Tom shouted. "Everything *London* wanted is history."

CB

Later, in the living room, I stared into the fire, which was now a glowing pile of embers. Tom was in the kitchen, seeming to want space to cool off. When he eventually came in to build the fire back up, I became uneasy about how similar the scene was to our night in the hotel. I couldn't imagine he wasn't struck by the same thought.

I stood up and started for the bathroom. "I need to try to get some sleep."

"I'm going to have to put the handcuff back on once you get upstairs," Tom said. "It's a safeguard for you, too."

I stopped and turned around. "What do you mean *for me too*?"

"Think about it," he said. "When I eventually let you go, don't you think you'll be better off if you can honestly say you were my captive?"

"*I am your captive!*"

"I agree, and I need to treat you like one. That's all I'm saying."

I considered what he was suggesting. "You think I'll be accused of staging this whole thing to sell a fucking book?"

"I don't know what you might be accused of, but I intend to ensure no lines get blurred."

I scoffed at the absurd notion he was protecting me. "That's ridiculous," I said, but I left it there. I had no desire to argue with him. I just wanted to get away.

̓̓

Tethered in the loft, I had a hard time putting my thoughts in order. Everything had changed so dramatically from the previous night; it was hard to process it all. Now, instead of anticipating serial rape and murder, I was looking at something very different. With London's voice still ringing in my head, it was a lot to assimilate as I struggled—for hours—to come up with some kind of plan. Some way out.

I'm reluctant to admit it, but once I let myself seriously think about the book, my resistance began to flag. I knew my family would be put through hell, and there was no way of knowing what unexpected, possibly horrible things might happen over the next few days or weeks. But in theory, at least, I agreed with Tom's premise. When everything was over, I'd be all but guaranteed a book deal. Probably a huge one.

The more I thought about it, the more I realized that a book blending London's story into my own could be good. Maybe even important. And I knew how to write it, starting with my first encounter with Tom at the hotel.

But what would it cost my family? On top of the grief and trauma my disappearance was inflicting on my kids, describing my part of the story—not to mention Steven's—would mean revealing details painful and embarrassing to us all. It was a high price to pay.

I went around and around, but, in the end, I decided to do what Tom wanted. What other choice did I really have?

CHAPTER SIXTEEN

IT WAS SEVEN O'CLOCK on a Wednesday evening, and London, who was by far the most studious freshman on the third floor, was sitting on her twin bed, knees up, with her nose in a biology book. She took constant flak for her devotion to studying, but what her roommate and others in her dorm didn't understand was she was pre-med, and that meant her priority had to be her grades and not partying, which appeared to be the sole interest of most of the first-year students she knew.

All of them, like her, had practically killed themselves in high school—taking rigorous AP courses and juggling their studies with team sports, academic club memberships, community service, SAT prep, and all the other activities that, these days, were necessary for acceptance to top universities. It was exhausting, so it wasn't surprising that so many were ready to embrace the "party hearty" philosophy that had become such an accepted part of the college experience. What did surprise London was the extent of it, and the hard-core nature of some of it.

"Work hard, play hard" was a popular credo, but, so far, she'd seen very little *work hard*—although the first semester finals week in her dormitory had been a chaos of all-nighters, cramming, amphetamine bingeing, and a general atmosphere of unadulterated panic. London had kept up in all of her classes, so she wasn't part of the bedlam, although a girl on her floor had come to her the night before her hardest final and threatened suicide, so she'd taken the test for that class on less than two hours of sleep.

London assumed that most everyone would throttle down and start hitting the books eventually, but, for the moment, heavy drinking and hard partying were still in high gear. As for London, she was focused on a three-point plan she'd been visualizing since she was six: Get an excellent undergraduate education, attend Stanford or Harvard Medical School, then embark on a career as a pediatric oncologist.

She couldn't remember ever not wanting to be a nurse or doctor. She was diagnosed with childhood leukemia at the age of four and had spent the better part of the next three years in the hospital, so it wasn't surprising she wanted to grow up and emulate the people who'd cared for her so tenderly. She'd initially focused on nursing, but her parents encouraged her to aim high, so at the ripe old age of six, she'd set her sights on becoming an oncologist, and they'd remained there ever since.

Nothing was going to keep her from reaching that goal, but the environment in which she was now immersed made it hard. So hard that most evenings, she'd been forced to walk clear across campus to study at the library because her room, and most rooms in her dormitory, were competing for the label of *party central*. London's roommate was one of the hardest partiers, frequently reporting, with a twisted pride, that she'd gotten "black-out drunk."

A shocking number of students appeared determined to break the record for most times inebriated to the point of insensibility. And they weren't just drinking hard liquor. They were taking drugs and smoking prodigious amounts of marijuana. All of this would have been bad enough, but London's roommate and others on her floor seemed hell-bent on forcing London down the same road. London wrote this:

> I'm sick of being badgered constantly for being so "straight." Riley and the others never let up trying to make me drink or smoke. But what's it to them? I keep telling them I'm not interested, but they refuse to back off. Last Sunday, Riley gave me a brownie containing weed without telling me. I should have known better than to eat anything from her, but I never thought she'd stoop that low. She knew I was in the middle of writing a paper due on Monday. She thought it was hilarious, but it was not funny spending the next five hours unable to do anything but lie on my bed. I can't even believe the way I used to picture college. What a joke. So far, the most interesting discussion I've had outside of class was with the homeless guy who hangs out by Starbucks.

> The homeless situation around here, that's a whole other thing. Yesterday I saw an old blind guy camped out in a covered bus stop who looked so sad that I bought him a sandwich and coffee. You would have thought I gave him a million dollars the way he thanked me, but I felt horrible not doing more. There are a shocking number of homeless people on the streets around campus, and all of them are sad, but being blind and homeless? That one killed me. All of them do, really. I honestly don't understand why there isn't more help for people. It's heartbreaking.

On the brighter side, Riley has a boyfriend now, so she's been spending a lot of time at his fraternity house, thank God. (She would go for a frat guy.) She stays overnight sometimes on the weekends, and most weeknights she's gone until late, so I can finally study in my own room. What a concept. I still have to wear the noise-canceling headphones Mom sent me, but it's much better than having to go to the library. Walking back by myself at night is scary.

London was wearing those headphones with her biology book open across her knees when she became aware of knocking at her door.

"Come in," she called, figuring it was probably someone looking for Riley.

The door opened, and a tall student she'd never seen before appeared, then took a few cautious steps in her direction. "Are you London?" he asked, narrowing his eyes under a disarray of curly hair.

"Yeah, hi," London said, pulling off the headphones. "Are you looking for Riley?"

A smile widened across his face. "No. You, actually. I hear you're taking Literature and Justice, and I wanted to see if I could maybe see your notes from today."

"Sure," London said, wondering how she'd never noticed him in the lecture hall. He was handsome, with olive skin and dark eyes. And he was taking Literature and Justice, which meant he might be interesting. "Do you live in this dorm?" she asked, her antennas raised.

"No, but I have a friend who knows your roommate, and she mentioned you might have notes I can borrow."

London wondered if he was in Riley's boyfriend's fraternity. She hoped not.

"I'm Jason, by the way," he said. "Nice to meet you."

"Nice to meet you, too," London said, and thus began the first night London and Jason stayed up late studying together.

CHAPTER SEVENTEEN

IT WAS NEARING THE end of the semester, and London and Jason had become regular study buddies, now with a weekly routine that London spent the rest of the week looking forward to. In addition to meeting once a week in her room, they also sat together in lectures on Mondays and Wednesdays, London being the designated note-taker. Jason, who was a weekend partier, was sometimes a no-show on Mondays, but London was inclined to overlook his imperfections.

At times she wished they could be more than friends. She liked his quiet intelligence and sense of humor, and he had a worldliness that reminded her of her father. He was also good-looking in a disheveled kind of way.

London wrote the following in her diary:

This place is getting to me. I need to make more of an effort to make friends outside the dorm so that next year I can move into an apartment and have decent roommates. At this point, Jason is probably my best friend. I like him, although I wish he wasn't in a fraternity. He claims he only joined because his father forced him to, so I guess I shouldn't hold it against him. He's definitely interesting. His mother's from Guatemala and his dad's Canadian, so he's spent a lot of time in both Guatemala and Canada. He also lived in Spain for a summer and took a gap year to travel around Europe, so he knows a lot more about the planet than most people our age. I guess he reminds me of Dad in that way. He's been making it pretty clear lately that he's attracted to me, and I'm starting to feel the same way, but he has a girlfriend back in his hometown who texts him about every two seconds, so I'm not sure what will happen. We'll see, I guess.

With their Literature and Justice midterm behind them and now only a final paper to complete, London and Jason were in London's room where, as always, he copied her notes, and then the two of them discussed the material and read together.

Around ten o'clock, Jason, who was stretched out on Riley's bed, yawned, then closed his book with a sharp crack, prompting London to look over with a questioning smile.

"There's a party at the house tomorrow night," he said. "You should come."

London gave him a look.

"I know you don't like the frats, but a lot of the guys are good people, and this party will be excellent. It's a birthday party, and the guy's parents are paying for live music and catered food. I saw the menu. The food's going to be great. If nothing else, you should come for the food."

He paused to flash a smile. "Seriously. It'll be the best party of the year."

London was skeptical but tempted to give in. It was the first time he'd invited her to do anything outside of studying.

"Come on," Jason said. "What's the worst that can happen?"

"I don't know..."

"If you aren't having a good time, you can eat and run. I'll even personally walk you home." He raised his eyebrows. "Just say yes. You can be my date."

At this, London's heart did a little dance. She wasn't sure it would be an actual date, but still...

"I'll think about it," she said. But even as she was saying the words, she knew she'd probably go. *What the heck,* she thought. *At the very least, I'll get to eat something besides dorm food.*

CHAPTER EIGHTEEN

ON MY FIRST DAY of writing, I was surprised that Tom had spent so little time looking over my shoulder. It was a relief. After he presented me with a laptop all booted up and ready to go, I expected him to stand behind me like a prison guard, wanting to approve every sentence. But he didn't. He did mill around and occasionally glance at the text I was working on, but under the circumstances, I considered his behavior restrained. He mostly puttered in the kitchen or sat reading in the living room. At one point, he went outside, and I heard him chopping wood.

Despite my decision to cooperate, I had a hard time starting. With so many fears, it was tough to focus. But as the afternoon progressed, sentences began to flow, and I managed to put myself into the mental state my kids called "the zone." In this state, practically anything could be happening around me, and I'd remain wholly immersed in what I was writing.

Tom was arranging wood in the fireplace when I decided to call it a day. I stood and stretched.

Noticing the movement, Tom looked over and nodded at the laptop, now closed on the table. "Finished for the day?"

I nodded.

While I rotated my aching neck and shoulders, he struck a match and lit the fire. "How'd it go?" he asked.

"I think I got a decent start," I said. It was true, but my words were freighted with anger. Now out of the zone and back in the present, my mood was dark.

"Good," Tom said, ignoring my tone. "Have a seat by the fire. I'm going to get started on dinner."

I was surprised by how relaxed he seemed. The way he sounded, you'd never know he was capable of all the terrible things he'd done. Our experience in Montana had set a congenial stage, and he seemed inclined to fall back into that rhythm—the non-sexual part, anyway. (To my great relief, I hadn't seen any indication he was interested in more sex. I prayed this wouldn't change.) It was obviously better for me that he wasn't hostile, but the situation was panning out to be extremely odd, and confusing.

I know it will be hard for some people to understand how quickly I rolled over and caved to Tom's demands. I suppose I could have bashed him over the head with a skillet or made a barefoot run for it when his back was turned. I could also have refused to write, or maybe refused to eat. But none of that seemed plausible. My instinct told me my best strategy was to cooperate, write as fast as possible, and keep trying to convince Tom to let me finish the book from home. But it wasn't easy. It was awkward and scary. And Tom was unpredictable.

○ॐ

During dinner, I decided to take a risk and introduce a topic we'd strangely avoided up to that point. I was nervous bringing it up, but Tom seemed to be on a steady keel, so I held my breath and took the plunge, hoping for the best.

"You don't ever talk about your ex-wife," I said. "I hope you don't mind me asking, but how is she doing?"

The question seemed to take him by surprise, although I don't know why it should have. It was an obvious thing to wonder. He didn't respond for several seconds, and I braced myself for an outburst. It didn't come. But neither did he answer my question.

"It's not an unreasonable thing to ask," he said finally. "You'll eventually need to know, but I don't want to talk about it now."

He stopped there, and I wasn't going to argue with him, but I did wonder about London's mother. Apart from a few tidbits I'd picked up in the diary, I knew nothing about her. She was undoubtedly devastated by what happened to her daughter, but I had no idea how long she and Tom had been divorced, if she had any other children, or anything, really, apart from learning from the diary that she liked to ski. (One of London's entries described skiing with her at Mammoth around Christmas time.)

After a couple of minutes, Tom broke the silence.

"I compartmentalize," he said. "When I don't want to think about something, I just wall it off and keep it separate. It's not the best thing, I guess, but it's a strategy that's helped me live through some tough times."

He picked up a glass of bourbon he'd poured for himself and took a drink. I prayed he'd stick to the one and not get drunk.

Placing the glass back on the table, he looked at me and frowned. "I have my ex-wife pretty walled off at the moment, but I will tell you this: *I failed her.*"

He shook his head, and his eyes beamed regret. "I failed both of them."

"London mentions you in her diary, and there's no indication of negative feelings toward you at all," I said. "Quite the contrary."

I figured being sympathetic wouldn't hurt. And it was true. London spoke of him only lovingly.

"You're probably being too hard on yourself," I added. "Lots of people get divorced these days. It's practically the norm."

"It's not just the divorce. Because of my work, I was almost never around, and when I was, I tried to make up for it with gifts and money—even with my wife, and she didn't deserve that. She deserved an equal co-parent."

He took a drink of the bourbon. "She and London both wanted another child, but I wouldn't agree. I was too selfish and self-important to care about what they wanted. By the time I realized what a mistake I'd made, it was too late."

I was struck by Tom's honesty. I supposed it was the alcohol.

We finished eating in silence, and my thoughts turned to my own considerable problems. Eventually, I had the impulse to tell him something I'd been thinking about, but I hesitated. The last thing I wanted was to endanger anyone else.

I took a deep breath and decided to proceed, hoping it wasn't the wrong choice.

"There's something I want you to know," I said.

He looked at me, his expression saying he was listening.

"It's true that London took a course from me, but I taught that course in an auditorium. That's why I didn't recognize her picture when you showed it to me. There were over three hundred students in that class, and the sections were conducted by TAs."

Tom stared back at me like he didn't understand my point.

"The TAs did all the testing and grading," I said. "I was just the lecturer."

Tom sat frozen, and I wondered if I'd made a mistake—if I'd lit a match where gas might be present. I was braced for an explosive reaction, but he sat silent, as though he were uncertain how to feel, or even if he believed me.

After what seemed like forever but was probably less than a minute, he stood up and took our empty plates to the sink. A moment later, he spun around to face me.

"When the time comes," he said, "tell it to Oprah."

CHAPTER NINETEEN

SATURDAY MORNING AROUND ELEVEN, London was reading in bed when she heard Riley's key in the door. She'd spent the night out, and it was apparent as soon as she stepped into the room that she was hung over.

"Hey," was all she said before immediately flopping onto her bed and falling asleep. London was accustomed to seeing Riley in this condition, especially after a Friday or Saturday night, but this morning she looked especially haggard.

London was worried about her. Her grades the previous semester had been terrible—mostly Ds—and there was no evidence to suggest this semester would be any different. Riley seemed perfectly content to trade the chance for a top-shelf education for the constant pursuit of inebriation. It was both hard to understand and painful to watch. London knew Riley's parents were worried about her, too. She'd overheard multiple arguments over the phone. But Riley didn't seem to care. She'd just roll her eyes and roll another joint.

With her roommate passed out next to her, London tried to concentrate on biology, but soon Riley began moaning, and London became nervous. Just as she was wondering if she should do something, Riley lurched and threw up. Then she continued throwing up until there was nothing left in her stomach to expel—at which point she began dry heaving, her face red and distorted with agony.

Alarmed and frightened, London ran to the door and called into the hallway. *"Help, someone! Can someone please come help me with Riley!"*

Not waiting for a response, she hurried back to where Riley was now writhing and groaning, her face, hair, and clothes a sickening mess of chunky pink vomit.

Holding her breath against the caustic smell that threatened the contents of her own stomach, London was resigned to becoming a stinking mess herself. It wasn't the first time she'd had to deal with someone drunk to the point of being sick, but this was the worst she'd seen, and it was her first time with Riley.

Looking around in a panic, she pulled the top sheet from her bed and placed it around Riley, hoping to get her to her feet and lead her to the bathroom down the hall. All she could think to do was put her in the shower, clean her up, and try to bring her to her senses.

"Can I get some help in here!" London called again, struggling to sit Riley up. Finally, two girls arrived on the scene—sophomores named Rachael and Malia.

"Ewwww, she stinks," Rachael cried.

"I'll help you," said Malia. "Are you trying to take her to the shower?"

"Yes," London said, straining to hold a barely conscious Riley, whose head was now lolling like a rag doll.

She turned to Rachael. "Can you at least get her a towel and some clean clothes?" She nodded at the closet and dresser on Riley's side of the room. "Her stuff's over there."

Rachael agreed but made a big show of plugging her nose and looking disgusted.

Soon several other girls were standing in the hallway looking in through the open door as London and Malia pulled Riley to her feet. She was shaky but eventually managed to stand up and, with support, shuffle to the bathroom past a line of girls who gawked and made faces as they went.

Once they made it to the bathroom, London and Malia helped Riley into the shower—first fully clothed because they wanted to rinse the vomit from her clothes before stripping them off.

"I don't feel good," Riley mumbled as the spray slowly rid her hair of morsels of food and pink goo.

"I know," London said. "But we'll get you cleaned up, and you'll feel better soon."

London was in the shower, too, helping Riley stand and needing some rinsing herself. Malia was just outside the curtain, ready to assist if needed.

Eventually, London and Malia removed Riley's clothes, which was no easy feat. Her shirt was simple enough, but her pants clung stubbornly to her legs, so they had to sit her down to pull them off. Once they had her stripped, London soaped her up and shampooed her hair. Twice.

When Riley was finally clean and rid of the smell, London and Malia stood her up, dried her off, and dressed her in clothes Rachael had heroically delivered before beating a hasty retreat. Afterwards, they walked her back and laid her down on London's bed.

When London was dried off and changed, she was exhausted but now faced the daunting task of dealing with Riley's soiled and stinking sheets and blankets.

As Riley slept peacefully in London's bed, London held her breath and took her bedclothes back to the shower and rinsed them before putting them, along with Riley's clothes, into a washer on the first floor. Her pillow was beyond redemption. That went into a dumpster behind the building.

London's biggest dilemma was what to do about Riley's mattress. Most of the vomit had remained on her sheets and blankets, but there was a spot on the mattress that would stink to high heaven if it wasn't cleaned. London felt like burning it, but since that wasn't an option, she went out and bought cleaning supplies, including dishwashing detergent, bleach, rubber gloves, Febreze (which billed itself as an odor remover), and a box of baking soda.

By the time London had made their room livable again, it was three-thirty, and she was so far beyond exhausted she could barely think. Riley, who'd remained oblivious through it all, was asleep in London's bed, her face turned to the wall.

Sitting at her desk, London was thinking about zapping the mattress one more time with the Febreze when Malia appeared in the open doorway. "Looks like you mostly got the smell out," she said. "I'm shocked. I didn't think it would be possible."

London smiled wearily. "It wasn't easy. It's taken me all afternoon."

Malia made a face in sympathy. "I'm sorry I bailed on you. I had plans with my boyfriend."

"It's okay," London said. "You helped a lot."

"How's she doing?" Malia asked, nodding at Riley.

"She's been in and out of it for most of the day, but she'll live."

Malia stared at the heap in London's bed and shook her head. "She's a hard case," she said, lowering her voice to a whisper.

"I don't understand her," London said. "She has an opportunity other people would die for, and she's totally blowing it."

"It's kind of shocking how many people are doing the same thing," Malia said. "At least two people on this floor will probably flunk out after this semester."

Riley moaned and turned over, then raised her head and squinted her eyes. "What time is it?" Her voice was weak and scratchy, and she looked like she'd been dragged to hell and back.

"It's three-thirty," London said.

Riley yawned, then laid her head back down. "Can you wake me up around six? There's a party at Kevin's frat house tonight, and I don't want to miss it."

CHAPTER TWENTY

BY THE MIDDLE OF my second week of writing, I'd pretty much made peace with what felt like complicity—or, at the very least, cowardice—where my captivity was concerned. I experienced bouts of guilt and remorse but largely accepted that the die was cast. Tom mostly left me alone, preferring to keep to himself. I sometimes wondered where he retreated to when he sat alone, with no book or task to attend to. Wherever he was, it was obvious a lot was happening inside of him.

I became fairly good at divining his moods, even when he wasn't speaking to me. I could tell by the quality of his breathing, the sound of his footfalls, and the manner in which he handled objects and closed doors that storms sometimes raged inside of him. At those times, I gave him as wide a berth as you can give in a five-hundred-square-foot space. Fortunately, he mostly kept the storms to himself. I presumed it was in the interest of the book. He wanted to keep me writing.

The weather had gotten colder, so he kept a fire going around the clock. Days blended together, and life became surreal, for lack of a better word. Under other circumstances, this would have been a fair approximation of my dream life: living in a cozy cabin in the mountains with nothing to do but write, with a man waiting on me hand and foot.

If not for the grief I was inflicting on my family, I might have been amused by the absurdity of the situation. Tom still had my shoes, and I expected to be chained to my bed every night. But, in all honesty, I didn't think much about getting away as the days turned into weeks. I was focused entirely on writing. When I did think about home, I couldn't help but fear what was waiting for me. For all I knew, I'd be arrested for murder. At the very least, I'd face a host of difficult and embarrassing questions. When it did eventually happen, I knew I'd be better off if I had a manuscript to sell, so I was doing my damndest to produce the best book I could.

"How's it coming?" Tom asked as I closed the laptop at the end of a long day. I was at the kitchen table, and he was in the living room, fooling with the fire.

"Pretty good," I said. "Today I wrote about London's roommate getting sick and her having to clean it up."

I made a face and shook my head in disgust. "I held the hair for a friend or two when I was in college, but I never experienced anything like that."

"If I'd had any idea, I would have yanked her out of that fucking dorm so fast," Tom said. "It's *ridiculous* what they let go on in college these days."

His temper flared hotter than the fire, and I felt a surge of guilt. It was no secret that student drinking and drug use were on the rise at the university—probably most universities—but it was mostly swept under the rug. I was as guilty as anyone of looking the other way.

Tom poked the fire hard, creating a spray of sparks that reminded me it was best to avoid subjects that aroused his anger. "We didn't pay enough attention. If I'd known half of what I know now..."

I braced myself for more, but he stood up and headed for the door, choosing to vent his rage by chopping more wood.

଼

That night after dinner, I was sitting on the sofa, hypnotized by the fire, when Tom gave me three diaries from London's high school years.

He settled into the chair by the fireplace. "I haven't read much of those," he said. "I've paged through them, but that's about it. I'm sure you'll find some of it useful."

"Did she ever have a boyfriend in high school?"

Tom thought for a moment. "I know she went to a couple of proms and dated a boy or two, but I don't think she ever had a serious boyfriend. My impression is she was picky."

As I nodded, the expression on his face changed. "You're probably wondering if she was a virgin." He turned his gaze to the diaries in my hand. "The answer may be in there, but I don't know."

"I wasn't thinking about that specifically, but do you want me to tell you if I find out?"

He considered the question. "Probably not. It's not the kind of thing a father really wants to know, I guess."

He pursed his lips, and his eyes glistened in the firelight. "It's still hard to think about her without falling apart." He crimped his forehead in a way he did when he was upset. "Maybe don't tell me anything for now. Just read those and write whatever you think is appropriate."

He stood up and headed for the kitchen. "I'm going to pour myself a drink," he said. "Want one?"

"No thanks," I said.

He returned and finished his drink in a few gulps, then got up and poured himself another one. I'd hoped he'd stop at two, but this time he brought the bottle back with him.

I had London's diaries in my lap but hadn't opened them. The light was too poor, and I wanted to read them when I was alone. I planned to take a look once I was back upstairs for the night.

After a long silence, I spoke up with a question that had been bothering me, hoping the bourbon might loosen Tom's tongue.

"Are you ever going to solve the mystery of why you were originally at the lodge? If you had the book idea after seeing me on the panel, what was your original plan? Why were you there?"

He filled his glass again. I held my breath, unhappy about his drinking but hoping he'd answer the question.

He stared at me, as if deciding. "I had it in my mind to show up at your conference and embarrass you," he said. "I was going to stand up and confront you."

I thought for a moment and was confused. "But how did you know about the conference? And what was in your head when you invited me to dinner that first night?"

"I wanted to size you up."

"You weren't trying to seduce me?"

"I only thought of that later."

I was dubious. "I don't know if I believe you."

"I don't care if you believe me or not," he said, the alcohol apparent in his voice. "What possible difference could it make to me? You asked, and now you have your answer."

He gave me a stern look. "No more questions."

I didn't respond. I simply stood up and got ready to head upstairs, anxious to both get away from Tom and dive into London's diaries.

◌

Cuffing me in the loft for the night, Tom nodded at the diaries on the table next to me. "If you read anything interesting, maybe let me know."

"I will," I said.

He started to leave, then turned around at the top of the stairs. "You probably think it's strange I haven't read them myself." He tilted his head, strong feelings simmering beneath a veneer cracking due to the whisky.

He exhaled a potent breath. "It still feels like an invasion of privacy, I guess." He sounded like he might cry. "I can't tell you how much I loved that girl. We didn't spend as much time together as I'd have liked, but she was everything to me. *Everything*."

"I'm sorry. I wish there were something I could say..."

His eyes filled with tears. "Just write about her. And do more than tell a fucking horror story. Show her goodness. Show how special she was. *Do her justice*."

123

"It would be a lot easier if I weren't so worried about my own family," I said impulsively. "Why not let me go home and finish? You *know* I'll finish it."

My heart thumped in my chest. I knew it was a risky moment to make him mad.

"It's not that simple," he said. "We need more time. You're not a big enough story yet."

"How can you possibly know that?"

"I just know," he said. "Accept it and let it go."

He turned and disappeared down the stairs, but I didn't want to let it go. "Can you at least find out what the news is saying? It might be nice to know if my husband is dead or alive."

"Let it go," he shouted back.

Deflated but relieved he hadn't gone sideways, I picked up one of the diaries and opened it to the first page.

It was a while before my heart slowed enough to concentrate, but soon everything but London faded into the background, and I entered the mind of a teenager whose writing and thinking were extraordinary. Having graded thousands of college essays, I was in a position to judge.

☙

Since I'd already read one of London's diaries, I expected a high level of writing, but what I found in her high school diaries was still a surprise. A lot of her entries were less personal than what she'd written in her latest. Many had to do with problems that concerned her, like homelessness and climate change. There was one on the need for universal health care that was as good as any editorial I'd read in a newspaper. She was a deep and compassionate thinker, with a breadth of knowledge far surpassing what I'd expect from a high school student, even an exceptionally bright one, making what happened to her seem even more tragic.

Mentions of Tom were mostly incidental, but I learned he'd had a career in the Army, which I hadn't known. It fit, though. I could picture him in the military. She also joked about him being in the CIA—although I wasn't sure she was joking. With all of his international travel, that kind of fit, too.

When she wrote about herself, it was also impressive, revealing a level of sophistication that was unusual, even for an only child. One of her entries recounted arguing with a teacher during a class discussion on the Second Amendment. (Someone recorded the altercation and posted it on YouTube.) Another described an intervention she organized for a friend who was abusing cocaine. Drugs were apparently a problem at her school. She wrote the following crushing pages on a student who'd overdosed on fentanyl:

> Today is one of the saddest days of my life. Over the weekend, Nathan Peterson, one of the nicest guys I've ever known, was found dead in his room from an overdose of fentanyl. His brother Cameron found him. Everyone is in complete shock because he wasn't a druggie at all. He was an athlete and one of the best students in the whole school. Just a week ago, it was announced in assembly that he'd gotten a track scholarship to Princeton. It's so terrible, and it doesn't make any sense. It definitely wasn't a suicide. He was a totally happy, well-adjusted

guy with everything to live for. All anyone can think is that he somehow took it by mistake. Ecstasy has been going around. Maybe that's what he thought he was taking. But even ecstasy is out of character. I guess you never know. But I feel so terrible for his parents, and poor Cameron. Nathan was his only brother. His big brother.

 According to what I've heard, his whole family is so devastated, they don't want to talk to anyone. The school sent out a bulletin asking everyone to give them privacy while they grieve. I told Mom today, and she went crazy. One of her oldest friends lost a son to fentanyl a few months ago, and she knows another family who lost a daughter, so she's totally freaked out. She made me swear never to take any kind of pill. I told her she doesn't have to worry. I despise drugs. Especially now, with fentanyl out in the world, I think anyone who takes anything is crazy. If it were up to me, there would be commercials on TV and all over social media warning people about it, because I don't think some people know what's going on. Anyway, the news about Nathan is devastating. He was one of the best guys in the whole school. I can't even imagine the pain his family is feeling right now.

The terrible parallel brought me to tears.

I read until my eyes were so strained I was forced to stop and turn off the light. But I couldn't quiet my mind. With London's thoughts in my head, I was overwhelmed by the magnitude of her spirit, and intelligence, and by the immensity of Tom's loss.

It took some time, but I know I slept because I was having a nightmare about Steven when I was awakened by Tom banging around in the kitchen. Soon I heard footsteps on the stairs. Tom was on his way up. I held my breath and pretended to be asleep.

After the first few days, I'd mostly put aside my fear of Tom coming to me for sex, but now—especially because he'd been drinking—I worried my trust had been misplaced.

Soon Tom was standing at the top of the stairs. My eyes were closed, but I knew he was staring at me. I remained still, fearing the worst, although I had no way of knowing what he was thinking. Maybe he was considering letting me go. He stood there, not moving, for a long time. I could hear him breathing. Then, finally, he turned around and tiptoed back down the stairs, leaving me wondering what he'd been doing there—or if maybe I'd been dreaming.

CHAPTER TWENTY-ONE

RILEY DID NOT ATTEND the fraternity party that night. When six o'clock rolled around, she was still so weak and sick she could barely sit up. London offered to bring her dinner from the dining hall, but she had no interest in food. Her stomach had been turned inside out and was still so tender, even soup was out of the question. She was a mess, and London wasn't surprised when she learned what she'd done.

"I woke up and had a horrible hangover," she explained. "Someone suggested the *hair of the dog* thing, and I ended up doing some shots of tequila. Then someone gave me a pill to settle my stomach, but it only made things worse."

"What was the pill?"

"I don't know. *How should I know?*" Riley replied testily.

London didn't bother to respond. She just marveled that someone who'd gotten a 1400 on the SAT could have so little sense.

London decided not to go to the party either. She called Jason and explained that she needed to stay in and take care of Riley.

"You can leave her for a few hours," he argued. "It's not like she's going to die. She's hung over."

"She's a lot more than hung over."

"Whatever," Jason said. "The point is, she'll be fine if you leave for a couple of hours. Just come for dinner. You can bring some food back to her."

"She doesn't want food. She can barely hold down a sip of water."

"So let her sleep. She doesn't need you to babysit her while she sleeps."

"I'm sorry. I'm not going to change my mind," London said. But she wasn't really sorry. Her distaste for the fraternities had been renewed, and the last thing she wanted after spending the day nursing Riley was to be around heavy drinking.

ж

Just after nine o'clock, Jason, refusing to give up, knocked on London and Riley's door and presented London with a plate of sliced brisket, barbecued ribs, and potato salad. A gigantic piece of chocolate cake was wrapped separately in aluminum foil.

Not wanting to wake Riley, who was sleeping peacefully, London led Jason to a common room down the hall, where she dug into the food. She hadn't eaten much all day, so she was hungry.

"This is delicious," she said, licking barbecue sauce from her fingers. "Thanks for bringing it."

Jason took a bite of the cake. "How's Riley doing?"

"She's fine. Out cold. But I can't believe she did that to herself. You'd think she'd be smarter."

"From what I heard, the tequila thing was meant to be a joke. No one thought she'd really do it."

London frowned. "People die of alcohol poisoning, you know."

"I guess," Jason said, "but no one forced her to drink it. She did it on her own."

"Yeah, well, I'd like to get my hands on the person who gave it to her. Was it Kevin?"

"I don't think so, but I'm not sure. I only heard about it third-hand. But listen," he said, changing the subject. "You want to take a walk or something? Get some air?"

London shook her head. "It's too late."

"It's Saturday night, and it's not even nine-thirty. Come on, take a walk with me. Riley's asleep, and you said yourself she's out cold. You can leave her for an hour."

London was unsure, but she'd been inside most of the day, and Jason was persistent, so she finally agreed to go out for a walk, but only a short one.

CHAPTER TWENTY-TWO

AS PER OUR NOW normal routine, Tom cooked breakfast, then left me alone to write. It was the last week of April, but it had snowed, and the weather was frigid, so he kept a big fire going, occasionally disappearing to chop or fetch wood. Most of the day, he sat in the living room and read. He'd brought an impressive number of books and seemed determined to work his way through the stack.

Toward the middle of the afternoon, he brought me a peanut butter sandwich, then sat down at the table next to me and studied the page I was writing. He smelled like wood smoke and sweat. He'd barely spoken a word all day, which was fine with me. Having him near me now made me nervous, reminding me of his late-night visit to the loft.

"Did you learn anything interesting last night?" he asked.

"Well, I learned some distressing things about her high school," I said. "About drug use and that kind of thing. But I was mostly just impressed by her writing and maturity. She was an amazing girl."

Tom fidgeted, and I felt uncomfortable singing London's praises—like I was rubbing salt in the wound.

"I learned you were in the military," I added, anxious to change the subject. "It took me a second to figure out who she was talking about when she called you *The General.*"

He scoffed and shook his head. "That was a family joke started by my ex-in-laws."

"But you were in the Army?"

Tom nodded. "It paid for my education. I got a PhD, then worked in a division involved with strategic global resources. But as soon as I qualified for a pension, I got out. And I was a lieutenant colonel, not a general—clearly. The name was facetious."

"I think London thought you were in the CIA," I said, curious to see what would come back.

Tom just rolled his eyes.

Later in the afternoon, something caught my attention. Tom had gone outside, but I heard none of the usual sounds I associated with his trips to get wood. This time, I heard murmurs that sounded like Tom was talking to someone. Reflexively, I jumped up and ran to the window by the front door, wondering if it might be the police. There were no police. What I saw instead was Tom walking in circles with a phone to his ear. He'd claimed there was no cell coverage where we were, but now I realized he was lying.

Only seconds after I arrived at the window, he put the phone back in his pocket, and I retreated—deflated, but still so charged with adrenaline that it was a good five minutes before I was able to steady my nerves.

Not long after, I began hearing the familiar sound of Tom splitting logs, but his ax had a rhythm and force different from its usual cadence. I got up and went back to the window, where now I could see him attacking the wood with a fervor that was fierce. Veins bulged on his neck, and his expression was savage.

When he came back inside, he dumped an armful of his spoils onto the hearth with uncharacteristic carelessness, then stomped into the bathroom. Soon, I heard the squeal of the faucet turning on. He emerged minutes later wearing a fresh shirt and went straight for his bottle of bourbon, then spent the rest of the afternoon brooding in front of the fire.

That night at dinner, I was wary of irritating him, but I finally gave in to temptation and raised the subject of the phone. "I know you were talking on the phone today. I thought you said there was no cell service here. Have you been able to check the news all along?"

"I never said there was no phone service," he said. "I said we can't connect to the internet. And, even if we could, I'm not stupid enough to use my smartphone here. It was a burner."

I wasn't sure I believed him. "Can you show it to me so I can see?"

"No, I'm not going to show it to you!" he erupted, and I was frightened by the intensity of his flare-up.

"Can you at least tell me if you learned anything?"

"It was nothing that concerns you, so you need to drop it. Understood?"

I sat silent, and he upped the severity of his stare.

I finally nodded.

Satisfied, he pushed away from the table and stormed into the living room, leaving me to wonder who he'd been talking to and what new thing was eating at him.

CHAPTER TWENTY-THREE

LONDON AND JASON HAD barely gone a block when Jason's phone began buzzing in his pocket. He pulled it out and looked at it. "Sorry," he said, "I'll only be a second."

He put the phone to his ear. "What? I'm busy." He listened for a few moments, then said, "All right. Be there in a minute."

He placed the phone back in his pocket and frowned. "I'm sorry, but I have to go give my keys to Dillon—my roommate. His little brother's waiting to get picked up at the bus station, and his car won't start. I'm going to let him take mine."

"That's fine," London said. "I'll see you on Monday."

She turned to start walking back to the dorm, but Jason stopped her. "Don't go. Come with me. It'll just take a second. Then we can keep walking."

"Wouldn't you rather just go to the party?"

"It'll be going all night," he said. "I can go later." He looked at her with a hopeful smile. "Come on. You've been cooped up all day in a room that smells like puke."

"Really? You can still smell it?"

Jason shrugged. "Little bit."

London shook her head and smiled. "All right. I guess it is nice being out in the fresh air."

As they approached the fraternity house, London could see that the party was in full swing, with music blaring and scores of people spilling out onto the porch and lawn—many holding the large red solo cups that were the staple of every student party.

Jason pulled out his phone and called his roommate. "I'm outside," he said.

He put the phone back in his pocket and turned to London. "Sure you don't want to come in for a while? I'm a crappy dancer, but we could dance."

London hesitated. "Are you and Amy not together anymore?"

Before Jason could respond, Dillon arrived and interrupted, looking and sounding drunk.

"Dude," Jason said. "You're crazy if you think you're driving my car, and your mom would kill you if she knew you were going to pick up your brother all fucked up."

"I can drive," he protested. "I've had, like, three beers. I'm fine."

He switched his gaze to London. "You must be the famous London," he said. "Did he tell you about the fight?"

"Shut up," Jason said. "What about your brother?"

"He's fucking waiting, man. I need to go get him."

Jason sighed in exasperation. "I'll take you. There's no way I'm letting you drive."

He looked at London. "I'm sorry. I don't know what else to do. Come with us. I'll drop you back on the way."

"I can walk," she said. "I'm fine."

"I didn't mean to ruin your thing," Dillon said. "But I'm telling you, I'm barely even buzzed..."

"Shut up, you're not driving," Jason said. "Just go to the car and I'll meet you there in a second. It's up the street in front of Rick's truck."

He looked back at London. "Let me drive you."

She was thinking about it when Riley's boyfriend, Kevin, walked up. "Hey, London," he said. "How's Riley doing? I called her around five, and she sounded pretty bad."

Jason put his hands up. "Hold on. We're in the middle of something." He turned to London. "Are you coming?"

"I'm good," she said. "Really. Go."

Reluctantly, Jason complied, leaving London in front of the house with Kevin, who immediately began making excuses about Riley.

"I told her she was being stupid, but she wouldn't listen." He smiled and raised his chin. "I'm not surprised she puked all over your room. Even I can't drink tequila without getting sick."

"I'll be sure and let her know how worried you are about her," London said.

She was going to start to walk back, but Kevin stopped her. "Hold on. I need to give you some stuff she left here."

"What stuff?"

"A notebook and a book I think she has to finish before Monday."

Fat chance, London thought, but she kept it to herself. "Alright," she said. "But hurry up. I need to get back."

"Come wait on the porch," he said. "Or come inside and get something to eat or drink. There's a lot of food and whatever you want to drink. There's some great pomegranate punch one of the sororities brought over if you don't like alcohol. Come on in and try it."

London shook her head. "I'm fine."

"Whatever," he said. "I'll go get Riley's stuff and be right back. But at least come sit down."

He grabbed her hand and pulled her in the direction of the walkway leading to the porch. She wasn't in the mood to yank her hand away and make a scene, so she let him lead her to the porch, where she immediately recognized a girl named Sheryl from her biology lab. At six feet, with the classic long volleyball ponytail (she was captain of the girls' freshman team), she was hard to miss. Kevin disappeared inside, and London walked over to say hello.

Not surprisingly, Kevin didn't come "right back," and he still hadn't returned after twenty minutes. But London was sitting with Sheryl, and they were having as good a conversation as you could have over the music, so she wasn't worried. Soon after she sat down, someone delivered big red cups of punch to both of them. It was fizzy and sweet, with pomegranate sherbet seeming to be the primary ingredient.

"Good, right?" Sheryl said. "One of the girls in my sorority makes this for all our parties."

"Delicious," London agreed.

Soon, nearby chairs filled up with friends of Sheryl's, and London began to worry about the time and whether or not Kevin had forgotten about her altogether. She was thinking about leaving when someone arrived with a pitcher and refilled her cup. She initially resisted, but Sheryl told her to "Sit back and have another one," so she did.

CHAPTER TWENTY-FOUR

THE DAY AFTER I heard Tom talking on the phone, he rushed me through dinner, then announced he'd be going out for a few hours. He ordered me to do whatever I needed to do in the bathroom, then head up to the loft. He said he'd have to cuff me while he was gone, but claimed he'd return before midnight.

"Where are you...."

"I'm not answering questions," he said. "Just go get ready. I want to leave in ten minutes."

The reality of being left alone hit me in the pit of my stomach. "You know I'll starve here if you don't come back."

"I'm coming back."

"What if you don't?"

"Don't be so fucking dramatic. I'm coming back. Now, go on." He nodded at the bathroom. "And while I'm gone, get some sleep. We'll be getting up early tomorrow."

"Why? What's going on tomorrow?"

"Nothing. I just want to start getting up earlier. Things are moving too slowly."

My fear of being abandoned chained to the bed mushroomed into panic. *"Please don't do this to me,"* I pleaded.

"Take me with you. You can lay me down in the back seat."

"This isn't a debate."

"Something could happen to you!"

"Just pray it doesn't," he said. "Now, go."

Terror-stricken, but understanding the futility of arguing any further, I slunk to the bathroom. Seeing my reflection in the mirror, I barely recognized myself. I looked worn down. Vacant. "Hang in there," I whispered to myself. "Someday, this'll be over."

Minutes later, Tom fastened me to the bed, then marched down the stairs and out the door, totally dismissive of my fear. His last words before closing the door behind him were, "I'll be back. Get some sleep."

I did not sleep. My imagination went wild wondering about the phone call that had rattled Tom.

Who'd he been talking to, and what had upset him so much? *Had Steven died? Was that it?* If so, maybe Tom feared a murder investigation would increase the likelihood we'd be found by the police. Or maybe he thought it would impact my cooperation with the book. Whatever it was, he obviously didn't want me to know.

I tortured myself picturing all the horrible scenarios that might be playing out, and I prayed the police had found my phone and listened to the recording. *Of course they would find it. Why wouldn't they?*

When I wasn't sweating over Steven and my family, I worried Tom might not return—might really leave me to die, whether deliberately or because something happened to him. The police were probably looking for him. *And Tom had a gun.*

Not knowing anything for sure was as maddening as the chain that bound me to the bed, and as time went on, I became more and more anxious.

I attempted to talk myself down. The call may have had nothing to do with me, like Tom said. He had a life, too, after all. He was probably talking to someone associated with his work, or a lover. He'd have his own disappearance to explain. Thinking optimistically, I figured that if the call *hadn't* been about Steven, and Tom did return, I'd probably learn Steven's condition when he got back. (Assuming he'd tell me the truth.) Surely Tom would check the news while he was out. I tried to hang on to this hope as each painful hour dragged on, but it was impossible to quell my fear, and I continued imagining the worst.

When Tom finally did return, it was well after midnight, and I was so relieved I wept. I called down and asked him what he'd heard in the news, and he said, "Nothing. I didn't hear any news."

"That's ridiculous! I cried. "Do you expect me to believe you've been gone all this time and didn't check the news?"

"I don't care what you believe," he said. "I'm tired and want to go to sleep."

And that was it. That's all he'd say—although a short time later he spoke to me again like he sometimes did when he was on the couch and I was in the loft.

"You know what hurts the most?" he said, totally out of the blue.

"What?" I said.

"The weekend of that fucking party, I thought about surprising her with a visit."

He paused, and I thought he was done, but then he went on, his voice catching.

"I ended up not going because I couldn't get a first-class ticket for the second leg of the trip. *Can you imagine living with that?*"

Ꮐ

The next morning, it was apparent that something was up. Something had changed. I could see in Tom's face and overall posture that wheels were turning in his head.

I asked him again about the news, and again he claimed he knew nothing—that he hadn't seen or heard any reporting on me, Steven, or anything while he was gone. I found it hard to believe, and it fueled my fear about Steven.

It wasn't until the middle of the afternoon that I learned we were leaving. I'd been writing all day, and things had settled into what seemed, on the surface, like our regular routine, but I could feel something was looming. Tom hadn't told me why he'd gone out, but eventually it became apparent he'd been shopping for supplies. Finally, around five o'clock, he informed me that, from here on, we'd be "camping."

Apart from learning Steven was dead and I was being charged with his murder, I don't know what could have been a bigger blow.

Tom behaved as if it were nothing. He poked the fire, straightened up, then casually informed me it was time to start packing up—that we'd be trading the cozy comforts of the cabin for the great outdoors.

"And I don't want to hear any crying about it," he said. "It's not a negotiation."

Alarmed, I asked him why we had to leave, but he refused to explain. He simply told me to get used to the idea—that we'd be leaving after sundown.

⊂∞

By the time we were ready to go, it was well into the night, and I was petrified. Tom seemed nervous, too. He'd been on a hair trigger all day.

Items I'd seen in the back of the SUV made it clear he was dead serious about camping. I could only hope it wouldn't be as bad as I feared. It had been cold enough to snow where we were, so I prayed we'd head down to a lower altitude. But I had no idea what to expect, and Tom was in no mood to answer questions.

When I was finally in the car and had my seat belt on, he handed me a small white pill. "Take this," he said.

"What is it?"

"Just take it," he demanded. "It's not going to hurt you. It'll relax you enough to sleep."

"Maybe I don't want to sleep."

"Look," Tom said, "we can do this the hard way if you want, but one way or another, you're taking it, so just do as you're told."

He reached into the back seat and grabbed a pillow. "Here," he said, placing it in my lap. "This'll help you get comfortable."

I thought for a moment, then looked him in the eye, understanding he might be doing me a favor. Maybe a little unconsciousness wouldn't be so bad. I popped the pill in my mouth and swallowed.

Tom started the car, and we headed back down the dirt road that had delivered us to the cabin almost three weeks earlier. I had no idea where we were going, but the farther we ventured into the blackness, the more my worries melted away. Soon, I surrendered to the softness of the pillow and seductive pull of sleep.

When next I was conscious, it was still dark, but the trees and mountains had given way to a vast scrubby desert. At least we'd left the snow zone. I lifted my head, which was still groggy, and squinted out the window. "Where are we?"

I tried to bring the passing scenery into sharper focus, but there was too little light to get more than vague impressions.

"Go back to sleep," Tom said. "We still have a long way to go."

"Where are we going?"

"You'll know soon enough. Just close your eyes and go back to sleep. I'll wake you when we get there."

Still feeling the effects of the drug, I obeyed.

When I woke up again, it was light out, Tom was gone, and we were parked in a rust-encrusted gas station that seemed so far removed from civilization, it was like waking up in *Mad Max*.

Everything appeared apocalyptic: the landscape; the yellowish pallor of the air; the ancient gas pumps and dilapidated building—even the old guy whose profile I could just barely make out through a dirty, cracked window. It occurred to me fleetingly that if I were on my game, he might be an opportunity for rescue, but before I even completed the thought, Tom emerged from the building and got in the car. Moments later, we were back on the road.

"I could have used a bathroom back there," I said after we'd traveled about a mile.

"If you need me to, I can pull over," he said.

"I can wait," I mumbled, praying it wouldn't be too long. I was still groggy, but I was awake enough to register a troubling pressure in my bladder.

As it turned out, we still had a long stretch to go, and we traveled the miles in silence, my fear growing sharper with each passing minute. Finally, panic got the better of me, and I cried out. *"Do you even know where we're going, or are you just randomly looking for the most godforsaken place possible?"*

With a knot in my throat, I could barely get the words out, but I kept going. "If you want me to write, why plant me in the middle of a burned-out desert? Why couldn't we stay where we were?"

"Calm down," Tom said. "If you can't, I'll be forced to give you another pill. But I'd rather have you conscious, so try to pull yourself together."

Staring out the window at a landscape more desolate than I'd ever seen, I shook my head in despair.

Moments later, just as the clock in the dashboard ticked up to 7:00, we turned off the highway onto a rough road heading into a rise of craggy hills. I couldn't imagine that Tom had any idea where we were going. He hadn't consulted a map or GPS. He'd just turned right, as if on impulse. But there was no point in commenting, so I kept my thoughts to myself.

As we passed scattered cactuses and black tangles of dead-looking shrubs, I thought wistfully of the warm cabin we'd deserted, and I wondered, with a sick stomach, what new brand of nightmare was in store. Under other circumstances, I might have found some beauty in the landscape, but with a gray sky overhead and little but parched earth in sight, all I could think of was death.

CHAPTER TWENTY-FIVE

LONDON FINISHED HER SECOND drink, then stood up to leave, explaining to Sheryl that her roommate was sick and she wanted to get back and check on her. It was just an excuse. She knew Riley would be fine, but raucous talk and behavior were starting to make her uncomfortable. She'd exchanged a couple of texts with Jason, and he'd asked her to stay and wait for him, but she told him she wanted to get back, that she'd see him next week.

As soon as she stood, she realized something wasn't right, and it hit her that she was drunk.

She looked at the empty cup on the table by her chair, then at Sheryl. "Is there alcohol in this punch?"

Sheryl nodded. "Vodka. Didn't you know?"

"No," London said, feeling like a fool.

"I'm sorry, I should have told you," Sheryl said. "You're not the first person to make that mistake." She looked at the drink in her hand. "This is a killer batch. I can tell."

London sat back down, deciding to wait for Jason after all. She didn't want to walk back alone if she was drunk, and she was definitely feeling it. It was starting to hit her so hard, she was surprised she hadn't felt it sooner.

She pulled her phone from her purse and texted Jason: "Staying after all so you can walk me home. I'll be on the porch."

Moments later, Kevin materialized, looking sheepish. "Sorry it took me so long. I didn't think you'd still be here."

London noticed he was empty-handed. "You didn't get Riley's stuff?"

He shrugged. "I couldn't find it. I guess she took it after all." He put his hands in his pockets. "Jason's not back yet?"

"Not yet," London said.

Her phone buzzed. "That's probably him."

She picked up her phone and read his text: "Shit. I figured you already left. I dropped those guys off and decided to head home for the weekend."

London's heart sank. "No prob," she texted back.

She looked up at Kevin. "That was him. He's decided to go home for the weekend."

Kevin rolled his eyes, then grinned. "Having a good time?"

"I had the pomegranate punch. I thought you told me it didn't have alcohol."

"I said it's good if you don't *like* alcohol." He chuckled like it was a joke. "A lot of girls like to drink vodka mixed with something sweet because you can't taste it."

He nodded at the cup on the table next to her. "Is that your cup? Want some water?"

"I'm fine," she said. She was thinking about calling an Uber.

"Bring her some water," Sheryl said. "Someone should have told her there was vodka in the punch." She held up her cup. "These are strong."

Kevin reached for the cup, then nodded to a stocky guy in a hoodie who'd just arrived on the porch from inside. "Grab some water for me, would ya?" He handed him the cup. "We have a lady here who's had too much punch."

The guy nodded and took the cup, then went back inside. When he returned a minute later, he handed the water to London without a word, then went off and blended in with a crowd congregated on the lawn.

London sat forward and took a long drink of the water. "Thanks," she said. "I probably do need this."

Kevin disappeared into the house, and London thought again about the Uber, wondering if she should use a bathroom first. She peered inside the open door. The dense crowd and loud thrumming music were anything but inviting.

She looked at Sheryl. "Do you know what the bathroom situation is like in there?"

"It's not *too* bad. There's one downstairs on the right if you go straight inside. Want me to go with you?"

"No, I'll be fine," London said. She took one more big gulp of water, then stood up, wishing she hadn't had the second drink.

After taking a moment to steady herself, she smiled at Sheryl. "Here goes nothing," she said, then she headed for the front door, smiling and nodding as she bobbed and weaved through the animated crowd of boisterous students in the foyer.

A band was playing, and people were dancing in a large room to the left. Ignoring it, London followed Sheryl's directions and headed straight ahead, easily finding the bathroom toward the middle of a long wood-paneled hallway. There was a short line, but she chatted with a couple of girls outside the door while she waited, feeling increasingly impaired as she struggled not to slur her words. She was surprised because she'd been to high school parties and knew what it was like to be drunk. This was different. Maybe, she supposed, because it was hard liquor. She'd only ever had beer and wine.

When it was finally her turn to use the bathroom, she peed, then stood at the sink and stared at herself in the mirror, shocked by her deteriorating state. Moments later, she exited and tried to make her way back to the porch, her legs unsteady and vision starting to blur. But she never got there—or if she did, she didn't remember it.

The next thing she remembered was the stinking hot breath of a nightmare.

CHAPTER TWENTY-SIX

TOM DROVE SLOWLY OVER the rutty dirt road, carefully steering around rocks and deep holes that would have meant disaster if we'd hit them head-on. Eventually, the road turned sharply to the left, and we entered a skinny passage through hills not visible from the highway. As we continued further into the ravine, the road became even rougher, and so narrow in most parts that turning around would have been impossible.

As we ventured further into what seemed like a road to nowhere, I began noticing patches of green, indicating water of some kind was present. I didn't see an actual stream, but it was clear there was a water source somewhere. Maybe an underground spring.

"Do you actually know where we're going?" I asked. I found it hard to believe that a road like this could be on his, or anyone's, radar, but Tom projected an air of confidence as we continued to wind our way deeper into the craggy gorge.

"I know where we're going," he said.

We bumped and swerved for probably ten more miles, and it was slow going, but eventually the land around us spread out, and we found ourselves in a slender valley surrounded by steep, jagged hills. Bushy creosote, sagebrush, and various types of cactus gave subtle hints of life, but the general color scheme was parched. Soon, old wooden and metal remnants of human activity became apparent, and I realized we were in the neighborhood of an abandoned mine. Squinting up at the rugged hillside to our right, I made out a dark area that I guessed might be the entrance.

"Was this a gold mine?" I asked, putting two and two together. *Tom was a geologist.*

He pulled off the road and drove to a wide area near a stand of disfigured trees. "Silver," he said. Then he pushed the shifter to Park in a clear signal we'd arrived.

"So this is it? This is where we're stopping?"

He unhooked his seatbelt. "This is it."

He opened the car door and pointed to a large boulder ten feet from where we were parked. "We'll camp on the other side of that rock."

He got out, stretched, then stooped down to look at me. "Get out and help me unpack the car. Then we need to get set up. For the next few weeks, this is home."

⚃

We had almost finished unloading, and I was surveying the heap of items that would provide the meager comforts of our new home when a hint of yellow drew my eyes to a bag of legal pads that would replace the laptop I'd been using. I'd argued the car should be able to charge the laptop, but Tom insisted it wasn't an option. "You'll be writing on paper from here on," he'd said. "Get over it."

Apart from an occasional postcard and edits in the margins of student essays, I hadn't written anything on paper in decades. I could barely even read my own handwriting anymore. The prospect of scratching out a book in longhand gave me heartburn, adding to my misery.

I was in the middle of mentally cataloging my degenerating circumstances when I heard Tom yell my name. He'd been doing something in the front seat of the car.

"Valerie," he called. "Here's your news. Listen up!"

As I bolted for the car, Tom turned the radio up high, and a male voice filled the air.

"According to police, there are still no solid leads on the fate or whereabouts of Valerie Hawthorn, the writer and university lecturer who raised eyebrows by releasing nude photos of herself over the internet, then disappeared days later after an altercation with her husband in which he was shot and near fatally wounded. The public is being asked to please contact local authorities if they have any information relevant to the investigation."

That was it. That was the whole story. By the time I arrived at the car, the newscaster had moved on to sports.

"So now you know," Tom said.

"*Know what?*" I said, frantic to hear more. "There was almost no information."

"Well, you know your husband is alive, for one thing."

I tried to remember what had been said. It had come so unexpectedly and ended so quickly, I wasn't sure. "What did they say exactly?"

"Near fatally wounded," Tom said. "I.e., he's alive."

"Near fatally wounded could mean practically anything," I said. "He could be in a coma, or brain dead, or paralyzed from the neck down. And we don't know if they think I shot him on purpose, or it was an accident, or what?"

I paused to think. "If Steven were conscious, I'm sure they'd have reported it was an accident. He can be an asshole, but he wouldn't claim I tried to kill him."

I looked at Tom earnestly and whimpered in frustration. "Did you hear anything else I missed? Have you seen or heard any other news you aren't telling me about?"

He shook his head. "Sorry. You know what I know."

"It's good news for you," I said bitterly. "It doesn't sound like they're thinking kidnapping. They think I'm some sex-crazed lunatic who shot my husband and left him bleeding on the floor."

"I don't think that was clear at all," Tom said. "They said you *disappeared*, which means they probably haven't ruled anything out. And, remember, I'm the one who called 911. That has to have them wondering."

⚃

As the day went on and I grudgingly helped Tom set up our camp, I continued to think about the news story and what I could and couldn't glean from what was said. I eventually reasoned that if Steven *had* been in a coma or some other dramatic condition, it would have been stated, so I felt easier about that. But I was worried about my phone. Judging from what was reported, it seemed clear it hadn't been found. The battery had been low, so I figured it must have died before the police had a chance to track it. I pictured it at the bottom of the vase by the stairs and cursed myself for not using the cable in my car to keep the battery charged up when I was driving home.

The more I thought about everything, the more certain I was that no one was going to rescue me. This was not a movie. No leading man and squad of devoted detectives were going to work night and day until I was found. My best hope for getting home safely was to keep doing what I was doing and hope for Tom's promised ending. I knew, of course, that things could go off-script. Anything could happen out in the middle of the desert. But I would do my best to finish the book. When I thought about the laptop and lost comforts of the cabin, I wanted to throw myself on the ground and cry. Everything was about to get a lot harder.

⁊

By late afternoon, our camp consisted of a blue and beige nylon tent that could easily sleep four, a Coleman stove, a sizable plastic cooler, multiple stacking milk crates filled with food and cooking utensils, two camping chairs, a small collapsible table, and a wooden bench fashioned from a relic of the mine. Tom had also designated an area not too far away as our official "latrine." His final project was a fire pit that would have put even the most decorated Eagle Scout to shame. As he artfully stacked rocks and piled wood he'd salvaged from the mine, he assured me it would be cold at night.

By the time Tom got around to building a fire and testing out the stove, I was exhausted and emotionally raw.

"We can have left-over ham for dinner," Tom said. "We also have some cheese and fruit and a few other things we can eat tonight and over the next couple of days, but soon we'll be living mostly on peanut butter and crackers, rice and beans, freeze-dried food, and canned goods, so enjoy the fresh food while you can."

Hungry enough to eat almost anything, I lowered myself into a blue canvas chair on the upwind side of the fire. There was still plenty of daylight, but the sun was starting to sink in a sky growing pale, and the air, which had been warm, was cooling down and becoming breezy.

Sitting in front of a can of black beans he was heating on the stove, Tom passed me an apple he pulled from one of the crates. I took a bite and savored its crisp sweetness, understanding that fruit would soon be off the menu.

Surveying our "camp," my eyes settled on the tent. I'd been trying to put it out of my mind, but now it was solidly in my thoughts. My chest tightened.

Tom noticed where I was looking. "Don't worry," he said, "I'll leave you alone."

"I'd rather sleep in the car," I said, my face heating up.

Tom looked down at the beans, then back at me, the fire reflected in his eyes. "I don't think that's a good idea."

"Why not?" I said. "I'm not going anywhere. Not in this fucking desert, and especially not in the middle of the night."

Despairing at my ever-worsening situation, I closed my eyes and fought the urge to cry.

When I opened my eyes, Tom was staring at me. With several days' growth of beard and loose skin circling his eyes, he looked uncharacteristically haggard.

"Sleeping in the car doesn't make any sense," he said, keeping his voice even. "That back seat won't be comfortable. I have air mattresses, and there's more than enough room in the tent for both of us."

He slapped at something crawling up his leg. "If it'll make you feel any better, I'll put some gear between us so you don't have to worry about *drift*."

He lowered his head and poked at the fire. "I promise you're not going to find me on top of you in the middle of the night."

He looked back up and straight into my eyes, and his expression was profoundly sad. "I might be a lot of things, but I'm not a rapist."

I thought about how he'd tricked me into bed, but the pain emanating from his gaze sent a wave through me. In those few moments, I could see both who he'd been and who he'd become, and I couldn't help but be struck by the wreckage and horror of it all. He'd said he was a ghost, and I knew what he meant. But I also knew and could see that his light was not entirely out. He flickered between essential goodness and a rage so corrosive it was eating him alive.

CHAPTER TWENTY-SEVEN

LONDON'S AWARENESS THAT SOMETHING terrible was happening began as a feeling of suffocation and immobilization. Struggling to breathe, then move, she felt a crushing weight followed by a wetness on her face and bitter taste that added a swell of nausea to her rising terror. Realizing, to her horror, that a large someone was on top of her, she attempted to scream, but her cries were quickly stifled by a rough hand over her mouth. She tried to lash out with her arms but found them pinned. It was dark, so she couldn't see, but she heard whispers. She and whoever was on top of her weren't alone.

Suddenly, her legs were wrenched apart, and she felt a shock of pain as her attacker forced his way inside her. Her clothes had apparently been removed because she felt a rough surface on her bare skin as she was pounded again and again, each thrust feeling like a fresh burst of fire. In excruciating pain and terror, she tried to remove herself from the attack. *Just get through it,* she repeated to herself, struggling to block it from her consciousness. But there was no blocking. There was only enduring and waiting for the nightmare to end.

Just when London thought the ordeal was over, she felt a jarring cold and wetness between her legs. A moment later, her attacker relinquished her to a second. She tried to cry out, but, like before, her mouth was covered, her arms were pinned, and she endured more pain and burning and terror, all while feeling the sweat and hot breath of someone on top of her. This one had a pungent smell that brought a renewed rise of nausea.

More whispering, a jolt, a prolonged shudder, a cry—then, again, the cold between her legs. To London's horror, a third now took his turn. This time, amid the pounding and burning, she vomited, then began choking until it seemed her captors got scared because they sat her up to help her breathe—all still in the dark, with whispering she couldn't make out. Afterwards, left alone, she lay stricken in the scratchy blackness— throbbing, despondent, and raw to the core, but knowing with crystal clarity that she would never again be the person she was when she woke up that morning.

Exhausted and emotionally ravaged, London fell into sleep, waking hours later to a world of pain and slivers of light shining down through high narrow windows. The windows were covered with sheets of black paper, but they were poorly enough fitted to give her a dim picture of her surroundings. Raising her head and trying to focus, she soon recognized her location as a large unfinished basement with a cement floor, furnace, and pipes and wooden beams overhead. Disheveled boxes and other miscellaneous items were stacked on metal shelves, and bicycles hung from rafters at the far end of the room.

To her great distress, she discovered she was completely naked. The scratchiness she'd felt during her attack was the rough pile of an ancient green couch, which was the only furniture she could see besides a set of folding chairs leaning against one of the cement walls. She was relieved to the point of tears to find her clothes and purse strewn on the floor near the end of the couch. Wooden steps to the left of the shelves were the way out, but the thought of passing through the first floor of the fraternity made her shake.

Desperate to retrieve her clothes, London attempted to sit up and was immediately hit with a pounding head and wave of dizziness and nausea that may have been partly due to a stinging odor and sour taste in her mouth, by-products of having been sick to her stomach. Pain between her legs and in the muscles of her thighs were terrible reminders of both what had been done to her and what she'd have to face going forward.

Not wanting to think about either of these things, she focused on getting dressed and getting out. She could worry about everything else later.

Sitting up and placing her feet on the floor, London again experienced dizziness and a terrible pounding in her temples and between her legs. She stopped and tried to steady herself with slow, deep breathing, struggling to endure the smell of the vomit that had soaked into the couch and was crusted on parts of her body.

Managing to stand on wobbly legs, she stepped to where her clothes lay in a pile on the floor and began to put them on, ignoring the stinking mess stuck to her flesh.

When she was finally clothed and ready to brave the stairs, she searched her purse for her phone, wanting to see the time. She had heard no movement overhead and hoped it might be early enough to slip out unseen. She found her phone and saw it was just after six-thirty. She also noticed several text messages, but she had neither the time nor the desire to read them. All she wanted was to get the hell out.

CHAPTER TWENTY-EIGHT

TOM HAD ERECTED THE promised divider in the tent. As days and nights passed, he kept his promise to leave me alone, but his proximity was still unnerving, making me acutely aware of the peculiarity of our situation as it was evolving.

Our "relationship," for lack of a better word, was built on such an odd mixture of contradictory events and feelings, it was difficult to know, from one minute to the next, what to think or how to feel. I hated Tom and everything he'd done to me, but at the same time, I pitied him and empathized with his grief. I also had vivid memories of Montana, which was disconcerting. I tried not to think about it, but it was always there—as were sporadic moments between us that contrasted starkly with the gruffness he seemed more comfortable displaying. The moments where he let his guard down were few, but they seemed somehow more sincere. At times, "Bad Tom" struck me as an act. But it may have been wishful thinking on my part. I wanted "Good Tom" to be real.

On his side, I couldn't fathom that he'd managed to behave with so much charm and vigor in Montana when his feelings were hostile. I could only conclude that men really are from another planet where sex is concerned. But, then, so much of what men are capable of is incomprehensible.

You only need to study war to understand that. And I'd seen plenty that was incomprehensible in Steven.

One night in the tent, I began wondering about the young men who'd raped London. Did they seem, to all the world, just like any other college students? Did they come from good homes? Chalk up their actions to "boys will be boys" or to having too much to drink? Did they wake up the next day horrified or at least *surprised* by what they'd done? Did they feel remorse or care that they'd shattered a life—a family?

It sickened me to think about it, especially knowing they'd probably go on to become wealthy and successful. To live seemingly exemplary lives.

Tom stirred. "Are you awake?" I whispered.

"I'm awake," he said.

"I'm thinking about the book. Can I ask you something?"

"Go ahead," he said.

"London never mentions the name of the fraternity in her diary. I might not be able to use it for legal reasons, but I'm curious because I know some of those kids. Which one was it? The only distinguishing feature she mentions is the porch, but most of the houses have porches."

"I don't remember the call signal, or whatever it is they call those ridiculous names, but it's that big brown one on University near the art gallery with all the banners."

"The one that had the fire?"

I wondered why I hadn't thought about it before.

"I don't know anything about a fire, but if it's the one by the art gallery, that's the one," Tom said.

"You didn't hear the news about the fire? It was a big story. The whole house was destroyed and two or three kids ended up in the hospital."

"Until you and I met up again, you may recall I was fishing, not following the news. But if that place went up, I'm not going to shed any tears. I'm glad the fucking thing burned down."

Tom rustled around, then said, "That's enough talking. Let's get some sleep."

But I didn't sleep. Not soon, anyway. I lay awake thinking about what he'd said and trying to remember exactly what I'd told him about the fire. I was sure I hadn't said when it happened, yet he somehow knew it happened when he was supposedly fishing. Which meant he *did* know about it—leading me to wonder why he'd lie. Had he had something to do with it?

I quickly realized that if Tom hadn't stayed to fish another day, he could have made it to town before the fire started. Of course, it didn't mean he *had* set the fire, only that it was possible. But why would he say he knew nothing about it if he did?

CHAPTER TWENTY-NINE

ACHING, SHAKING, AND BARELY able to think, London tiptoed up the stairs. When she arrived at the top, she held her breath and turned the knob on the door. To her great relief, the door was not locked. Opening it slowly, she peeked out, praying no one would witness her departure. Even in her weakened state, with a pounding head and legs that could barely carry her, she knew she should *want* witnesses—that the responsible thing to do would be call 911 and summon the police. But she couldn't bring herself to invite all the terrible new traumas that would entail. She just wanted to run—to wash, sleep, then try to forget.

With the door open and no one in sight, London stepped into a hall, and it was not what she expected. To her considerable shock, she had not been in the basement of the fraternity as she'd assumed. She was in another building altogether, which added to her disorientation. She had no recollection of leaving the fraternity house and no idea where she was.

As she passed through a dim hallway toward the front door, she soon realized—owing to a large bulletin board and other obvious clues in the foyer at the end of the hall—that she was in a student housing co-op. Anxious to escape, she took no time to study any of it. She simply opened the door, rushed out, and got her bearings, seeing almost immediately that she was only three blocks from her dorm.

Relieved not to have to call an Uber, she kept her head down and headed straight to the things she wanted now more than anything in the world: hot water and her bed. Minutes later, she arrived back at her dorm, limped up the stairs to the third floor, and went straight to her room, staying there only long enough to drop her purse and retrieve a towel and toiletries.

Still in bed, Riley mumbled something in London's direction, but London ignored her and headed for the bathroom, single-minded in her desperation to wash herself. When she arrived, she turned on the shower and stepped under a stream of near-scalding water, not even bothering to remove her clothes. It was only then, with the blessed water flowing over her, that she allowed herself to break down and cry. She tried to do it quietly because she didn't want anyone to hear, didn't want anyone to know what had happened. She felt deeply ashamed—both for the rape and for being too cowardly to call the police.

Eventually, she peeled off the clothes clinging to her trembling body and scoured herself with soap and shampoo—noticing, as she did, that her inner thighs and more sensitive areas were bruised and raw. When satisfied she was clean, she lowered herself to the floor and wept, soon falling into convulsive sobs at recalling how she'd always imagined her "first time" would be. She'd been waiting for the right person, the perfect time. The thought made her want to curl up and die.

When she was cried-out and exhausted, she wrapped herself in a towel, placed her wet clothes in the trash, then crept back to her room and got into bed. It was not yet eight, and Riley was still asleep.

Once in bed, London found it impossible to achieve the comfort she desired. Terrifying visions spun in her head like a merry-go-round. She tried to blot them out—to think of *anything* else—but nothing worked. When she closed her eyes, the horror of the night before played and replayed, only interrupted by bouts of shame for running to the shower instead of the police.

She considered calling her best friend, Sara, back in Seattle, or her mother, but she couldn't bring herself to call either of them. She *really* wanted to talk to her mother, but she and her father had suffered so terribly when London had cancer. They'd spent three straight years worrying about her, having no lives outside their fears for her well-being. She didn't want to put them through any more heartache. Also, she knew they'd be shocked and disappointed by her destruction of evidence. She didn't want to deal with that or risk being pressured to go to the police. She knew it was wrong to give her attackers a pass, but she knew with even more conviction that doing anything else would prolong her trauma and ruin her life—all for the highly predictable outcome that no one would be held to account.

Finally accepting there was no blanking her mind, London tried to remember all she could about the party. The last thing she recalled was going to the bathroom and feeling dizzy. She'd had two large cups of "punch." Could she have consumed enough vodka in those two drinks to become drunk to the point where she'd been taken some-where with no memory of it? Considering it unlikely, she wondered if someone had drugged her punch or the water she'd consumed before going to the bathroom. It probably wasn't too late to request a tox screen, but she shut the thought down. She knew the only thing that could help her feel normal again was enough time to allow the experience to fade. It might take years, so the clock had to start now — *immediately*.

For the moment, with everything still so raw, including the places on her body that were a throbbing reminder of what had been done to her, she would remain in bed. She had things to do for her courses, but she'd worry about them tomorrow, or the next day. For the time being, she would be down with the flu. Too sick to get up.

She wished she could sleep. She was desperate to find some peace, some escape. But sleep wouldn't come. All that would come were flashbacks that played like reruns from hell.

CHAPTER THIRTY

DAYS PASSED, AND TOM kept his distance. We spoke to one another in passing during the day and slept just feet from one another at night, but, for some reason, he'd decided to start behaving as though we were strangers. We inhabited the same physical space, but he had retreated to some mental universe from which I was barred.

The silences weren't like the ones I'd sometimes endured with Steven when we were too angry and alienated to even look at one another. Tom demonstrated no visible animosity or "coolness" of the type Steven often exhibited. He just refused to engage with me on any but the most superficial level. He even refrained from looking at what I was writing. I tried several times to bring him back, but I wasn't successful. It was like he'd flipped a switch and turned himself off. What was left was an autopilot program that was little more than an empty shell.

Finally, one night I couldn't take it anymore. I had so many questions, both for the book and about my own situation. I *needed* him to talk to me, so I decided to try again. I'd been thinking all day about what kind of approach to take. I ultimately decided to do it in the tent. I wouldn't be able to look him in the eye, but I'd learned from experience that the tent was where he was the most relaxed — the most apt, I believed, to let his guard down.

We'd just settled in, and it was almost completely dark. The air was cold, and a brisk wind was vibrating the nylon walls, creating an effect that made the tent seem alive. It had been over a week since either of us had bathed, so we were starting to smell ripe. Tom, in particular, was emitting a delightful medley of armpit sweat, wood smoke, and foot odor.

I turned on my side and faced his direction. An ice chest between us prevented me from seeing him.

"Tom," I said. "I don't know where you've been for the last few days, but I need you to come back to earth and talk to me. There are a whole set of things I need to discuss with you for the book, and I also need to know what you're thinking about how this thing with us will end. Have you heard any more news?"

I'd seen him occasionally enter the car and turn on the radio, but if he'd heard anything besides the one report we'd listened to early on, he hadn't shared it with me.

He didn't answer.

"*Please*," I said, trying to sound compassionate. "I have questions about London. I know it's hard on you, but I need more than what's in her diaries, and you know what I mean."

I paused, understanding I was in sensitive, possibly volatile territory. "I need you to tell me what happened. I don't know the ending."

"You know the ending," he said abruptly, his voice sharp. "You just don't know you know."

Disturbed and confused, I wanted to ask him to explain, but I was hesitant now that he seemed angry.

After a few moments, I braced myself and continued. "I know it's painful to talk about, but soon you're going to have to talk to me if I'm going to do this right."

I waited, and Tom was quiet. I took it as a good sign because he seemed to be considering instead of simply lashing back. As he was ruminating, I was thinking about the fire. I wanted to ask him about that too, but I was even more hesitant to go there.

"Tom," I ventured finally, "I need your help. I have questions. For example, after London... After it happened, did you or your wife notice she was different? Did you suspect there was something wrong? You must have at least talked to her on the phone."

"It kills me to say it, but I didn't talk to her at all," he said, seeming to come back from wherever he'd been. He sounded like the old Tom. The good one.

"I was in the Middle East, and we weren't in the habit of talking on the phone much when I was out of the country." His voice was plaintive. "We sometimes shared pictures and texts, and we occasionally did FaceTime, but with the time difference and all, it's just the way it was. We loved each other. That was never in question. Everything just happened at the worst possible time."

He stopped, and I didn't say anything, hoping he'd go on. After a few moments, I heard him take some deep breaths, and then he did.

"Lauren talked to her," he said, "but she didn't pick up on anything that set off alarm bells. London told her she was sick, and she believed her. Later, she went crazy with all kinds of second-guessing. *She should have known* and all that. But I didn't blame her. London deliberately kept it from us—wanted to spare us—which was just like her."

His voice trembled. "I can't stand that she went through all that alone."

I tried to think of something comforting to say but had nothing.

"I swear to God, if I knew who to go after, I'd ring their *fucking* necks," Tom said, his temper rising.

"I'm so sorry," I said.

"Can we go to sleep now?"

His voice had fallen into a whisper, but I could hear he was quietly seething. "I'll tell you what you need to know, but later."

"Okay," I said. "And thank you. I know it's hard."

"*You have no idea*," he said. And, of course, he was right. I'd never know the darkness of the place he now lived. How could I possibly?

CHAPTER THIRTY-ONE

LONDON DID FINALLY SLEEP, but it ended with a nightmare in which she was being suffocated in the dark. She tried to scream, but she was paralyzed, unable to move or make a sound, no matter how hard she struggled. When she did finally manage to cry out, it woke her up, and she wasn't sure if she'd really screamed or if it had only happened in the dream. Riley was gone, so if it had been real, no one was there to hear it.

Sweaty and shaking, London sat up and tried to calm herself, but the reality that set in once she regained her senses was as terrible as the dream. It was more terrible, really, because it was nothing from which she could wake up. It was her new life.

She fell back and closed her eyes, wanting to retreat back into sleep, even at the risk of more nightmares. She turned over, then spent a good twenty minutes tossing and turning until she finally gave up, deciding to look at her phone and check the time. She also recalled vaguely that she'd received a spate of texts. She'd check those, too.

She picked up her phone. It was ten-thirty. When she looked at her messages, she was shocked by what she found. At first, she had a hard time comprehending what she was seeing. But soon, as her pulse raced and she was struck breathless with rage and fear, she got it. Whoever had raped her had taken photos of her breasts and texted them to Jason from her phone. And not just Jason. Pictures had been sent to others in her text history as well. All male, and all now in various states of surprise and confusion—and, in the case of Jason, anger because his girlfriend had seen the text and accused him of cheating.

London fell into the fetal position and sobbed, wishing she could go to sleep and never wake up. Exhausted from crying, she finally did sleep, but she was eventually awakened by another nightmare—the second in a seemingly endless series that would punctuate the remainder of her life.

"What are you still doing in bed?" Riley asked when she arrived back at their room late that afternoon. Observing that London was in bad shape, she chuckled. "I heard you were at the party last night. Looks like it was your turn to drink too much."

Not wanting to engage, London turned over and faced the wall. "I have the flu," she mumbled, hoping Riley would go away. "I need to sleep."

"I saw the picture you sent Jason," Riley said. "Everyone's seen it." There was cruelty in her voice. "I'm surprised you did that. You know he has a girlfriend."

She made a scoffing sound. "You *must* have been drunk."

London's stomach churned, and she wanted to lash out, but she held back, silently willing Riley to shut up and leave her alone. But Riley wasn't finished. The roommate that London had spent the previous day caring for like a baby appeared bent on making her suffer.

"Do you know how dumb it was sending a photo like that to someone in a fraternity?" she said. "There's no way everyone in the house hasn't seen it by now. It's probably in all the other fraternities, too."

Not satisfied, she kept on. "I can't believe you were that stupid. I don't care how drunk you were."

Unable to take it anymore, London turned over and sat up. "I was *raped* last night. And I didn't send that picture."

London's voice and face were shaking, but she held Riley's gaze.

"I don't believe you," Riley said after a moment. "You just drank too much and now you're sorry. It happens all the time."

She collected her backpack from beside her desk, then stepped to the door and opened it. Just before disappearing, she stopped and turned around. "You should be careful what you say. You can ruin someone's life making accusations like that."

The words hit London like a punch in the stomach. She and Riley had never been friends—they had almost nothing in common apart from their room—but she could never have imagined this. And learning Jason had shared the picture was like a knife to the heart.

 beta

Feeling the heat of a growing rage, London began to rethink everything she'd done and hadn't done since the rape. Soon, with regret and anger compounding her trauma, she turned the rage on herself. *She was weak. She was a coward. She had done everything wrong.* She wrestled with thoughts like this for hours, pin-balling between guilt, shame, fear, and flashbacks she felt in every cell of her body.

With so many caustic emotions coursing through her, she became physically and mentally depleted. But despite everything, by the end of the longest, bleakest, loneliest day of her life, she redoubled her resolve to muscle through it. What else could she do? She'd done what she'd done, and there was nothing she could do to change it. All she could do now was put it behind her and focus on school—on her goals. Her "flu" would end the next day. *It had to*. She couldn't afford to let her classes slide.

That evening, London sent a brief text to each of the people who'd received the picture, explaining it had been a cruel prank and asking them to delete it. She considered sending a different kind of message to Jason, but she resisted, hoping what she wrote would shame him for what he'd done. Soon after she sent the final message (there were four), her mother called, and it took every speck of willpower London had to both answer and not break down.

"Hi, Mom," she said, struggling but failing to sound normal.

"London, is everything all right? You sound funny," her mother said.

London let out a long slow breath. "I picked up a bug that's been going around, but it's not a big deal. I'll be okay in a day or two."

"Well, that's a bummer. I'm sorry to hear this. Do you have a fever?"

"Maybe a low one. I haven't taken my temperature. But, seriously, I'm fine. I slept most of the day, and I'm starting to feel better."

"Well, make sure you eat," her mother said. "Can you get food brought to you from the dining hall?"

"My roommate's been bringing me food," London said, and the words tasted bitter in her mouth.

"Well, that's good. It's important not to let yourself get too run down. Make sure you eat even if you don't feel like it. Soup's always good. Do they have soup?"

"Yeah, they do," London said, fighting back tears. She sniffled and took some deep breaths.

"It sounds like you have a cold," her mother said.

"I've had a little cold for a while. You know what it's like living in the dorms. Hopefully, next year I can leave this Petri dish and move into an apartment."

"We'll see. Have you had to miss any classes?"

"No, and I'm sure I'll feel well enough by tomorrow or Tuesday to go to class. All I have on Mondays is one lecture and a lab, and I can miss those if I have to."

"Well, call me if you get any worse. And if there's anything I can do, let me know. I can have food delivered if you need it."

"Thanks, Mom, but I'm fine. Don't worry about me."

"I'm your mother. That's my job. I love you so much."

"I love you, too," London said, and now it was taking everything she had not to fall apart.

"Bye-bye, sweetie."

"Bye, Mom," London whispered, then she hung up and cried until she could barely breathe, promising herself she'd get strong in the morning.

∞

When London woke up the next day, it had been more than thirty hours since she'd eaten, and she was weak with hunger. She slunk to the bathroom, hoping not to be seen, and was aghast when she saw her misshapen face in the mirror. With her eyes discolored and swollen, she resembled a prizefighter. Upset but not surprised, she splashed cold water on her face. *"No more crying,"* she whispered, even as she fought back another round of tears.

She peed and showered, then returned to her room, wondering what to do about food. She couldn't bring herself to go to the dining hall. She felt terrible, and her eyelids looked like red balloons. Riley hadn't come back, or if she had, London hadn't heard her. In any event, she wasn't around, and London was glad. Just the thought of her sent her heart racing.

Wondering who else on her floor might be able to bring her some breakfast, she turned on her phone. She'd turned it off after talking to her mother, not wanting to deal with any more messages about the photo.

With her phone slowly coming to life, she dreaded the texts that might be waiting for her. To her relief, she mostly found sympathy and assurances that the picture had been deleted. Jason's response was a different story: "Okay. But I had to promise Amy I won't see or talk to you again. I'm sorry."

Wounded and angry, London was tempted to write back and tell him the truth. And why shouldn't she let him know what her little visit to his "house" had cost her? Deciding to consider the question later, when she was more clear-headed, she lay down and curled up. But soon she was forced to turn her thoughts back to food. Putting Jason out of her mind, she texted the only two people on her floor whose numbers she had, but neither panned out. One didn't answer, and the other was clear across campus.

She ended up calling a nearby cafe with a to-go order. Then she dressed, combed and tied back her hair, put on some sunglasses, and went out to pick it up. Being outside among people was disorienting. Shaky and wrung out, she felt completely alienated from the life flowing around her—as if what she'd experienced had cast her into a different reality. She knew it was probably exaggerated by the dark glasses, but it was like a barrier now separated her from everyone else who had *not* been violated, *not* been damaged to their core. And she thanked God for the glasses because they gave her a sense of privacy. She didn't want to be seen or interact with the world while her wounds were still so fresh.

After picking up her order, she hurried back to her room and attacked the food like a starving dog, praying that having something in her stomach would make her feel more like herself. It didn't. She did regain some strength, but she still felt blanched, obliterated. She tried to read, then tried to solve a set of math problems, but nothing stuck or computed. Her mind was hopelessly muddled— as though trapped in a fog from which she couldn't escape. She understood she was shell-shocked. This was classic

PTSD. But the knowing did nothing to fix her. She was broken, and there was nothing she could do about it. So she decided to sleep. To give herself another day.

CHAPTER THIRTY-TWO

LONDON DID GIVE HERSELF an extra day to recover, and then another, but as the days passed, she was so plagued with terrifying memories and flashbacks, she was unable to read or complete any of the problem sets that were due, despite repeated efforts.

She knew her classes were getting away from her, but she couldn't focus or think with any measure of clarity. It was all she could do to secure food each day, and when she did, she had to force herself to eat. She'd already been thin. Now, with a total lack of appetite, she was starting to appear anorexic. She thought about calling her mother, or maybe her friend Sara, many times, but, for various reasons, she couldn't bring herself to do it.

Wednesday morning, as she examined her emaciated frame in the bathroom mirror, she considered seeking counseling. She'd seen mental health services advertised around campus. She made a promise to herself to find out how to make an appointment. Maybe she could at least talk to someone on the phone. In the meantime, she wrote in her diary. It was difficult, but it somehow put the experience at a distance—as if she were writing about someone else. But as soon as she put down the pen, the distance diminished, and, once again, she was the girl in the basement—the girl unable to move or cry out.

Riley hadn't returned to their room for more than a quick in-and-out in days, and her obvious desire to stay away struck London as suspicious. When she did make an appearance, she wouldn't look London in the eye. London wrote this in her diary:

> Riley's been acting really weird. It could be she feels guilty about the way she treated me when I told her what happened, but it seems like something else. Like she might know something. Maybe even who did it. If she does know, she's definitely not going to tell me. She's so desperate to keep her stupid boyfriend, she'll do any-thing.

Despite suffering from another night of little sleep and bad dreams, London woke up determined to go to class. First, she had an early lunch in the dining hall. *Enough was enough.* It was time to jump back into her life before she let things slip too far and jeopardized her grades. She still had to force herself to eat, and she was unable to make eye contact with anyone, but it was progress. She attended a chemistry lecture at noon, and although she absorbed very little, she at least managed to take notes.

That afternoon, as she headed for Literature and Justice, she wondered if Jason would be there. They'd made a habit of sitting together, so when London arrived, she couldn't help but look at their regular seats as she entered the auditorium. He wasn't there, but she spotted him sitting alone near the end of a high row. Not wanting to meet his gaze, she looked away, then found a seat down near the front on the opposite side of the hall.

When the lecture was over, Jason surprised her by crossing the auditorium and heading in her direction as she made her way up the stairs toward the exit. Even from fairly far away, she could tell by the look on his face that he was unsettled by her appearance. Her weight loss was noticeable, and she had dark circles under her eyes.

As he was starting to get near, he made eye contact for an instant, then quickly looked away. When he was within arm's reach, he stopped and handed her a folded piece of notebook paper. Then, without so much as a nod or hello, he turned and went back up the stairs.

With a sick feeling in her stomach, London opened the note. The words she read hit her like a slap in the face.

London,

I know what you told Riley about the other night, and I just wanted to say that if it's true, I'm really sorry. According to what I've heard, a bunch of guys no one recognized crashed the party. I hope you're okay.

Take care,

Jason

That was it. After weeks of studying together—not to mention what had seemed, on the night of the attack, like a play to get closer to her—this was his response to learning she'd been raped. A note essentially designed to divert blame away from his fraternity.

Shocked and hurt, London had to leave the stairs and sit down, both to keep from falling and to get out of the way of other students who were still flooding out around her. She had a Literature and Justice discussion section she was supposed to head over to next, but she sat frozen in place, incapable of moving, much less facing a group. Instead, she spent the next hour sitting alone in the empty auditorium, wishing she'd never gotten out of bed.

∛

Later that day, London was struggling to start a paper on the impact of the Communist Party on mid-twentieth-century African American literature when Riley made an appearance. As usual, she ignored London, and London did her best to ignore her back, hoping she'd leave after collecting whatever it was she needed. But she didn't leave. Instead, she settled on her bed and obsessed on her phone, her mere presence feeling so toxic that London considered going to the library rather than subjecting herself to what felt like quiet torture.

Not lifting her head, London shifted her eyes from her laptop to Riley, finding her utterly inscrutable. She was Central Valley working class—by her own account, the first in her family to go to college. But now that she'd made it, she seemed content to piss it away. And for what?

"What are you looking at?" Riley said when she noticed London's eyes on her from across the room.

"Nothing," London said. "I was just wondering who you talked to about what I told you the other day."

"You mean who did I tell that you claim you were raped at the party?"

"You know that's what I mean," London said. "Did you tell a lot of people? Because Jason seemed to know about it."

Riley shot London a look of annoyance at having her busy schedule of Instagram scrolling interrupted. "I told Kevin, and he may have told a few people."

185

"What did Kevin say?" London asked, and she was genuinely interested because he was one of the last people she remembered seeing before everything went to hell.

"Whatever happened to you had nothing to do with Kevin or anyone else in the fraternity," Riley snapped. "He told me to tell you the party was crashed by a bunch of losers they didn't even know. It was probably one of those guys."

She turned her eyes back to her phone. "And, anyway, you shouldn't have had so much to drink. From what I hear, you had at least two big cups of punch that was mostly vodka. Just one of those gets me drunk."

She looked back over at London. "Besides that, it didn't even happen at the house. It had nothing to do with them."

London stared at Riley in shock, almost not believing what she'd heard.

"What?" Riley demanded, clearly having no idea what she'd just let out.

Momentarily speechless, London didn't answer.

"What the fuck is wrong with you?" Riley said, it still not dawning on her. "Why are you looking at me like that?"

"How do you know it didn't happen at the house?"

Riley looked confused, then nervous. "Of course it didn't happen in the house. I told you, they didn't have anything to do with it."

"But I never said it didn't happen in the house," London said.

Riley picked up her backpack and started for the door. "It doesn't matter what you said. It didn't happen in the house because the house had nothing to do with it."

CHAPTER THIRTY-THREE

ANOTHER WEEK PASSED, AND with each day, the temperature rose until soon the desert heat became stifling. It was only the middle of May, but already the daytime temperatures were probably in the upper nineties. Luckily, it was a dry heat. But, still, it began to feel like we were living in an oven.

Tom set up a small collapsible table under an umbrella he attached to one of the skeletal trees in our camp, and that, at least, gave me a place to work out of the direct sun. But nothing brought relief from the scorching afternoon highs, and each day it got worse.

By this time, Tom and I had developed a pattern with one another that hovered between total estrangement and careful congeniality. It was a strange dance, but I stopped worrying about Tom and became single-minded in an effort to get to the finish line. I couldn't have been more committed to the task at hand, but the sweltering conditions made it increasingly hard to think.

One especially blistering day, as I was cursing the sweat on my wrist for making my paper soggy, Tom hollered at me from the car. *"Valerie!"* he commanded with urgency. "Come listen to this."

As he turned up the radio, I rushed to where he was sitting with one leg in and one leg out of the SUV's passenger side.

"...meantime, the mystery surrounding Valerie Hawthorne continues to deepen. According to a police spokesman, newly discovered phone evidence suggests she may have been abducted by a third party present at the shooting who is believed to drive a dark late-model Toyota 4Runner. Investigators are asking anyone with knowledge relevant to the investigation to please contact local authorities. In addition, the victim's family is offering a twenty thousand dollar reward for information leading to the discovery of Ms. Hawthorne's whereabouts."

"Wow," I said, stunned and also relieved by what I'd heard. "Was there anything I missed? Anything about Steven or my kids?"

Tom killed the radio and shook his head, his eyes narrowing as he digested what we'd learned.

"You didn't miss anything," he said. "The crucial part was the *phone evidence*, whatever that is, and the fact they're looking for an abductor now. They must not have my license plate, or they'd have mentioned me by name."

His face was red and shiny with sweat. "Now you can at least stop worrying that they think you fled the scene."

"What about you?" I said. "Are you worried?" It looked to me like he was.

He began thinking out loud. "Maybe one of your neighbors saw you getting into my car."

More thinking.

"They might have heard the shot, started watching your house, and then seen us and taken a picture. But if that's it, I don't know why the police didn't have the photo sooner."

Of course, I hoped the police had finally found my phone and listened to the recording. They may have questioned my neighbors and gotten a description of the car that way.

Tom got out of the SUV and pushed the door closed. He looked weary and overheated, with sweat dripping from his grizzled hairline. He lifted his right arm and pressed the sleeve of his t-shirt to the side of his face, then repeated the action on the other side, his skin a dark bronze against the white of his shirt.

"Even if they don't have the license plate, we both know the book will identify you," I said. "Then what? What are you going to do?"

I was looking directly into his eyes, but he didn't answer.

"If you turn yourself in, you're bound to get a lot of public sympathy once we tell the story about London. They'll probably go easy on you."

But, then, I thought, *there was the fire*—which may have accounted for the grim look on his face. If he was responsible for that, it changed everything.

I'd been tempted several times to revisit the subject of the fire, but I hadn't yet found the courage. I guess part of me didn't want to know. Now my desire for the truth was greater than my fear. "Can I ask you something?" I said impulsively.

"You can ask me whatever you want. Doesn't mean I'll answer." He pulled a bandana from his back pocket and wiped his face. "Some things are best left alone."

"I understand," I said, and I wondered if the fire was one of the *things* he was thinking of.

He put the bandana back in his pocket.

"I'm thinking about the fire," I said.

He stood rock still, and I braced myself for a bad reaction, but he didn't explode. Instead, he looked down, kicked at a stone underfoot, then looked back up and nodded at the hillside. "Let's take a walk up to the mine and get out of this heat."

Minutes later, after collecting a lantern, a bottle of water, and two camp chairs, Tom led me, heaving and sweating, to the entrance of the mine. There, he lit the lantern as I stared breathlessly into the depths of the cavern, envisioning bats, rattlesnakes, and scorpions. Once the lantern was glowing, I reluctantly followed him inside, where my dread was quickly replaced by amazement at how much cooler it was.

"Oh my God," I said, feeling a flash of annoyance. "Why haven't I been in here before?"

Not far from where I was standing, I could see where Tom was using the mine for food and water storage.

"Do you think we can set up a work area in here for me?" I said. *Bats and snakes be damned,* I thought. It was great to be out of the blast furnace.

Tom ignored me and set up the chairs, then nodded for me to sit down. I did as I was told, first inspecting the ground for anything moving.

Placing the lantern between us, Tom lowered himself into the other chair, then opened the bottle of water and took a long pull. After closing it, he tossed it to me. As I opened the bottle and drank, Tom wiped sweat from his brow and stretched his long legs out in front of him. I screwed the top back on the water and looked at him expectantly.

With sweat reappearing below his hairline where he'd just wiped it away, he stared back, seeming to wonder at the wisdom of what he was about to do. Just when I thought he might be having second thoughts, he took in a long breath and blew it out slowly. Then, in a surprisingly straightforward manner, he commenced talking, not stopping until he'd told me the whole terrible story.

CHAPTER THIRTY-FOUR

THE SUN WAS RISING in a cloud-filled sky when Tom turned left onto the highway, still smelling vaguely of the woman he'd just betrayed. The air was cool, but his thoughts were heated as he barreled in a direction he knew would shred what was left of his life. But he didn't care about his life. Not anymore.

In the wake of London's death, grief and rage were an all-consuming torment—which is why he didn't blame his ex-wife for choosing to go to sleep and escape the pain. It was also why, as he headed full speed in the direction of trouble, he wasn't worried about himself. As far as he was concerned, his life was finished. Whatever lay ahead was simply an epilog whose consequences for him personally were of little importance.

He hadn't originally planned to target the fraternity. The urge had struck him and gathered steam in the middle of the night when he was thinking about the woman. Now in the car, he wondered if she was still asleep—blissfully unaware—or if she'd already awakened to find him gone and her life changed forever.

He felt a pang of guilt. Under other circumstances, he'd have liked her. He'd certainly had no trouble performing with her sexually. She was an attractive woman, and he was no stranger to shepherding people into his trust only to use them for other purposes. His work for the CIA had made him adept at deception. Of course, playing Valerie Hawthorne had been different. This was personal. If he managed to achieve what he was shooting for, it would be the most important mission of his life.

His idea was brilliant, although it wasn't what he'd initially envisioned. It had evolved from what started as little more than a prank to humiliate her. It all began one day when he googled her name and discovered she was slated to appear at a writing conference near one of the most beautiful fishing spots in the country. On impulse, he contacted the woman in charge of the event and asked for a hotel recommendation. A few phone calls later, and with just an amateur level of deception, he knew exactly where Valerie Hawthorne would be staying.

His original intention was simple. He'd stand up in an audience and expose how her callousness had contributed to his daughter's death. But as he was waiting for the right moment, he'd thought of something much better.

The book.

Targeting the fraternity house was just an afterthought. He was heading in that direction anyway to take Valerie once she returned home. (Kidnapping her from the hotel would be too risky.) As long as he was lighting the fuse on his own life, why not light another and burn down the monument to London's suffering? He thought the idea had a nice symmetry.

⊳

The drive was long to do in one shot. By the time Tom arrived in town, he'd been on the road for almost seventeen hours, stopping only briefly for coffee, gas, and fast food. He'd planned to drive straight to the fraternity, but he was exhausted, so instead, he checked into a motel near the freeway and crawled into bed.

Before closing his eyes, he plugged his phone into the lamp by the side of the bed and checked on Valerie. He'd placed a tracking app on her phone. She was in Salt Lake City. His plan was to follow her progress and grab her shortly after she returned home and faced the inevitable fallout with her husband. Tom wanted to add as much drama to Valerie's story as possible. A fight with her husband would be perfect, with the added benefit that he would be a suspect once she disappeared. Thinking about it brought a smile to Tom's face before he turned off the light and went to sleep.

When he woke up the following day, the first thing he did was check on Valerie. She was still in Salt Lake City. This made him happy because the longer it took her to arrive home, the more time he had to prepare for the next few weeks and for visiting the fraternity.

He regretted not following through with his plan for the fraternity the night before. Had he been thinking straight, he'd have realized that the timing of Valerie's homecoming would almost surely screw up his plan to set the fire. He was, therefore, delighted when, later that day, it became clear that Valerie was going to spend another night on the road—this time in Las Vegas.

She's afraid to go home, he thought with pleasure, so now he was free to carry out his vision for the fraternity.

ᚼ

Parked up the street from the frat house, Tom waited for the right time to execute his plan. It was well past midnight, but lights were still visible on both floors and even from a fair distance away, he could hear the deep throbbing base of music. Determined to be patient, Tom drank a Red Bull to keep himself alert. Around two a.m., the music and lights downstairs finally went off, but there were still a couple of lights on upstairs. That was both good and bad. It was good because it wasn't his intention to kill anyone. Once he started a fire, anyone still awake could help get everyone out. The downside was obvious. He didn't want to be seen.

With these things in mind, he waited another fifteen minutes, then reached back and collected a baseball cap and dark windbreaker from his back seat, wanting to make himself as unidentifiable as possible. He also pulled his fishing gloves from his coat pocket and put them on.

He had no expectation he could simply walk into the house, but he decided to check the doors anyway. He started with a side door on the north side of the house. It was locked. Next, since the street was deserted, he tried the front. Approaching the porch, he checked for video surveillance cameras but didn't see any. To his surprise, when he tested the heavy front door, it opened. Pulling his cap down, he opened the door further, then peered inside. The foyer was dim and deserted, so he crept in, pushing the door closed behind him but not clicking it shut, aware he might need to make a quick getaway.

The house smelled of old wood over a sour mixture of stale food, beer, and the musky odor of young men. It was mostly silent, but Tom heard occasional low murmuring from both upstairs and the far right of the house. He was surveying his surroundings, contemplating his best move, when he heard voices and footsteps coming toward him from what he supposed was the kitchen.

Moving swiftly and quietly, he fled just a few yards up a hallway and opened the door to what turned out to be a large walk-in closet under the stairs. He stepped inside and closed the door. Moments later, the voices grew more audible as two young men approached and then stopped near the front door. They spoke in hushed tones, so much of what they said was unintelligible, but Tom could hear their language was crude.

Just before one of them left and the other locked the door and sprinted up the stairs, the volume went up, and Tom heard what seemed like a fitting preamble to what he was about to do: "I swear to God I'm going to fuck her before the end of this year. I'm sick of this dick tease shit. What does she think this is, fucking high school?"

Ϗ

When Tom was sure no one was left downstairs, and there had been no noise or movement upstairs for approximately fifteen minutes, he slipped out of the closet and unlocked the front door. Next, he found two other doors on the downstairs level and unlocked those as well.

Stepping quietly through the different rooms, using a small penlight attached to his keychain for light, he noted all the places where it would be easy to start a fire. Large banners and tapestries hung on various walls throughout the house. Scattered closets and hat racks contained clothes that would be trivial to ignite. He consciously excluded areas near the stairway, wanting to make sure there was a safe exit path from upstairs.

The most promising candidates for easy ignition were the numerous sets of tall curtains in every room with windows. The large paneled room to the left of the foyer had three floor-to-ceiling sets. There were also sizable curtains in the dining room and in a messy booze-bottle and beer-can-littered game room that held a pool table, bar, and several overstuffed couches and chairs. In the game room, which smelled of cigars and a hint of vomit, he examined rows of group photographs going back generations. Studying the faces of the men—many long dead—he felt sure they'd be shocked by the current crop of students sharing their legacy.

Once he had a fair picture of the layout and flammable contents of the first floor of the house, Tom pulled a lighter from his pocket and began setting things aflame, doing so in a pattern and order that would both maximize the impact of the fires and minimize the risk that anyone would be unable to escape. He was careful to avoid areas too close to smoke detectors. He wanted them to go off, but not right away. He needed enough time to start a sufficient number of fires, then get out undetected.

His strategy worked. By the time the detectors started going off, he was already out of the house and hiding at a safe distance. But he was close enough to see lights turning on and hear the first cries of *"Fire!"* from upstairs. Now all he had to do was wait and watch the show.

Almost immediately, total pandemonium broke out. Young men and even a few women began flooding out the front door in various states of undress and panic as the house behind them belched smoke and lit up with flames that were visible through the windows on both sides of the front porch.

As Tom watched the terrified stream of bodies fly out the door and onto the lawn and sidewalk—yelling, cursing, and most everyone clutching phones and laptops—he couldn't help but wonder if the monsters who'd raped London were among them. He wished he were close enough to see their faces, to relish their terror more intimately, but he had to keep a safe distance, especially because now multiple people were filming the spectacle on their phones. He couldn't risk being noticed.

In just a matter of four or five minutes, as more of the house combusted and flames were starting to lick at the second-story windows, sirens rose in the distance. Tom was enjoying the mayhem, but he knew it would be dangerous to watch much longer, so he stepped out of the shadows and headed back to his car.

By the time the fire and police departments arrived on the scene, Tom was already miles away. It wasn't until the next morning, when he turned on the news in his motel room, that he learned two or three students had been pulled out on stretchers, and one was apparently missing. He was stunned. He'd wanted to destroy the fucking *house*, not kill anyone.

He switched off the TV and collapsed into an armchair. Trying to make sense of what he'd learned, he wondered if maybe the victims had been passed out—too intoxicated to get out of the house on their own. It was the only thing he could think of that made any sense. It may have been his military training, but he couldn't imagine a group of men running out of a burning building without making sure no one was left behind. But, then again, this group had demonstrated they were capable of much worse.

He felt a swell of revulsion, then agonizing shame. Regardless of whatever cowardice might have been demonstrated by the so-called frat brothers, Tom knew he'd come close to murdering those kids. Maybe he'd even killed one or two. If he'd thought his life was over before, it was really over now.

He remained frozen in place for a good hour, determined to get his emotions under control and put the fire out of his mind. Over the years, he'd become an expert at compartmentalizing—at diminishing anything that prevented him from moving forward or doing his job. He needed to do that now. He didn't have the luxury of being sidelined by guilt or remorse. He had a mission to complete. He closed his eyes, breathed slowly in and out, and tried his best to focus like a laser on one thing only—taking Valerie Hawthorne.

When he'd achieved the desired level of calm, he opened his eyes and checked his phone. According to his tracking device, Valerie was still in Vegas. That was fine. He could use the time to purchase extra provisions. But he hoped she would leave soon. Now, especially, he needed to move the ball forward as quickly as possible.

CHAPTER THIRTY-FIVE

TOM HAD TALKED WITHOUT pause for more than twenty minutes, recounting his role in the fire in a strange amalgam of stoicism and raw emotion. Now he stared at me in silence, as though awaiting a verdict.

I remained still, my head swimming with mixed feelings. I knew his remorse was sincere. I also understood for the first time that his ex-wife had died of suicide, which deepened my sympathy for his suffering. I had no sympathy for setting fire to a house filled with sleeping kids.

I didn't know what to say, so I let his last words hang in the air while I tried to collect my thoughts.

"Go ahead and write it," he said finally. "I'm not asking you to keep any of this secret."

He sighed, and his features collapsed into an expression so dark, I wondered what he was thinking.

"There's more," he said. "I might as well tell you."

He stared at the ground, then shook his head before raising his eyes back up to mine.

"Turns out a kid did die in the fire after all," he said. "The body wasn't found right away, which is why neither of us heard about it."

He paused and stared down at his feet again. "That phone call you heard? It was my ex-wife's sister." He looked up. "She thinks I'm in South America."

He scratched at the beard on his neck. "She left a weird message on my service. When I called her back, she told me about the fire. She doesn't think I had anything to do with it. She just figured I'd want to know since, you know, that was the house..."

As I was digesting, everything in Tom's bearing spoke of defeat. He'd told me repeatedly that his life didn't matter to him anymore, and it was never more clear to me that he meant it.

Motes of dust sparkled around his head in the light of the lantern. "I made a fucking mess, and I know I'll have to pay for it one way or another," he said.

We sat without talking for a long time after that—Tom lost in a sea of pain and regret, and me not knowing what to say.

Finally, I ended the silence. "Can I ask you something?"

He raised his eyes, and I took it as a yes.

"Are you really in the CIA?"

He scoffed, seeming surprised by the question.

"It's complicated," he said after a moment. "I've been what they call an *asset*, which means I'm not employed by the CIA, per se, but I sometimes help with intelligence gathering and recruiting other assets."

His eyes drifted like he was remembering. "Most of what I've done is mundane compared to what you might think. And I never did anything particularly dangerous, or that I'm ashamed of. I felt I was serving my country."

"And I can mention it?" I asked.

"I don't give a shit," he said. "Anything I did is old news by now."

He looked at me sardonically. "They won't like it, but I'm way past caring at this point. Any way you look at it, I'm fucked."

"You honestly thought you could burn down that old house and no one would get hurt?"

"I guess I wasn't thinking," he said. He tilted his head in the dusty light. With his sunburned skin and recently acquired beard, he resembled a world-weary Ernest Hemingway.

He mustered a sad smile. "I know it's hard to believe, but I used to be a pretty respectable fellow. You'd have probably liked me."

"As you may recall, I did like you."

We locked eyes, and I felt for a moment like we shared a deep understanding of how truly strange and tragic life can be.

"Can you please let me go home now?" I said. "You know I'm serious about the writing. But you also know my kids are being traumatized."

He didn't react.

"I promise I'll finish the book. You know I'll finish it. And I'll do it a hell of a lot faster with a computer to work on. I'm terrible writing in longhand, and I can't think straight in this heat."

I appealed to him with my eyes. *"Please? I've been missing long enough."*

Tom picked up the bottle of water that sat half empty between us and screwed off the top. He took a drink, put the top back on, then tossed it to me. "Kill it."

As I was finishing the water, he stood, then bent down and picked up his chair, folding it in a crisp motion before knocking dirt from its base. "I'll think about it," he said.

I started to press my argument further, but he stopped me. "I said I'd think about it."

He nodded at the lantern. "You can hold on to that and stay here out of the heat if you want. You can even get your things and work in here if that suits you better."

He paused and stared at me with what I took to be a sympathetic look. "I have some things to do back at camp. We'll talk more later."

He nodded in a way that gave me hope. Then his expression darkened, and he strode out of the mine, vanishing into a mirage of wavy lines.

☙

I did move my writing table into the mine, but I had a hard time concentrating, despite the cooler conditions. All I could think about was returning home.

I had no idea what kind of news splash my homecoming might make. Tom believed I'd be a big story, but with so many crazy things happening in the world, I wasn't convinced he was right. But I honestly didn't care one way or the other. All I cared about was reuniting with my children and ending their suffering.

Thinking about Steven upset my stomach. Not so much because I was worried about him. I was reasonably sure he was fine. I just dreaded seeing him. It was pathetic, and he was the father of my children, but after living with him for more than half my life, I had no desire to spend another second with him. When I thought about all the years I'd sublimated myself to such a terrible marriage and selfish man, I felt nothing but regret and shame. But I wasn't going to shame myself anymore. Of this, I was certain, no matter what.

When I eventually emerged from the mine and returned to camp, Tom was starting a dinner of rice, red beans, and Spam. Moving slowly and looking tired, his demeanor was aloof, so I left him alone, quietly hoping he was considering letting me go. He was definitely thinking about something, and I couldn't help but wonder if he was plotting how his own story would end.

I didn't like imagining what would happen to Tom. Despite everything, I didn't relish picturing him in prison or taking his own life, which I recognized as a distinct possibility. As crazy as it sounds, I might have preferred a daring escape. But, frankly, he didn't seem up to it. He didn't look that different from the man I'd met in Montana, but mentally, it was starting to seem like Elvis had left the building.

When dinner was ready, we ate quietly together, only commenting on the food, which was more or less what we ate every night. As we were scraping our dishes, Tom finally opened back up.

The sun was starting to sink beneath the hills behind him, and the sky was streaked with dramatic cloud swirls of orange, gold, and purple. The air had cooled, and a soft breeze carried the scent of scrubby creosote, which grew in low bushes over the desert floor and across the rocky slopes. "I've decided to give it one more week," he said. "Then we'll start thinking about wrapping things up."

My heart sank. He might as well have said *one more year*. I closed my eyes and wondered at the wisdom of arguing with him.

Opening my eyes, I gave him a pleading look.

"I said I'd think about it, and I did," he said. "You've got my decision. One more week. Then we'll see."

He scratched his chin, then softened his tone. "Before the week's up, I'll tell you what happened. Give you the ending."

"Why not just tell me now," I said. "It'll be so much easier for me to finish at home."

"It won't," Tom insisted. "Once you're home, you'll have all kinds of demands on your time. Your life will become a circus. I need you to write *here*. If a week isn't enough time to make good progress, we'll stay as long as it takes, but that's the deal."

"I'll make progress," I said, and I promised myself as I was saying it that I'd do my damnedest to make it true.

∞

Like every night, we went to bed as soon as the sun went down. Normally, we did very little talking, and I was always surprised by how quickly Tom's steady breathing indicated he'd gone to sleep. But this night, as I lay awake for what felt like hours, Tom's steady breathing didn't come, and I could tell by subtle noises and movements coming from his side of the divider that something was bothering him.

"Are you awake?" I whispered.

"Yes, Valerie, I'm awake," he whispered back, and with just those words, I could hear something was different about him. There was despondency in his voice.

I wondered if our conversation earlier had started him thinking about what would happen to him when everything was over. He claimed he didn't care, but the reality of his predicament may have been starting to sink in. Or maybe he was just thinking about London. I knew he dreaded talking about her death. He'd just barely managed to tell me about his ex-wife's. (His mention of her suicide was so oblique I almost missed it.)

"You know, if you ever feel like you need to talk, you can talk to me, and we can keep it off the record," I said.

He didn't initially answer, but a change in his breathing told me he was struggling with something.

"I've been thinking about conversations I had with London," he said finally. "It's my fault she didn't go to the police. If she had, she'd be alive today. It's just that simple." He let out a long sigh. "I warned her about the fraternities, and about drinking too much and making herself vulnerable to rape. But I also told her that when those types of kids get accused of rape, they don't get convicted. At least not if they're white. And university students? No."

He stopped, and I thought he was finished, but then he went on, his voice vibrating with regret. "I told her defense attorneys always find a way to turn the rapists into the victims and blame the girls. We had the discussion more than once." He sounded close to tears. "*I'm* the reason she didn't go to the police."

"She might not have gone anyway," I said. "Most rapes go unreported. Women just want to forget."

"I don't want to talk anymore," he said. "There's nothing more to say. I just have to live with it."

I respected his wishes and left it there, but I continued to think about London and how her story would have changed if she'd gone to the police. Tom was right. She'd probably be alive. But he was also right about how rape victims are treated. If London had reported the rape, she'd almost certainly have gone through a whole different kind of hell. Women paid a steep price for doing the right thing.

Tom woke up first the next morning, and it was evident by the way he went straight back into *I'm the boss* mode that he was more comfortable keeping a distance between us. Although he'd talked about giving me the end of the story, he didn't do it that day, and I decided not to push for it. Instead, I took my cue from him and steered clear, spending most of the day writing in the mine while he read, prepared food, and collected wood for our evening fire.

When the sun eventually gave way to stars, and we retired for the night, we remained distant, the only sound between us being our breathing and the swish of our sleeping bags as we adjusted positions. I lay awake a long time, thinking about home and what awaited me there. When I finally fell asleep, it was to the strong, steady ruffling of our tent. I dreamed of London that night, but when I woke up, all I could remember were visions of her face and the precipitous rise of the wind.

CHAPTER THIRTY-SIX

LONDON TRIED TO PUT Jason and Riley out of her mind. She suspected they both knew more than they were saying. For all she knew, what happened to her was common knowledge. But she was determined not to think about it. She needed to focus only on her courses and how to start feeling like herself again.

She thought about the counseling she'd been considering, but decided talking would make her feel worse. She wanted to forget, not remember. Also, she had a paper to write. It had to be finished and uploaded no later than eight o'clock the following morning.

She stared at the open file on her laptop. All she'd written so far was the title: *The Communist Party and Mid-Twentieth Century African American Literature*. It only had to be ten pages, and she had a strong enough understanding of the topic to write much of it off the top of her head. That is, if she'd been in her right mind. Unfortunately, she wasn't. But she forged forward anyway, telling herself to pretend she was taking an essay test, which had always been one of her strong suits.

She began writing and got off to what she thought was a strong start, but less than two pages in, her concentration began to falter, and she found herself reading and re-

reading what she'd already written, unable to move past what seemed like a wall.

Realizing she was weak and needed to eat, she took a break and went to the dining hall for dinner. She still had very little appetite or desire to be around other students, so she planted herself in a far corner and force-fed herself a grilled chicken sandwich and green salad. She ate quickly, then returned to her room, where she found Riley and two other girls from her floor smoking weed and listening to loud music.

London wondered politely if they could take their party to another room. "I need to finish an important paper," she informed them.

"This is my space, too," Riley said after taking a long gurgling hit on a bong. "You've had the room mostly to yourself for weeks. You can go to the library for a change. Or go see if anyone's in the common room. Maybe you can work in there."

London glanced at the other girls, hoping one of them might offer to move the party to her room. All she got back were blank stares.

Disappointed, London loaded her laptop into her backpack and headed for the common room, which turned out to be occupied by a mixture of boys and girls who, not surprisingly, were both drinking *and* passing around a large joint. Just an ordinary evening in the dorms.

Resigned to a long night, London headed to the library, which was a considerable distance across campus. The sun was still out, but she knew she'd be returning in the dark. She'd taken late walks back from the library many times with only slight trepidation. But now... Now, just thinking about it filled her with terror. Even so, she pressed on with only one thing in mind: finishing her paper.

When she got to the library, she found a free table and set up to work, but concentrating was even harder now that she had the added worry of her walk home. She looked at the time. It was six-thirty.

By eight-thirty, she hadn't made much progress, and mounting anxiety made it impossible to think, much less write. In an act of desperation, she decided to do something she'd never done before. She'd look on the web for material already written on the subject and then rewrite it to make it her own.

Lots of students did this kind of thing, not considering it plagiarism if they rewrote the passages they "borrowed." They just had to be careful to rewrite every sentence because the university used computer programs to scour uploaded papers for plagiarism, and the programs were reportedly good at finding even the smallest instances of copying.

London took pride in never resorting to "rewriting." Everything she wrote was strictly original. In this case—which she considered an emergency—she decided to make an exception, promising herself she'd use whatever she found only as a roadmap. She'd rewrite every word.

She did manage to find useful passages for each of the authors she was focusing on: Richard Wright; Langston Hughes; and Ralph Ellison. She pasted the passages into her essay, then set about meticulously rewriting, rearranging, and deleting. It wasn't difficult, and the relief she felt at seeing the composition come together allowed her to think more clearly. So clearly, she managed to add a lot of material on her own. By the time the paper was finished, she was satisfied that not a single unoriginal phrase remained.

The paper was due early the next morning, so she proofread it several times, did a bit more editing, then sent it off, feeling, as she was clicking Send, as if a mountain had been lifted from her shoulders. Now all she had to worry about was getting home in one piece. She checked the time. It was just after eleven o'clock.

She glanced around the room, wondering if there might be someone she could walk with—at least part of the way—but there were just a few stragglers left, and no one looked ready to go. She took some deep breaths and resigned herself to setting out alone.

There were lights on campus and normally at least a few people around this late, but she was flush with fear as she walked out the door of the library. She wished there were someone she could call, but there was no one, spurring a feeling of loneliness—friendlessness, really—that made her feel even worse.

With her throat tightening, she remembered fantasizing about the friends she'd make in college. She scoffed, then recalled her mom telling her she'd eventually find her people. She hoped she was right.

Be patient and take things one step at a time, London told herself, channeling her mother. At the moment, those steps needed to take her back across campus like she'd done, without incident, dozens of times.

She did her best to quell a burgeoning sense of danger that manifested partly as a racing heart and partly as an extreme tightness that moved between her chest and throat, making it hard to breathe. Each shadow and every male whose path she crossed—whether it was a student with a backpack or a homeless guy pushing a shopping cart—exacerbated her fear and made her want to run. But she didn't run. She walked as steadily as she could, all the while hoping her legs wouldn't buckle and leave her collapsed in the street.

She was two blocks from her dorm when a Mustang slowed down next to her and someone on the passenger side rolled down the window.

"Want a ride?" said a bearded young man in a baseball cap. As he spoke, another car raced by with several people in the backseat whooping out the window. "You shouldn't be walking by yourself so late," he said over the din. "We'll give you a ride. Where do you live?"

He didn't seem especially menacing, but London's adrenaline was sky-high. "I'm fine," she said, increasing the length of her strides.

She walked by someone sleeping in a doorway, and the smell of rancid sweat and urine stung her nostrils as she passed. The Mustang was still beside her, and now the driver leaned over and called out the open window. "I'm sorry. We didn't mean to scare you."

London looked over and nodded but didn't reply. Instead, she increased her pace even more.

"You have a good night," the driver said, then he sped up and disappeared around a corner, leaving London with her heart in her throat.

When she was finally back in her room, she was happy to find no party and Riley already asleep. She was also proud of herself for finishing what she believed was a good paper. *One step at a time*, she reminded herself.

Mentally and physically exhausted, she made a quick trip to the bathroom, then collapsed into bed. She slept deeply, not waking until the next morning when she was struck by the latest variation of her standard nightmare. In this one, she was being passed, like a crowd surfer, over hundreds of grasping men. She wore nothing but an open hospital gown and was unable to move a muscle. With each hand that groped and grabbed her, she felt her flesh separating from her bones. As always, she tried to cry out, but she couldn't utter a sound.

CHAPTER THIRTY-SEVEN

TWO WEEKS PASSED, AND London was slowly starting to heal. She still had bad dreams and a long way to go, but she was heartened by the fact that she was increasingly able to study and concentrate in class. She'd managed to complete problem sets in math and chemistry, get As on a couple of quizzes, and was even caught up on most of her reading. She was far from a hundred percent, but as finals approached, she felt she'd be able to complete the semester without taking too big a hit on her grades.

She was preparing to head out to a chemistry lab when her phone buzzed with a text. It was Susan, her Literature and Justice TA. "Can you come see me at my office today?" she wrote. "I'll be there between two and four."

"Sure," London replied. "What's up?"

"We'll discuss it when I see you," came back, giving London the feeling something was wrong.

London entered the TA's small office at two o'clock. Susan had only just arrived herself. Barely looking at London, she instructed her to sit down while she booted up her laptop and arranged some things on her desk.

As Susan fiddled with her computer, it occurred to London that maybe she'd seen the photograph that was probably still circulating. London had tried to put the picture out of her mind, but she knew that, by now, almost anyone might have seen it.

All kinds of rape and photo-related explanations began flowing through London's mind. Any of them, London reasoned, would account for the TA's serious demeanor. And her demeanor was deadly serious. Something was definitely wrong.

As London sat waiting for Susan to solve the mystery, she got increasingly nervous that she'd be put on the spot for not reporting the rape. It would be hard to justify her inaction to anyone, but in Susan's case, it would be especially uncomfortable because social justice was the theme of the course. What kind of justice was served by allowing rapists to remain free to rape again?

London was feeling a rush of shame when Susan finally spoke up. "I've been struggling with how to talk to you about this," she said, "because I've always liked you. Unfortunately, the only way I can really deal with it is to put my personal feelings aside and go by the rules."

London stopped breathing as Susan turned over a set of loose papers she'd pulled from a folder and placed on her desk. Next, she spun the open laptop around so London could see it.

London recognized the pages as the essay she'd written in the library.

"This is the paper you turned in," Susan said, placing her right hand on top of the pages. She nodded to the screen on the laptop. "This is one of the places we know you copied text."

London's heart began to race.

"That's impossible," she said, but she already had a terrible feeling she knew what had happened. She picked up the pages, and it took her only a few seconds to recognize that what she was holding was one of the early drafts she'd saved while working on the paper.

Whenever she wrote essays, she routinely saved early versions in case she later wanted to go back and retrieve something she'd pulled out or changed. She always added x's to the filenames to identify the documents as old drafts.

"This isn't the paper I meant to send you," London said in a panic. "I sent this by mistake. I can show you the final paper. There's nothing in the final version that contains a single sentence that's copied. This was just an early draft containing some of the source material I used in my research."

She leafed through the pages. "If you read this, you can tell it's not finished. *This is just a mistake.* I can show you. My final paper is nothing like this."

"I'm sorry," Susan said, "I really am, but it's too late. This is the draft you sent. It's a department policy not to accept do-overs, no matter what the explanation. And, unfortunately, because of the university's zero-tolerance policy on plagiarism, there are strict guidelines on how we have to deal with it."

She frowned. "All incoming students are warned about the consequences if they're caught plagiarizing. With the internet, and AI, it's become a big problem. But, in any case, it's out of my hands. You're in the system now. And I have to be honest; there's a chance you'll be expelled."

Dizzy, London bent over her lap as hot tears flooded her eyes. She wanted to explain about the paper, about the rape, about how much she'd been suffering and struggling to hold herself together, but her throat closed up and she couldn't talk. She could barely even breathe, and her pounding heart seemed ready to burst from her chest.

"I'm sorry," Susan said.

London let out a gasp, feeling as if she were back in one of her nightmares, powerless to help herself. She raised her head, trying to regain composure, but her face burned with shame as water fell from her eyes and nose.

Susan opened a drawer and handed London a tissue. "I'm sorry," she repeated. "But it truly is out of my hands. You can try talking to Valerie, but I doubt it'll do any good. The policy's dictated by the university."

London closed her eyes, understanding that a Hoover-sized dam of pent-up emotion was in danger of bursting. She wanted to explain so many things, but she couldn't. All she could do was get away.

Barely hanging on, she stood up and whispered, "I understand. Thank you."

In a state of near delirium, she fled to the ladies' room. Once inside a stall, the dam broke, and she sobbed until she was red-faced and raw and so spent that it was another hour before she had the legs to stand up, wash her face, and make her way home.

CHAPTER THIRTY-EIGHT

TOM HAD SOMEHOW MANAGED to bring thirty gallons of water in one and five-gallon containers. We'd been using it so sparingly that we were constantly underhydrated, and I spent a good part of every day fantasizing about taking a shower and washing my disgusting hair. Even so, it was running dangerously low. Tom had chosen our camping spot partly because it was close to one of the few known springs in the Mojave desert. Unfortunately, it turned out to be depleted to the point of being useless.

It was around seven o'clock, and we were eating our nightly rice and beans when Tom informed me that he was going to have to go out and find more water. I argued aggressively that instead of getting more water, we should abandon *"Camp Hellscape"* and he should let me go home, but I only aggravated a foul mood I'd seen building all day.

"I'll be leaving as soon as the sun starts going down," he pronounced, making it clear the subject was not up for debate. "I can probably pick up some jugs at that gas station where we stopped on the way in. I don't know how many. I'll just have to see."

"I want to come with you," I said.

"That station's not more than forty miles from where we turned off," he said. "I'll be back in two or three hours.

You'll be fine, so just calm down. Besides water, I'll bring you some goodies."

"I'm sure they have really great food in that place," I said bitterly. "You can bring me some Twinkies and a ten-year-old hotdog."

He ignored me, took a last bite of beans, then stood up and stretched. The sky overhead was still blue, but it was starting to fade, and the ghost of the moon was visible over the hills.

"Please don't leave me alone out here," I said. "If something happens to you, I'm dead for sure. You *can't* leave me here by myself."

"You said the same thing at the cabin, and I came back. Nothing's going to happen."

"No one was looking for you then. For all we know, your face has been all over the news. What happens if the gas station guy recognizes you, or some trucker? Or a highway patrolman?"

The more I thought about it, the more worked up I got. "You could get killed in a shoot-out with the police and they'd never find me!"

"Don't be so fucking dramatic," Tom said. "Nothing like that's going to happen."

"You can't possibly know that! You have no idea what might happen. *Anything could happen.* Just take me with you. You can duct tape me from head to foot and throw me in the back seat. Just don't leave me here. *Please.*"

Tom responded with an eye roll and shake of his head.

"I haven't wanted to say this," I pressed, "but the police probably know who you are by now. Because of the pictures. Don't you think they'd have checked the hotel registration and put two and two together? The whole country is probably on the lookout for you."

"I wasn't registered at the hotel," he said. "I lied about that."

"What are you talking about? I saw you check in."

"You saw me making a dinner reservation. And if you recall, I paid for dinner with cash. There's no way they can connect me with the hotel."

I was quiet for a moment while this sunk in.

"Look," he said before I could react. "You're just going to have to trust me on this. I'm coming back."

"*Why should I trust you?* What have you done to make me trust you? All you've done from the moment we met is use me, and humiliate me, and order me around like a dog!"

Tears of pent-up fear and frustration were now streaming down my face. "I've done everything you've asked, and now I'm asking *you* for something." I wiped my face with the back of my dirty hand. "Why can't you just once think about what I want? I don't want to be left out here by myself!"

"I'm sorry, but having you in the car would be too risky. It's not going to happen."

"You're not thinking of leaving me tied up, are you?"

He looked like he was considering the question.

"Please tell me you're not going to do that. I swear to God I won't try to leave. You can take my shoes if you don't believe me."

With my face heating up, I looked into his eyes and held his stare. "I can't believe that after all I've been doing to cooperate, you don't trust me."

"*Why should I trust you?*" he shouted, and I was surprised by the force of the outburst. "You lied to me." He wasn't yelling anymore, but his temples were pulsing on his sweaty forehead like a flashing red light.

"What are you talking about? What did I lie about?"

"You said you didn't recognize London, but I know you talked to her after she met with her TA because she called my ex-wife right after."

I grew even hotter, and I was momentarily speechless.

"I didn't lie," I said finally. "The picture you showed me didn't look like the girl who came to my office. I only realized I'd spoken to her later—after I read the diary."

My heart pulsed in my ears. "I told you what I did about the grading because I was afraid. I thought if you knew I wasn't the one who read her paper, you'd be less inclined to hurt me."

Tom stared at me in silence, his expression hard to decipher.

"If I'd known what was going on, I'd never have treated her with so little thought," I said. "She just caught me at the worst possible time."

"*Stop!* I don't want to hear it!" he shouted. "You're staying here. Just clean up, settle down in the tent, and I'll be back as soon as I can."

☙

An hour later, I watched Tom get in the car and drive off, deaf to my protests—although he did leave me both untied and in possession of my shoes, which was, at least, something. But as he disappeared behind a billowing curtain of dust, I had a knot in my throat like a walnut and a rising feeling of terror that I couldn't shake.

Of course he's coming back, I told myself. He wouldn't leave me alone in the desert with almost no water. But I wasn't convinced. As much as I wanted to believe it, I knew Tom's dark side was unpredictable.

As my fear compounded, I thought about him starting the fire, pointing a gun at me, playing me at the hotel. I thought about the pictures, the video (*oh my God, the video*). I remembered each and every time he'd been short with me, discounted me, fastened a chain around my wrist. How he'd made me live no better than an animal in extreme heat, with very little water and minimal food.

As the minutes ticked by, my thoughts spun relentlessly in the direction of doubt and panic. By the time the stars came out and I retreated to the tent, I was close to hysteria. I closed my eyes and tried to calm down, telling myself to go to sleep, that when I woke up, Tom would be back. *Of course he'd come back.* He needed me to finish the book. The book was all that mattered to him.

I finally managed to reduce my fear from a solid ten to a five or six, but when I did, my thoughts turned to my interaction with London. I'd been trying for weeks not to think about it, but now it was impossible to repress.

I prayed that once Tom learned the whole story, he'd find me worthy of some measure of forgiveness.

CHAPTER THIRTY-NINE

IT HAD BEEN A long terrible day, and I was in my cramped university office trying to get through a stack of bureaucratic paperwork that seemed custom-designed to dissuade anyone from ever contemplating a leave of absence. To the left of the stack, an even taller pile of English 1A essays waited to be graded. On days like this, I cursed myself for signing up for a job in the English department. I'd been warned that grading papers would destroy my personal life and reduce my hourly wage to mere pennies, but I'd considered the warnings to be exaggerations, not understatements.

My life had become an endless game of catch-up, and I was beginning to resent my students, many of whom were such poor writers that grading their papers took forever. It was tempting to simply circle big red Cs and Ds at the top of some essays, but instead, I spent hours meticulously editing and commenting in the margins. I sincerely wanted to provide this kind of guidance to my students, but it was consuming my life—which is why I was applying for time off. Unfortunately, the leave-of-absence deadlines on top of my grading deadlines were stressing me to the breaking point.

I was trying to understand some confusing health insurance forms when my phone rang. It was Steven. I considered letting the call go to voicemail, but we'd recently agreed not to ignore each other's calls, so I picked up.

"Hi. What's up?" I said, not taking my eyes off the form in front of me. I figured it would be his typical *I'll be working late, don't worry about dinner*. I couldn't have been more wrong.

"I know it's late notice," he said, "but remember the tall guy you said looked like Sting at my last high school reunion? He and his wife are in town, and I told him they could stay with us for a couple of days."

This got my undivided attention. "What are you talking about?"

"Look, I'm sorry," he said. "I meant to tell you a few days ago but forgot. He just texted me, and they'll be arriving around six-thirty. I told him to come for dinner."

"*Tonight?* Steven, no. *No way!* I can't possibly deal with this today."

"I'm sorry, but it's too late. It's happening."

"I can't believe you're telling me this now!" I said. "Even if the house were in shape to have guests, which it's not, I've got a million papers to grade! If you tell them it's a bad time, they'll understand. Offer to find them a hotel."

"They don't care what the house looks like or if you disappear to grade papers. They just need a fucking place to sleep for a couple days."

"Then how about this? *You* can go home and clean up the guest room and make the bed and clear off the dining room table and go shopping and do the cooking."

He was silent, and I knew damn well there was no way he'd do any of it.

"That's what I thought," I said.

"If you want, I can pick up some wine on the way home."

I felt like screaming. It was so typical. "Can you at least take them out for dinner?"

"You can cook. It doesn't have to be anything fancy. If we go out, I'll feel like I have to pick up the check."

"You're unbelievable," I said, but I wasn't in the mood for a fight I wouldn't win, so I left it there.

"I'll make it up to you," Steven said. "I promise." Then he hung up, knowing I'd rush out and take care of everything while he resumed his strenuous day of pointless meetings and talking on the phone.

Fuming, I gathered up all my papers and placed them in my briefcase, worrying over all the things I needed to get done before six-thirty—not to mention the traffic I'd have to battle on the way home.

I was heading for the door when my desk phone rang. I wanted to ignore it, but my office hours weren't quite over, so I figured I'd better answer.

I picked up the phone. "This is Valerie," I said, simultaneously eyeing the time. It was three-fifteen.

"Hey, Valerie," said the voice on the other end. "This is Adele in the Dean's office. I wonder if you can come by the office later today. There's some confusion regarding your leave. It's nothing we can't get cleared up, but I'm going to need you to come in. Can you possibly swing by before five?"

"Can we do it next week?" I said, wishing I'd let it ring.

"I'll be out on maternity starting next week, so we should really take care of this now. If we leave it to a temp, things could go sideways."

"Can we deal with whatever the problem is over the phone?" I said. "I'm kind of in a rush."

"I need you to sign a couple of things," Adele said, "so you really need to come in. It shouldn't take too long."

"Okay," I agreed, although I knew it would add at least twenty minutes to the time it would take me to get off campus.

I was just heading out the door when I was greeted by a student who had come for my office hours. Strictly speaking, I was supposed to be available for another fifteen minutes.

"Did I miss your office hours?" she said. "I was hoping I could talk to you about my last paper."

"I'm sorry, something has come up, and I really have to run," I said. "Can you talk to your TA or come see me next week?"

I forced a smile, waited for a beat, then turned and headed down the hall in the direction of the Dean's office.

I should have seen something was wrong. She was painfully thin, and her carriage was timid. Under normal circumstances, I'd never have paid her so little mind. I was just so preoccupied that I barely even noticed her, except as an impediment. It's only in hindsight that the red flags seem so obvious—the pallor of her skin, the condition of her hair, something in her eyes. But none of it registered at the time. At least not to the level it should have.

When I turned her away, she didn't argue or make any kind of fuss. She didn't say anything at all. Then I was off, and I'm ashamed to say I never gave her another thought.

Well, that's not quite true. I did read something about her in the newspaper, but I didn't recognize her as one of my students, and my TA never said a word. If I'd known she was the girl who'd tried to speak to me, I'd have been devastated.

CHAPTER FORTY

IT WAS THE MIDDLE of the night, and Tom still hadn't returned. I had no idea what time it was, but I was certain I'd slept because I'd been dreaming about food, which had become an almost every-night thing. Before falling asleep, I'd been awake for hours, so I was sure Tom had been away much longer than he'd promised. I unzipped the tent and poked my head outside, trying to get a sense of the time. The stars were still bright, so it was far from dawn. Judging by the feel of my bladder, I guessed it was two or three in the morning. *So where the hell was Tom?* Earlier, I don't think I'd really believed he'd abandon me. But now... Now, I began to fear in earnest.

Nervous about what might decide to crawl into the tent, I zipped it back up and lay down, trying not to let my imagination get the better of me. But it was hard to quell a growing sense of terror. Something had happened to Tom. *It must have.*

In an attempt to ward off all-out panic, I began thinking about what it would take to get back home if I really were on my own.

Soon, it began to seem more doable than it had before. Despite all my protestations to Tom about dying if he left me alone, I figured I could make it to the highway if I had to. The dirt road we came in on was probably no longer than ten or fifteen miles. It had some steep ups and downs, but if my life depended on it, I could do it. And if Tom had really deserted me, my life would depend on it—of that I was certain.

Walking it in the daytime would be brutal, making me wonder if I should start out in the evening, as terrifying as that seemed. Either way, if I were going to do it, I'd have to do it soon because I was almost out of water.

For the rest of the night, my thoughts bounced back and forth between plotting my escape and assuring myself that Tom *would* be back, that he was simply delayed. I reasoned that he wouldn't abandon me because he wouldn't abandon the book. But if he hadn't left me, where was he? What had happened?

I eventually fell back to sleep, only waking when sunlight and the inevitable heat began turning the tent into a sweathouse.

Emerging from my cocoon, the harsh reality of Tom's absence hit me with an intensity I hadn't anticipated. This was real. I was alone. There was no Tom presenting me with a cup of coffee. No breakfast waiting for me, meager as it might be. No grumpy presence I'd relied on for a sense of security.

As all the implications of being truly alone began to stack up in my mind and sink in, I became so filled with dread that I might have retreated back to the tent if it weren't so hot. It was probably only seven or eight o'clock, but the sun was already oppressive, promising another day of unrelenting heat.

Focusing on keeping it together, I forced myself to zip up the tent, step away, and think as calmly as I could about what I needed to do to prepare for a walk out.

I sat on the bench near Tom's fire pit, and the first thing I needed to do became evident. I needed to visit our camp "bathroom," which was a rocky area on the other side of a stand of cactuses where Tom had stationed a shovel and box of toilet paper.

As I set out for the task, a swell of empowerment began to rise inside of me. Stepping cautiously over the desert floor, I pictured myself walking the road, making it to the highway, flagging down a passing car, or maybe a highway patrol. The more I thought about it, the more I believed I could do it.

I wondered if Tom had planned this all along. He'd have a substantial head start for a getaway, and I'd have a dramatic ending for my story. It occurred to me that he hadn't given me London's ending, and that surprised me, but I knew I could figure it out for myself once I was home.

I had just completed my bathroom activity and was treading carefully around rocks and shrubs on my way back to camp when a chilling sound stopped me in my tracks.

Looking ahead and to the left, I froze upon seeing a large dirt-colored rattlesnake in striking position. With its tongue darting and rattle waving like a flag, it had only just registered in my consciousness when it struck, becoming a blur that, in a split second, lit a fire in my calf. Then it flew off at a speed I'd never have imagined possible.

As I stared at two neat holes now burning electric in my leg, the wound began to pulse, and I knew this was probably it. There would be no long walk out. No return to my family. No book. No questions to answer. No anything but slow death. In an instant, everything had changed.

I had no idea how long I had or how much pain I might suffer before it happened. I only knew I would almost certainly die. But the concept was still so new that strong emotions hadn't yet hit me. The main thing I felt at that point, apart from the burning, was astonishment that my fate could be decided so randomly and so quickly.

Understanding that panic might set in at any moment, I cautioned myself to remain calm. Maybe I didn't have to die. Maybe Tom would arrive back any second and save me. For the present, I needed to head back to camp, collect some food and water, and set myself up in a place out of the sun. The mine was the best place to shoot for, but I wasn't sure I could make it that far. I was already starting to feel faint, and my leg was throbbing and beginning to swell, so even the twenty or so yards back to camp would be excruciating.

Concentrating on my breathing, I slowly navigated the uneven terrain, telling myself to take it one step at a time. But with each step I took, the fire in my leg grew hotter, and my fear grew harder to suppress. When I finally arrived back, I unzipped the tent and retrieved my sleeping bag. It was tempting to simply lie down, but fearing I might fall into unconsciousness at any moment, I determined that the better course of action was to drink some water and seek shade.

I limped to where Tom had created storage for some of our provisions under a stand of dead-looking trees near the boulder that separated our camp from where the car was normally parked. It was the only semi-shaded spot in the area. Pulling a mostly empty jug of water out of a milk crate, I looked longingly at the mine, where most of our food and water were stored. I wondered if I could make it that far.

I looked down at my leg. It continued to swell, and a frightening shade of purple was beginning to rise around the wound. Telling myself to focus for the moment on the water, I placed my sleeping bag on the ground, lowered myself onto it, then took a long slow drink, savoring the way the wetness soothed my throat.

I closed my eyes, and almost instantly, emotions I'd been suppressing hit me like a deluge. Tears flowed, and I fell into convulsions of grief, thinking about my kids and wondering which would run out first, my water or my life.

CHAPTER FORTY-ONE

TOM HAD INTENDED TO secure as much water as possible, then head straight back, but when he got to the gas station where he'd planned to purchase the water, a sign in the window indicated the station was closed due to illness. Based on his recollection of the ancient proprietor, he wasn't surprised.

Thinking about the empty water jugs he'd brought with him, he investigated a water faucet outside and to the back of the station, but what emerged when he finally managed to turn the rusty handle was a trickle of brown water he wouldn't wish on a cockroach.

He considered what to do next. He could head back, and they could pack things up—call it a wrap. That would make Valerie happy, and he knew she'd finish the book. That wasn't a question. What was in question was her current newsworthiness. Out in the middle of nowhere, he had no way of knowing what was going on with her case. He couldn't access the internet, and the news he was able to hear in his car was minimal.

He had an ace in the hole he'd been holding, and he wondered now if he should use it, just in case. It would require finding a motel with Wi-Fi. A motel would also be a source of water—and a shower, which appealed to him more than anything. Unfortunately, there was no telling how far he'd have to travel before he came to one.

He got back in the SUV and only had to think about it for a minute before deciding to drive up the highway and stop at the first motel or gas station he found. If it were a gas station, he'd gas up, buy some water, and drive back to camp. If it were a motel, he'd get a room for long enough to take a shower, fill some bottles, and execute his ace in the hole. He might get lucky and find a gas station and motel together. Maybe alongside a diner where he could get some real food. Thinking about a hamburger made his mouth water. He knew being gone so long would send Valerie into a tizzy, but it wouldn't kill her. He'd be back soon enough.

☙

Tom started back in the direction of their camp. To his delight, he only had to drive another twenty miles past their turn-off before hitting the jackpot—a truck stop diner and gas station combo right next to a motel that, despite its tired appearance, had a large billboard promising *Cable* and *Wi-Fi*. He was leery of the motel, knowing it might require a credit card, so first he went into the diner, which also turned out to have Wi-Fi, so he was able to both eat and check the news.

To his great relief, he had *not* been identified as Valerie's abductor. However, it was evident, based on the dates he saw, that her disappearance was no longer a big story. It was time for his ace in the hole. But, first, he had a steak and baked potato, green salad, and a big piece of banana cream pie. He ordered the same—to go—for Valerie.

Thinking about a shower, Tom decided to try to get a room for a couple of hours and execute his plan from there. But, first, he put gas in his car and bought eight gallons of water in the attached mini-mart. He was tempted to buy more but didn't want to attract attention. If he managed to get a motel room, he could fill additional bottles there.

Putting on his ball cap, he pulled into the motel parking lot and went in, hoping to get a room with cash. He was fairly confident the police weren't looking for him by name, but he wanted to be cautious all the same. He stepped up to the counter and nodded a greeting to a young man who looked to be Native American.

"I need to take a shower and rest up for a couple of hours before getting back on the road," he said. "Can you help me out?"

Barely looking at him, the young man nodded, then began punching keys on the computer. "I'll need an ID and credit card."

"I'm more of a cash guy," Tom said, pushing a hundred-dollar bill across the counter. "Will this be enough?"

"That'll work," the young man said.

He took the bill, then, a moment later, handed Tom a key. "Room ten. When you're ready to leave, drop the key in the slot by the door."

"Is there a password for the Wi-Fi?" Tom asked.

"*Desert1*. No space, capital D."

"Thanks," Tom said, feeling a lift by how smoothly everything was going.

Three minutes later, he was out of his clothes and standing under a welcome stream of hot water, lathering away weeks of sweat and grime. It felt so damn good, he'd have paid a thousand dollars for the luxury.

He lingered in the shower, not knowing when the next opportunity might come and wanting to savor the experience. With Valerie in mind, he finally stepped out and dried off. He didn't want to stay *too* long. It was one thing to make her sweat. It was another to scare her into doing something stupid.

He wrapped a towel around his waist, then retrieved his pre-paid phone from his pants pocket and settled himself onto the bed, first pulling off the dubious brown spread that probably held the sweat and skin cells (and God only knew what else) of hundreds of truckers.

After connecting to the motel Wi-Fi, he did another search for news on Valerie, just in case he'd missed something in the diner. He didn't find anything new. He did another search and, within seconds, located a Los Angeles Times website offering a secure encrypted messaging system citizens could use to anonymously report news leads.

"Got a tip?" the page asked in enormous bold letters.

I've got a tip, alright, Tom thought.

He typed a simple message:

I have Valerie Hawthorne. To prove this isn't a hoax, I posted a video of our first meeting on YouTube. Search for "Good clean fun with VH." To authenticate, look for a thumb drive buried in the soil to the left of her front door. I put it there before taking her. It contains the same video and pictures. Check it out and stay tuned.

He pressed Send, then smiled at recalling how, before taking Valerie, he'd posted the video and set it all up as a way of spicing up the story, if need be.

He didn't feel great about causing Valerie even more humiliation, but he reminded himself that she stood to gain handsomely from the deal. Quite handsomely if she wrote a compelling book, and he had confidence she would. Despite the one-star review of her last novel he'd posted on Amazon as a lark, he knew she was a good writer. At least London had thought so.

With bitterness, he remembered London talking about her—being excited about her course.

Stretching out on the bed, Tom felt pressure building in his head and a familiar pain in his stomach. He recalled the conversation vividly because it was the last time he and London had been together. It was the Saturday after her second week of classes. She'd had on a blue and white top, and her hair was clipped up, with loose strands falling just so around her face. As always, she was beautiful, without a hint of makeup. She'd beamed with enthusiasm as she talked about her pre-med courses and the extracurricular she was taking from a writer she admired. Tom had wondered aloud if London was taking on too much, but she told him not to worry, that she could handle it.

He was so proud of her, so thrilled to see his daughter finally launched on the journey she'd been dreaming of since she was a tiny girl. He could never have imagined on that perfect day that he'd never again see her smile. That she'd be gang raped by drunken thugs, then pushed over the edge by the teacher she'd so glowingly described.

ᦓ

Tom hadn't meant to fall asleep, so when he woke up the next morning, he was both disoriented and surprised. He sat up and looked at the time. *"Shit."* It was almost ten o'clock. He couldn't believe he'd slept so late.

He thought about Valerie and considered the situation. She would be feeling abandoned and afraid. By now, she was probably thinking about trying to walk to the highway. Maybe she'd already set out. What other choice would she have if she believed he'd really abandoned her? But it would be a long slow walk, so if she had started, he'd find her on the road. He supposed, in some spots, she'd be able to hide if she heard him coming, but he didn't think she'd hide. More likely, because of the heat, she'd welcome a ride back to camp, although he knew she'd be angry. *Really angry.* But he could deal with that.

Looking on the bright side, it would make for a better story, which was a good thing. The more drama and suspense, the more marketable the book. He decided he was glad he'd fallen asleep, and it was nice to sleep in a bed for a change. He might even take another shower.

He thought about the text he'd delivered to the LA Times and decided to check the news before showering. It was probably too early for any new reporting, but it wouldn't hurt to look. He'd also check YouTube to see if the video had any views. Views would indicate they'd at least seen his message.

Tom did not find any new reporting, as expected, but the video now showed seventeen views, so his message had been received and was generating interest. Tom smiled. Soon, Valerie would be back in the headlines.

He was tempted to extend his stay in the motel to keep tabs on the news, but he couldn't risk giving Valerie enough time to get to the highway. He'd just have to keep checking the radio in his car.

It was shortly after eleven and probably at least ninety degrees when Tom finally dropped the room key in the slot by the office door. Eyeing the diner, he decided to go in for breakfast. He simply couldn't resist the chance for some bacon and eggs. Or maybe a big Denver omelet with fried potatoes and sourdough toast. And coffee. He needed coffee. He'd pick up some coffee and breakfast for Valerie, too. That and the previous night's steak might improve her disposition once he made it back.

He took his time over breakfast, savoring every bite of his omelet, which was surprisingly good. The potatoes, toast, and melon he ordered were also good, and the coffee was strong, the way he liked it. He had to hand it to the place. It didn't look like much, and it was out in the middle of nowhere, but it wasn't bad.

He was done eating and had just ordered some food to go for Valerie when he noticed a highway patrol car drive up and pull into a space in the parking lot. There was only one officer in the car, and he didn't get out. He just sat in the car and intermittently talked on the radio. He also appeared to be reading something, but Tom wasn't able to look too closely at what he was doing because he didn't want to be noticed glancing over.

Valerie's food arrived, and he thought about standing up and leaving, but instead, he asked for a refill on his coffee. He doubted the patrolman posed a serious risk but decided, in the interest of caution, to stay put until the officer either drove off or entered the diner—at which point he'd either leave or reassess.

He thought about the pre-paid phone that connected him to the LA Times message. He'd pulled out the SIM card after he did it, but could it have been used to trace his exact location? He wasn't sure and regretted his technical knowledge wasn't better. Things were changing so rapidly it was hard to keep up.

With the patrolman still in his car, Tom began thinking of ways to destroy or dispose of the phone inside the diner. He ran some scenarios but eventually decided he was panicking for nothing. The SIM card was out, so it was back to being untraceable. *Just sit tight and don't act nervous,* he told himself, forcing himself not to look out the window.

After fifteen minutes, the patrolman entered the diner. Tom kept his eyes down as he stepped up to the counter, greeted the waitress like they were old friends, then ordered a coffee and blueberry muffin to go. Not long after, he threw a five-dollar bill on the counter, told the waitress to "keep the change," and returned to his car for another few minutes before finally driving off.

By this time, it was almost twelve-thirty, and Tom's anxiety was moving into the red zone. He hoped Valerie hadn't gone off the deep end, but he knew he needed to be prepared for anything.

CHAPTER FORTY-TWO

MY LEG THROBBED WITH searing pain as it became more and more swollen. It was also turning a frightening shade of purple. Despite my best effort to keep a cool head, I couldn't think straight.

I'd once read something on the "dos and don'ts" of rattlesnake bites, but in my harried state, I couldn't remember the details. I did recall that *"suck out the poison"* is a myth. Apart from that, I remembered you should either raise a leg or *not* raise a leg if bitten. I also seemed to recall that a tourniquet was not advisable—or maybe it was the opposite. It was emphatically one or the other, but which was it?

Using logic, I worked out that I should probably apply a tourniquet and *not* raise my leg, but I wasn't sure. In short, I was staring death in the face but paralyzed with uncertainty about what to do. It had been maybe two hours at the most since I was bitten, and already my leg was twice its normal size. I was also swinging between chills and sweats and dangerously close to throwing up— which I knew would make my water situation more dire.

To make matters worse, it was already hotter than hell. I knew I should try to get to the mine where it was cooler, but under the circumstances, the exertion it would take seemed unthinkable. It might as well have been at the top of Mount Everest.

Deciding to simply rest and focus on breathing, I remained flat and immobile on the sleeping bag. I was certain that *"stay calm"* and *"remain immobile"* were on the snakebite "Dos" list, but the *"stay calm"* part was easier said than done. When I closed my eyes, I felt like I was floating in a strobe-lit universe of throbbing, all-consuming pain.

In time, virtually all my thoughts were obliterated by an overpowering sense of being burned from the inside out. But even in that altered state, I managed to retain enough presence of mind to know that, mine or no mine, my survival depended on Tom coming back. In that flashing space of pain and uncertainty and fear, that single towering truth remained clear. Tom was my only hope, and he needed to return soon.

CHAPTER FORTY-THREE

BACK ON THE HIGHWAY, Tom drove briskly in the direction of their camp, but he kept an eye out for the highway patrol, not wanting to be caught in a speed trap. Upon arriving at the turnoff, he was forced, by the condition of the road, to reduce his speed to a relative crawl. It was frustrating because he was increasingly nervous about how long he'd been gone, but there was nothing he could do. The road was so littered with rocks and holes, he would lose his oil pan if he wasn't careful.

When he was maybe halfway back, he started surveying the surrounding area for Valerie. He was still fairly certain that if she saw him coming, she'd be disinclined to hide. According to the thermostat in his car, it was 95 degrees. But, just in case, he watched for her. He also tried to mentally prepare himself for the onslaught of rage that would hit him once he found her, whether she be on the road or still in camp.

It was pushing two o'clock when he finally arrived back, and there was initially no sign of her, which surprised him. He expected that, upon hearing him drive up, she'd come running from wherever she was to assault him with expletives. He looked up at the mine, where he guessed she'd be, and figured she probably hadn't heard him.

He stepped out of the car and, with his eyes on the entrance, slammed the door as an announcement of his arrival. The sound reverberated through the surrounding terrain, but Valerie didn't appear, causing Tom to wonder if he'd missed her driving in. He reached through the window and sounded the horn. Still nothing.

His thoughts began to race. He needed to take a quick look around, then, if he couldn't find her, go back and search for her on the road.

"*Fuck,*" he yelled, regretting he'd left her for so long.

He was still standing next to the car, mentally berating himself and trying to think ahead, when he heard a sound coming from the direction of their camp.

Not sure what he was hearing, he stepped around the boulder and was shocked to find Valerie lying just on the other side, barely conscious and with a leg that screamed *rattlesnake.*

As she moaned and gazed at him with pleading eyes, he picked her up and carried her to the car, gently placing her in the back seat. After checking to make sure the rear air conditioning vent was open, he started the car and turned the fan up high. He then retrieved a bottle of water, climbed into the back seat, and pulled Valerie into his arms. "Drink this," he said, placing the bottle to her lips. "*Slowly.*"

Desperate, Valerie drank, but she tried to take the water faster than she could swallow and began choking.

"Easy," Tom said, pulling the bottle back and waiting for her to resume breathing normally. Inside, he was screaming at himself for his negligence.

Once she settled, he put the bottle back to her lips and let her take more. "Slowly," he repeated, and as he was speaking, he was eyeing her leg.

He wasn't an expert on rattlesnake reactions, but he knew enough to know this was serious. Extremely serious. She had to get to a hospital soon or she would die. He couldn't imagine there being a feasible hospital within driving distance. She needed a helicopter.

"Where were you? What happened?" Valerie whispered, then she almost immediately broke into tears.

"I'm sorry," Tom said. "The gas station was closed, and I had to go somewhere else for the water."

Valerie groaned, and he put the bottle to her lips once again.

"I'll explain everything later," Tom said as she was swallowing. "For now, I have to get you out of here. I need to grab a few things, and then we'll go. Is your latest work in the mine?"

Valerie took some gulps of air. "Everything's in the tent," she said. "But please hurry."

She strained to raise her head and look at her leg. Now her foot was also grotesquely swollen. Her toes looked like fat purple sausages. "I don't want to die..."

"You're not going to die," Tom said, but as he was saying the words, he wasn't sure they were true. She looked and sounded terrible.

◌੪

Minutes later, they were bumping and swerving slowly toward the highway. Tom didn't know where, in the long run, Valerie would be headed. He only knew she needed a doctor or hospital as soon as possible. The best course of action he could think of was to drive back to the motel, drop Valerie in a room, and have her picked up from there. He guessed the closest hospital was in Needles. He just had to hope they were equipped for helicopter transport.

Tom had given Valerie some extra strength Tylenol, which was all he had in the way of pain relief. He also gave her the bags of food he'd purchased at the diner. Reclining in the back seat with her head and shoulders against a pile of gear, she gobbled food with her bare hands as her leg continued to swell. When food and water eventually buoyed her up, the anger Tom anticipated finally flared.

"What happened? Where were you?"

Tom filled her in, and she started to respond, but he stopped her. "We need to forget all that," he said. "We have more important things to talk about. I need to tell you what happened to London so you'll have your ending." He looked at her in the rearview. "Once I drop you, you won't see me again, so we need to do this now."

"What are you going to do after you leave me?"

"Stop talking," Tom said. "Just listen."

He reached over into the passenger seat and pulled a yellow pad and pencil from an open backpack. He handed the items back to Valerie. "I know you're in pain, but if you can, take notes. I'm only going to tell you this once, and I want you to get it right."

CHAPTER FORTY-FOUR

AFTER A NIGHT OF almost no sleep, London forced herself to get up and go to her classes, first visiting the dining hall for a badly-needed breakfast. Her appetite was still poor, but she understood she had to eat. She was starting to become so skeletal, she barely recognized herself. She knew her parents would be horrified if they could see her, but she put it out of her mind, simply focusing on getting through the day until she could meet with Valerie Hawthorne. She'd decided to go to her and tell her the simple truth—about how she sent the wrong paper, but also about the rape. If anyone in the university would understand and be sympathetic, it would be Valerie. Maybe she'd intervene and save her from being expelled. It was worth a try.

Her office hours overlapped with a class London had on the other side of campus, but London figured if she hurried, she could catch her. As it happened, she managed to get to the brick building housing the English Department with fifteen minutes to spare. As she entered and headed up a flight of stairs, she tried to calm her nerves and remember what she needed to say. She'd been rehearsing a speech in her head all afternoon. Now that the time had come, she was afraid she'd be too nervous to deliver it.

She was approaching the office door, hoping to find the courage to knock, when it abruptly opened, and Valerie

Hawthorne emerged in such an obvious hurry she almost bumped into London.

Wobbling on a shaky bearing, London gulped air and greeted her. "Did I miss your office hours? I was hoping I could talk to you about my last paper."

Her heart was racing so fast her chest ached, and she was short of breath.

"I'm sorry," Valerie said, barely looking at her. "Something important has come up, and I really have to run. Can you talk to your TA or come see me next week?"

London nodded and forced a smile as Valerie hurried off down the hall and disappeared around a corner.

Pulling out her phone, London lowered herself to a bench, deciding on the spot that it was finally time to talk to her mother. She understood the hallway of a campus building wasn't optimal for the conversation they needed to have, but she didn't care. She needed to hear her mother's voice. With her heart thumping in her ears, she dialed her number, but there was no answer. The call went straight to voicemail.

London hesitated to leave a message. Her throat was so constricted she wasn't even sure she could do it if she wanted to. After inhaling a deep breath, she gave it a try.

"Hi, Mom," she managed. "I really need to talk to you. Can you call me back as soon as you can? Thanks. I love you."

She remained on the bench for several minutes, trying to regain her composure as a parade of people walked past—including, at one point, Susan, her TA, who gave her a quick nod of recognition but didn't slow her stride as she hurried by.

London had hoped her mother would call her right back, but she didn't.

As she was getting up to leave, she considered calling her father, but after thinking about it for just a few moments, she realized it was a bad idea. Once he learned what had happened, he'd take the first plane out and probably threaten to kill someone. He wasn't the type to take a gang rape of his daughter lying down. The more she thought about it, the more she wondered if she should even talk to her mother. If her father got wind, there was no telling what he might do.

扲

London was on her way down a flight of stairs when her phone rang. Seeing it was her mother returning her call, she was seized with panic. She didn't know anymore what she wanted to tell her—or, more precisely, what she *should* tell her. She didn't want her father to know about the rape, but she wasn't sure her mother would agree to keep it from him if she told her.

As her uncertainty rose, so did her emotions, making her wonder if she'd even be physically capable of talking. Her phone's continued ringing echoed in the stairwell, each peal making London less sure what to do. When she reached the bottom of the stairs, she finally answered.

"*Mom,*" she said, but she was barely able to squeeze out the word.

"What's wrong, London? What's happened?" said her mother. There was fear in her voice.

London was now descending the steps of the English building, tears streaming down her face.

"*Mom*," she repeated, "I need to tell you something."

"What is it? *Where are you?*"

Turning onto a path that led off-campus, London broke into sobs. She knew she was creating a public spectacle, but she was unable to stop the torrent of emotion unleashed by her mother's voice.

"London," said her mother, her fear skyrocketing. "What is it? Please talk to me."

London continued to bawl as students passed her on both sides, some on bicycles and skateboards. One of them was Sheryl, the girl she'd sat with on the porch the night of the party. Sheryl called out to her, but London didn't answer. She just rushed past as though fleeing some unseen monster. Over the phone, her mother continued to say her name and ask questions.

All London could manage as a response was, "*I'm sorry, Mom, I'm so sorry...*"

Her mother persisted. "Where are you, London? Are you somewhere safe? I'm going to come as soon as I can, but I need to know you're safe. Can you tell me where you are? Are you in your room?"

"I think I'm getting expelled," London finally managed through her tears.

"What do you mean? Why would you be expelled?"

"*I made a stupid mistake. I tried to explain what happened, but it's too late. They won't listen.*"

London's words were barely discernible.

"Who won't listen?" said her mother. "I don't understand what you're saying, London."

"My TA. And I just tried to speak to my professor, but she wouldn't talk to me."

"Listen to me, sweetheart," said her mother. "I don't know what's going on, but the instant I hang up the phone, I'm going to make arrangements to jump on a plane. I'll take the first flight I can find. Until I arrive, is there any friend or someone in your dorm you can talk to? I don't want you to be alone."

London decided in that moment to tell her mother everything, but thinking about it made her cry even more convulsively.

She was oblivious to the people around her, but they weren't oblivious to her. Her feverish distress was noticed by a number of students who would later describe seeing her stumbling down the street, sobbing into her phone.

None of them thought her stepping off the curb was a deliberate act of suicide. It was believed by everyone who witnessed the accident that she was simply so distraught and blinded by tears that she didn't see the car coming.

On the other end of the phone, the last sounds London's mother heard before she collapsed into hysteria were the screech of tires and screams of terrified onlookers.

London's final words to her mother, which she choked out between sobs, were, *"I have to tell you something, but I don't want you to tell Daddy..."*

♈

It was a twenty-hour flight between Abu Dhabi and California. On the Abu Dhabi side, Tom's plane had been de-

254

layed by four hours, so by the time he arrived at the hospital, it had been two days since he'd received the frantic call about London from his ex-wife. He was a wreck, but Lauren was much worse. When he met her in the waiting area of the ICU, she was inconsolable.

Tom had received little specific information about London's condition up to that point. All he knew was she'd been hit by a car, and her condition was critical. Now, with Lauren collapsed and disconsolate in his arms, he feared the worst.

"Is she gone?" he whispered when she began to regain some composure.

"No," she said, her face collapsing into a grimace. "But it's bad. *Really bad*. I don't think she's going to make it."

Tom gave her a handkerchief, and she blew her nose. Then she took in a deep breath and blew it out in a long slow stream. Her face was red and misshapen from crying.

"She called me and left a message," she said, "and I could tell something was wrong. When I called her back, she was crying. And I've *never* heard her cry like that. She was saying something about being expelled, which seemed ridiculous, but that's what she said."

She paused to inhale more air, unable to breathe through her nose. Tom's heart pounded as he struggled to make sense of what she was saying.

"I didn't know where she was or what was going on, but it turned out she was on the street," Lauren said.

She closed her eyes and shook her head as though unable to say what came next. "She was crying and saying she needed to tell me something..."

She paused, and tears were streaming again.

"Then she walked out in front of a car."

Tom put his head in his hands and wept, unable to process, much less accept, what he was hearing.

"Can I see her?" he asked, raising his head. He wiped his face with the back of his hand.

"A doctor's in with her now," Lauren said. "We can go in when he's finished."

Her face trembled as she looked into Tom's eyes. "Can you believe we're back here again? And this is so much worse. *I just can't believe this is happening.*"

Moments later, a grim-looking doctor entered the waiting room. He nodded at Lauren, then turned his gaze to Tom. "Are you the father?"

"Yes," Tom said. He stood up and shook the doctor's hand. "How is she?"

"I'd prefer to talk privately," the doctor said. "Can you both come with me?"

Tom and Lauren followed the doctor down a hallway and into a small office, where he gestured for them to sit down. He took a seat on the other side of a wooden desk.

"This is the type of conversation no doctor wants to have," the doctor started, his pale face furrowed in genuine grief.

He looked at Tom. "As I've told your wife, your daughter's injuries are critical. About as critical as they get, I'm afraid. She's stabilized for the moment, but we don't anticipate her being able to survive once she's removed from life support."

He paused, and he was squeezing his hands folded in front of him so tightly, his knuckles were white. "Even if she were able to eventually breathe on her own," he said, "her lack of brain function means she's essentially gone."

He frowned, and his expression became even more grave. "I'm sorry, but I'm afraid we need to have a conversation about the possibility of her being an organ donor. And there's something else I wish I didn't have to tell you, but I'm afraid I have no choice."

His eyes narrowed, wincing at what he was about to say next. "One of the nurses noticed, while she was washing her, that she shows signs of being raped."

Lauren gasped, understanding now what London had wanted to tell her and why she was so distraught. She turned to Tom, and they shared a moment of horror.

"I'm sorry," the doctor said. "These situations are hard enough without this kind of news. By law, we need to contact the police. They'll want to investigate."

He unfolded his hands. "I know this is a lot to process. We can continue this conversation later. For now, I'm going to give you some time alone. You can stay in my office as long as you like. When you feel ready, you can go in and see London. She won't know you're there, but we encourage families in these situations to talk to their loved ones. It seems to help."

A moment later, he stood up and nodded a look of compassion. Then he stepped out of the office and silently closed the door behind him, leaving Tom and Lauren so frozen in grief, it was several minutes before either of them could speak.

CHAPTER FORTY-FIVE

WHEN TOM PAUSED TO take a breath and get a grip on his emotions, we were still a long way from the highway. The electric pain coursing through my leg had now spread to my whole left side, and the constant winding and lurching of the car was making me sick to my stomach. But none of it was as terrible as what I'd just learned.

I remembered reading about the student who'd walked in front of a car just a block from campus, but I had no idea she was the girl who'd come to my office hours. In truth, I was so stressed and under the gun with my classes and trying to shore up my leave, I paid the story almost no mind except to think it was sad. Now that I understood what had happened, I felt as though I'd pushed London in front of the car myself.

I stared at Tom's face reflected in the rearview. "I don't know what to say," I said. "I had no idea..." I struggled to think of words that would express how sorry I was. Just as I began to choke something out, he stopped me.

"Save it," he said. "The important thing now is to get you some help."

"Did the police end up doing an investigation into the rape?" I asked. I hated probing when he looked so bereaved, but I needed to know, and we were running out of time.

"If you can call it that," he said. "They dicked around for a day or two and questioned a few people, but they didn't try very hard, and it didn't amount to shit."

His voice and eyes were bitter. "We gave them London's diary and pushed them to do more, but, in the end, they claimed there wasn't enough to go on. And, of course, they blamed London for that. Once they learned she destroyed the forensic evidence, they said there was no case and seemed perfectly happy to leave it there."

He went silent for a few moments, and I was still so filled with shame and horror by what I'd learned that I didn't know what to say. *The ending* was so much worse than I could have imagined. *How could I have been so self-absorbed? So thoughtless?*

"We appealed to the university to do something about the fraternity," he added finally, "but they were just as bad as the police. They ended up sending some kind of bullshit letter and putting them *'on probation,'* whatever the fuck that means, but it was barely a slap on the wrist. They might as well have done nothing."

He scowled. "I was in everyone's face hard about that fucking fraternity. It's only a matter of time before they connect me with the fire if they haven't already." He looked in the rearview and our eyes met.

"Are you really okay with me writing about the fire?" I said.

"You want to be an accessory?"

"Of course not."

"Then leave it in."

We passed over a large rock in the road and the car bucked, causing me to cry out in pain.

"Sorry," Tom said.

When the pain leveled out, I asked, "Why did you tell me you set the fire?"

"I don't know," he said.

We were on a short straightaway, and he sped up and rubbed the back of his head.

"Are you going to turn yourself in?"

"Not sure."

"Seriously? It doesn't seem like you not to have a plan."

His eyes were in the rearview again. "If I had one, do you think I'd be wise to tell you what it is?"

"Good point," I said.

He nodded at me in the mirror. "How do you feel?"

"Well, apart from being destroyed by what you just told me about London, my head hurts and my whole left side feels like it's been dipped in boiling oil."

The car gave me another big jolt and I winced in pain. I glanced down at my purple manatee appendage and couldn't imagine it ever being normal again. "I think my leg might be infected because it's oozing and starting to smell."

"We'll get you some help soon," Tom said. "And be prepared for a lot of attention."

The thought of facing the media made me feel even worse. "The last thing I want right now is attention," I said. "I just want to see my kids."

"Well, whether you want it or not, you're going to get it," Tom said. "And, I hate saying it, but the snakebite's going to work for you. It'll make you more sympathetic and definitely be good for the book."

"Everything is not about the fucking book!" I cried. "Believe it or not, I have an actual life I care about, and it's been totally destroyed. My kids probably hate me, my husband could be paralyzed for all I know, and I'll be shocked if I still have a job. Also, I don't know how I'm going to live with myself now that I know what happened to London." I shook my head and tears began streaming down my face.

Tom swerved around a hole, then glanced up at the mirror. "While I was gone, I did something you're not going to like, but it was necessary."

I wiped my face with a napkin and stared down at my leg, which sent a fresh flare of pain at a sudden bump in the road. "I don't even want to know," I said, feeling too depleted to deal with one more thing. "Please just get me to a hospital before this thing kills me."

ଔ

When we finally turned right onto the highway, it was such a relief, I broke down again.

"How much farther now?" I said, my fear starting to balloon. I had a rising fever and could feel the poison working its way to my heart. My pulse had become erratic, and I was sweating even as cold air blew on me from a vent.

"How much farther?" I repeated. I gazed out the window at the desolate landscape, and the world had never looked bleaker. "Can't you drive any faster?"

"I'm doing ninety," Tom said. "Hang on. We'll get there."

I must have gone unconscious after that, because the next thing I remember, we were turning left into the parking lot of a scruffy-looking motel. The Bates Motel came to mind, but even so, I was overjoyed.

I looked down at my leg, and my stomach heaved. Parts of it were now almost black, and it was oozing even more yellow goo. "Please hurry," I whined. "It's getting worse."

Tom pulled into the parking lot one space away from an open door with a housekeeping cart stationed out front. He nodded at the door. "I'm going to take you to that room. We'll call 911 from there."

He leaned over and pulled a gun from the glove compartment.

"What do you need that for?" I cried. "Are you planning to terrorize some poor maid now? Just take me in and explain I need a doctor. You don't need a gun."

"Don't worry, it's not even loaded," he said. "Just be quiet and let's get you inside."

He stuck the gun down the back of his pants and pulled his shirt down over it. Then he picked up the backpack in the passenger seat and nodded back at the yellow pad he'd handed me earlier. "You didn't take notes?"

"I don't need notes," I mumbled, my stomach sinking at the reminder.

Tom zipped up the pack, then placed it over his shoulder and did a quick survey of the area before leaving the car and opening my door.

Looking down at my leg, he tried not to react, but I saw him flinch. "It's bad, but you'll be all right," he said. "We can probably get a chopper here in less than an hour." He leaned over. "Put your arms around my neck."

I obeyed, but as he began lifting me, pain sliced through me like a knife, causing me to cry out.

"Quiet," Tom said. "I don't want to attract attention."

As I held my breath, he pulled me from the car, then leaned against the door to close it before carrying me to the room where the housekeeping cart was parked.

When he stepped around it to get inside, we came face-to-face with a middle-aged Latina housekeeper. "We need to call 911 and get some help," he said.

He moved past her and placed me onto the freshly made bed as the startled woman looked on, seemingly in a state of horror at the sight of my leg.

"Do you speak English?" Tom asked.

The woman nodded.

Tom gestured to the bedside table. "I need to use the phone."

"Of course," she said, nodding nervously.

Tom picked up the receiver and dialed. A few moments later, he was speaking to a 911 dispatcher.

After giving our location and identifying the problem as a rattlesnake bite, he gave a description of my leg and overall assessment of my condition. If anything, he overstated the urgency, describing me as near death. When he was probed for personal information, he gave my name, which surprised me. But he refused to identify himself.

As he was talking, I reached out for the receiver. "Let me talk."

Reluctantly, he handed me the phone.

"Please send help right away," I pleaded. "I don't want to die."

"We already have people on the way," a woman said. "Am I speaking to Valerie Hawthorne?"

"Yes, that's correct."

"Are you aware the police are looking for you?"

"Yes," I said, looking up at Tom.

Tom pulled the phone from my hand. "Just send a helicopter as soon as you can or she's gonna die."

He hung up.

"Why did you do that?" I said. "What if they don't believe you? They might think this is a prank!"

"They're coming," he said. "But, trust me, the police are coming first."

He looked at the housekeeper, who appeared frozen in place. "You can go," he said, glancing at the door.

Looking confused and scared, she nodded and fled.

"What are you going to do?" I said.

"I'm leaving. When they come get you, make sure you take this with you." His hand was on the backpack, which he'd placed next to me on the bed. "Everything's in here. The laptop and all your legal pads. I put your wallet in here, too. Whatever you do, *do not* let this out of your sight."

"I won't," I said. "But why not just wait for the police and turn yourself in? If you don't, they're bound to find you."

"I don't have time to argue with you," he said. "I need to go."

He held my gaze for several seconds, and it felt like he was trying to communicate something, but I wasn't sure what it was. *That he was sorry? Goodbye and good luck?* I had no idea, but I knew what I was thinking. I was thinking about the gun.

"I might know what you're planning, and I don't think you should do it," I said. "Just turn yourself in. You'll go to prison, but you'll also have a chance to say *why* you did everything. Isn't that what you want?"

"That's *your* job," he said, and his voice and eyes were steady. "I'm not going to prison."

He glanced at the backpack. "Just finish the book. That's all I care about now."

He reached down and squeezed my shoulder. An instant later he disappeared out the door and was gone.

CHAPTER FORTY-SIX

TOM WAS RIGHT. A policeman arrived on the scene before the paramedics. When he did, I didn't feel like answering questions, so after confirming my identity, I used my deteriorating condition as an excuse to remain mostly silent, although I did, with some trepidation, give the officer a description of both Tom and his car.

Strangely enough, I had never learned Tom's last name, but I told the policeman that if he looked up the story about London's accident, he'd be able to find it there. I debated mentioning his unloaded gun and intention, I believed, to provoke a "suicide by cop." I ultimately decided to hold my tongue, figuring that the mere mention of a gun—even an unloaded one—might make a violent outcome more likely.

It didn't occur to me then that Tom might have lied about the gun or that he could have loaded it later, but in any case, I didn't say anything, and I was never asked by the policeman if Tom was armed. I simply left whatever was going to happen to fate—or to Tom, really, because I figured that whatever happened would be his choice.

One of my last thoughts before the paramedics arrived was that whatever he decided to do, it would probably be at least partly motivated by what he thought was best for the book. With that in mind, I tried to brace myself for a violent ending.

The paramedics arrived not long after the policeman, and almost the instant they walked in the door, they shot me up with antivenom and morphine. The next thing I knew, I was strapped to a gurney and loaded into a helicopter, where I was hooked up to an IV, fitted with an oxygen mask, and fussed over until I was eventually delivered, barely conscious, to an intensive care unit in the closest hospital, which turned out to be in Needles, as Tom had predicted.

It wasn't until I'd been in the ICU for two or three hours—during which time my wound was cleaned and bandaged, and I was fastened to various drips and monitoring devices—that I thought to inquire about the backpack. They'd given me strong pain medication, so I was groggy, but I was aware enough to wonder where it was.

As a sturdy white-haired nurse was changing my IV bag, I raised my head. "Do you know where they put my things?" I said. "I came with a small backpack."

"I'm sure that whatever you arrived with is somewhere safe," she said. "Don't worry about that now."

I looked down at my leg. With the benefit of drugs, the pain had subsided, but it was still massively swollen. It was covered in bandages, so I couldn't see most of it, but I could see my monstrous purple toes. They were enough to turn my stomach.

"Am I going to lose my leg?"

"No, no," the nurse said. "It'll take some time, but you'll be fine."

She fiddled with the IV. "You were lucky, though. If you'd gotten here any later, it could have been much worse. It was starting to go septic."

She looked at me soberly. "People die of rattlesnake bites."

"Has anyone contacted my children?" I asked. My head was starting to be clear enough to feel panic on various fronts, and my kids were way up on my list of worries.

"I need to talk to my children."

The nurse patted my hand, which was covered in tape and attached to two skinny tubes that snaked up to bottles hanging next to the bed. "Your family's been contacted," she said. "I'm sure they're relieved to learn you're safe. We all are."

She gave me a motherly smile. "I don't know if you realize what a stir you created with your disappearance. There's a whole slew of reporters outside right now just waiting to get a glimpse of you."

She raised her eyebrows. "You're going to need to be prepared for that."

Trying to put that particular worry out of my mind, I glanced around the room for a phone but didn't see one.

"Is there any way you can bring me a phone?" I said. "I need to call my kids."

"I'm sorry," she said. "We don't allow phones in the ICU. Not even cell phones. But I'm pretty sure your family's on their way here right now. We'll send 'em back as soon as they arrive."

The reality of facing Misha and Sam terrified me, but I was anxious to see them just the same. I couldn't say the same for Steven, although I was eager to learn his condition.

"Do you happen to know anything about how my husband is doing?" I asked.

"I'm sorry, I don't know anything specific. I haven't really been keeping up."

My face grew hot thinking about the news and all the embarrassing questions I'd soon have to deal with.

"I guess you probably don't know too much about what's been going on in the news," the nurse said. "You'll find out soon enough, I suppose." She tilted her head and gave me a look. "It's been a lot."

"Have you heard anything about the man who took me?" I asked. "Any news about whether or not they've found him?"

"I haven't heard anything, but then I haven't seen any news since I arrived on my shift early this morning. They keep us pretty busy here."

"When do you think I'll be moved to a regular room?" I said, desperate for both a phone and TV.

"I don't think it'll be too long. In the meantime, there are some people here waiting to talk to you. We've been keeping them away, but I think you're probably alert enough now to let them in."

"Is it the police?" I asked.

She nodded and patted my hand again. "We won't let 'em stay too long, but they're anxious to speak to you."

Fear gripped me. I knew the police would have a lot of questions, but I had no idea if they'd be asked with sympathy or suspicion. It was a strange situation. I knew I was a victim, but somehow I felt like a criminal.

"You'll do fine," the nurse said, noticing the look on my face. "If it gets to be too much, just press the call button wrapped around the bar down on your right, and I'll come shoo 'em out."

The nurse disappeared, and just a few moments later, two plain-clothes police entered my room—a man and a woman, both seeming to be in their early forties. They greeted me, informed me they were police detectives, and introduced themselves. To my great relief, their eyes were filled with kindness.

"A lot of people have been worried about you," the woman started. "It looks like you've had a pretty rough time, and I'm sorry about that, but we need to ask you some questions."

The man stepped closer. "We'll keep it short for now, but we'd like to start a conversation. Are you up to talking for a few minutes?"

I nodded.

"Can you start by maybe just telling us very simply where you've been and what's been going on?" he said.

"First, can you tell me how my husband's doing?"

"He's fine," said the woman. "He was shot in the shoulder, but he's explained the incident was an accident—and his fault—and we have a recording on your phone that bears that out."

"That part of all this we think we understand," the male detective said. "What we don't understand, and what we want to know, is the rest of it. We're confused about your relationship with your abductor. Are you aware of the video that was just released?"

My heart jumped into my throat. "No. What video? What are you talking about?"

"Yesterday, someone sent a video to the LA Times claiming it's you, and it appears to check out," the woman explained.

Something in her voice smacked of judgment, and I flashed on Tom telling me he'd done something I wasn't going to like.

"What was in the video?" I asked, praying that maybe he'd filmed me at our camp or in the cabin when I wasn't aware.

"It's you in the shower," the other detective answered.

My stomach went upside-down as I remembered the lie I'd told about my encounter in the hotel. "Has this been shown in the news?"

"I'm afraid so," said the woman.

As my heart raced and I struggled not to throw up, I silently cursed Tom for being so cruel.

"Have you found him yet?" I asked.

"Not yet," the woman responded, which surprised me. I figured that, by then, he'd either have been apprehended or killed in a shoot-out.

The male officer spoke up again. "We know who we're looking for, but what we don't know is what this was all about. I'm sorry to ask you this, but is he a sexual predator?"

"No, it wasn't like that," I said, trying to put the video out of my mind. "It had to do with his daughter, who was one of my students. She was raped and then died after stepping in front of a car."

I took a deep breath and tried to clear my head, which was muddled with both adrenaline and morphine.

"I know it sounds crazy, but he took me because he figured that if he made me famous—you know, turned me into a big news story—I'd be able to sell a book about what happened to his daughter."

The detectives both wore puzzled expressions.

"That's what I've been doing all this time," I said. "Writing the book."

CHAPTER FORTY-SEVEN

BY THE TIME THE nurse arrived back and announced it was time for the police to leave, I'd explained most everything in broad strokes, including what I'd learned about the fire. This particular revelation was met with interest and no small measure of surprise.

What surprised *me* was that I found myself not exactly defending Tom, but soft balling to an extent that was hard to fathom. I hated what he'd done to me, and to my family—and setting the fire was indefensible—but all my feelings were so marbled with sympathy and guilt that nothing seemed clear cut, especially after learning I'd been the straw that propelled London to her death.

The last thing I remember before the police left was promising to show them what I'd written about both the fire and the rape, which reignited my anxiety about the backpack. I asked the nurse about it again but was told she hadn't seen it.

I was soon moved to a private room where I slept until I was eventually awakened by a nightmare in which I was being slammed like a rag doll against a concrete wall. When I woke up, the pain in my dream manifested as pain in my leg.

I opened my eyes, and a grim-faced Misha slowly came into focus. Sam materialized next, and his even-darker expression provoked so much fear inside of me that I couldn't utter a word. Instead, weeks of pent-up anguish poured out of me as sobs.

The reactions on their side were hard to decipher. Both of them were now on their feet, but the looks on their faces were so foreign that my fear compounded.

Misha took my hand. "Don't cry, Mom, it's okay," she said, but something I saw in her eyes seemed to be saying that it *wasn't* okay—that she was confused, and probably angry, and definitely not sure who I was anymore. All of this and more filled up the room, but the only response I could manage was to cry.

A tall male nurse passing in the hallway stepped in. "You okay, hon?" he said.

The compassion in his voice made my tears flow even more.

He walked over and adjusted one of my drips. "I know it hurts. You should start feeling better in a bit."

He glanced down at my leg, then up at Misha and Sam. "Y'all are lucky they found her when they did."

He pulled a tissue from a box on the table by my bed and handed it to me. As I blew my nose, he bent over and gently pulled up the bandage covering the wound where I was bitten.

"It looks bad, and I know you probably think you'll never have a beautiful leg again, but it'll be fine in time. The body has a remarkable ability to heal itself."

He smoothed the bandage back down, then placed a thermometer in my ear. After examining the results, he pulled a plastic cover from the tip and tossed it into a canister on the wall.

"Hundred and one, but it's nothing to worry about."

He wrote something on a clipboard attached to the end of the bed. When he was finished, he gave Misha and Sam a knowing look. "Be easy on her," he said.

Turning to me, he smiled warmly. "I'll be back in a little while with some dinner."

When he disappeared back into the hallway, I was left, once again, to face the terrifying specter of my children's judgment.

Misha sat down and pulled the chair up close to the bed. "*Mom*," she whispered. She leaned forward and placed her head softly on my shoulder. "We've been so scared and worried about you. I can't even tell you what it's been like."

She lifted her head and grimaced at the grotesque bruising partly visible on my swollen leg. The colors now ranged from putrid yellow to almost black. "Where were you? What happened to you?"

I didn't have the energy to try to explain—there was so much—but some of my fear abated as I looked into a face that now seemed less like a stranger and more like Misha.

I turned to Sam, who was still standing, and when I held his gaze, his lips began to tremble.

"It's okay. You don't have to talk about it now," Misha said. "We're just so glad to have you back."

She reached up and brushed back a strand of my filthy hair. To my great relief, her eyes were filled with love. "I can't even imagine what you've been through," she said.

Sam nodded and swallowed hard. A moment later, he was wiping his eyes.

"Dad wouldn't come," Misha said. "There's been some weird stuff in the news, and he's screwed up right now. But I know he's sorry about the way he acted. He just needs some time."

I knew the "weird stuff" was the video, but I couldn't bring myself to think about it, much less talk about it, so I let it go. And I was relieved Steven hadn't come, although I wondered where I'd go when I was released from the hospital. Did I have a home anymore? I supposed not, but that was something else I didn't want to think about.

"We've all been afraid you were dead," Sam said. "And Dad getting shot. And that video…"

He shook his head and appeared overwrought. "It's all so fucked up."

"I'm sorry," I said. "I hope someday you can forgive me."

"You wouldn't believe how many fucking reporters are outside right now," Sam said.

"I'm sorry," I said again, but the morphine was making me feel like I was being pulled underwater.

"Everything's fucked up," Sam said.

"*Stop!*" Misha said. "Can't you see she's in a lot of pain?"

I started to tell Sam that it was all right. That I understood. But Misha stopped me.

"Don't try to talk," she said. "For now, just sleep and focus on getting well."

Sam was nodding, and I remember thinking how handsome he was. Both he and Misha were so beautiful, so good...

I had just closed my eyes and was on the precipice of sleep when I had a thought that pulled me back. I raised my head and looked around the room.

"I had a backpack."

I looked at Sam, who was near a narrow closet. I nodded at the door. "Can you check and see if it's there?"

Sam looked at Misha, then reached over and pulled the door open. "There's nothing here," Sam said.

"Do you see it anywhere?" I said, adrenaline now battling the morphine. "It's a blue day pack with black straps."

"Don't worry about it now," Misha said. "Whatever was in it can be replaced."

"You don't understand," I said. "It can't be replaced. Can you please call a nurse and see if someone can find it?"

I closed my eyes and felt myself falling into a black hole of drug-addled despair.

"*Please*," I said. "*I have to find it...*"

Ω

When I woke up, it was dark outside, and Misha and Sam were gone. A tray of food covered with plastic sat on a table swiveled away from the bed on my right. I looked to my left for a phone and was relieved to see one within reach.

According to a clock on the wall, it was just after ten o'clock. I thought about Sonia, my agent, and realized I couldn't call her because I didn't have her phone number. How ridiculous, I thought, that no one memorizes phone numbers anymore. Without my phone, I was screwed.

I remembered the backpack and wondered if my kids had found it. I tried to sit up, but moving my leg sent a bolt of pain shooting through me, so I lay back down. When the pain subsided, I surveyed the room as best I could but didn't see it. What I did see was a note next to my dinner with handwriting I recognized as Misha's.

Moving carefully, I reached over and picked it up, then settled back to read it.

Mom,

Sam and I have gone out to check into a motel up the road. Afterwards, we'll probably get some dinner. I'm not sure what time visiting hours end. If we don't make it back tonight, we'll see you in the morning. I'm sorry, but we didn't find your backpack. We did look.

Love you,

M & S

Trying not to panic, I told myself it had to be somewhere. It might still be at the motel—or in the helicopter. *I had to find it.* Maybe I could offer a reward.

I had about a million things to worry about, but the thing that stressed me most was the possibility I'd lost everything I'd written. And I wasn't just thinking of myself. I was thinking about London, and maybe mostly my kids. I believed the only chance I had of regaining their respect was to explain everything to them as honestly as I could, and the book seemed like the best way to do it.

I made a pact with myself that night that no matter what lay ahead, I'd toughen up and deal with it. And if that meant I'd have to start writing again from scratch, I'd start from scratch. But I prayed I wouldn't have to.

CHAPTER FORTY-EIGHT

I SPENT THE NEXT four days in the hospital. With the help of antibiotics, pain medication, and additional doses of antivenom, I slowly began to recover and regain my strength. My leg continued to look like something from a horror movie, but the swelling was slowly subsiding, and, starting on the second day, I was able to get up and hobble up and down the hallway outside my room. By the third day, I was off morphine and weaned down to extra-strength ibuprofen. I missed the dreamy escape of the opiate, but I benefited from thinking more clearly.

Tom hadn't underestimated the celebrity status I'd gain from all that had happened. When I was finally able to see the news, I was shocked by both the breadth of the media coverage and by some of the absurd conjectures with respect to my relationship with Tom, who, surprisingly, was still at large. His responsibility for the fire wasn't yet being reported, but I figured it would break at any moment.

I saw the first report early on my second day in the hospital, and I don't think I'll ever forget the feeling that took hold of my stomach when I watched the clip of myself in the shower. Seeing it on television was so much worse than seeing it on my phone. My body was still mostly blurred by the glass of the shower door, but my gung-ho spirit was in full display.

"Care to jump in and join me? I'll wash your back or any-thing else you can think of that might enjoy a little soap."

It was gut-wrenching to hear myself say those words, and to know that everyone I knew would hear them, too, and see me like that. Thinking about my kids seeing it brought both tears and the strong urge to throw up.

I was thanking God they hadn't come to the hospital yet when the recording of Steven screaming in a drunken rage was suddenly playing.

"You (bleep)! Do you think you can go off and behave like a whore and then come back and turn my kids against me? You're a (bleep) joke, and now the whole world can see what a goddamn pitiful joke you are!"

It sounded far away, but then, after a time, got louder as he got closer to the recorder.

"What are you doing with that? You have no right to touch that!"

It went on from there, escalating until the gun went off, and ending when Tom and I left the house.

Watching that first report was gruesome, and it was painful each time I saw another one. I never turned on the TV when Misha and Sam were with me, but whenever they left, the first thing I did was turn on the news.

I might have stopped torturing myself, but I was dying to learn the latest on Tom—who, against all odds, contin-ued to be "at large." More than once I had a nurse do a search on their phone to see if anything new was being re-ported. I was too ashamed to ask my kids to look.

I knew my homecoming would be hard, but it was even worse than I expected. Not surprisingly, the video was shown again and again, and so was the photo Tom had sent to half the world. With the blurring that was added for TV, the picture appeared more pornographic than it really was, which added to my humiliation. But I was, at least, somewhat prepared for this. What I hadn't anticipated was the extent to which the absolute ugliest version of Steven would be part of the story. It was no wonder he didn't want to see me. He wouldn't even talk to me. The recording had destroyed his life and seriously damaged his relationships with Misha and Sam. It had even cost him his job.

And poor Misha and Sam. I knew they'd be frantic with worry while I was gone, but I don't think I fully understood how damaged they'd be after I returned. They stayed with me while I was in the hospital and eventually drove me to my friend Carol's apartment (where I intended to stay until Steven and I could come to an agreement about the house), but they weren't themselves. They were relieved I was back safe, but still in a state of shock and confusion about what our family would be like going forward. They needed comforting, but I didn't know quite what to say. No explanation was going to give them back the family they now saw as "turned to shit," as Sam put it. Nor could it give them back the parents they had before. Steven and I were now so diminished in their eyes, we might never be able to redeem ourselves.

It was tragic all the way around. But there was no disputing that Tom had been right. By nine o'clock on my second day in the hospital, Sonia was already negotiating with several publishers interested in a book, and she hadn't even spoken to me. When she did eventually call and I gave her a quick rundown of the story, she was ecstatic. Her exact words when I finished were, *"Oh my God, I'm going to get you at least another half million for the movie rights."* She also promised to contact the motel and company that did the medivac and leave no stone unturned until she found the backpack. The last thing she told me before I was released from hospital was to keep things close to my vest. "If we want to get the big money, you can't give too much away."

I agreed to say as little as possible to the press. When I finally did leave the hospital and was confronted by throngs of screaming reporters—both outside the hospital and later when they followed me to Carol's house—I simply repeated some variation of the same simple statement: "I'm happy to finally be home and I would appreciate some privacy while I try to recover and repair things with my family. I might have more to say later."

I did have more to say. A lot more. But I feared I might never be able to repair things with my family.

CHAPTER FORTY-NINE

WEEKS PASSED, AND EVERY day that I woke up in Carol's periwinkle guest room felt like the first day of a life sentence. Sonia was busy mediating bidding wars for book and movie rights, and I was looking at having more money than I could ever have imagined, but no amount of money or success could make up for the mess I'd come back to. Carol assured me again and again that Steven had made his own mess, but I felt physically sick every time I thought about the recording. Who among us would want the lowest moment of our life held up for public ridicule? I was living through a similar nightmare myself, but it didn't make me feel any better about Steven.

I hadn't yet seen him or exchanged more than a few words with him over the phone, but I knew he was a wreck, and I felt horrendous guilt. The kids were better, but mainly because they were busy with lives that didn't revolve around their trauma. They were moving on, but it was clear they might always be scarred by the loss of something impossible to recover.

Despite Sonia's best efforts and the offer of a ten thousand dollar reward, we hadn't located the backpack, so I was having to rewrite everything I'd lost. This would have been maddening under the best conditions. With all that was weighing on me, it was so far beyond maddening that

I could barely bring myself to think about it. But I had to start—I had no choice—so with the help of both Carol and Sonia, I was writing within three days of being released from the hospital.

I kept one eye on the news. Tom still hadn't been found, but a few days after I left the hospital, his car was discovered in the desert not too far from the motel and truck stop. He'd pushed it into a deep gully out of view of the road. The police had a theory that he ditched the car and escaped in one of the big rigs parked at the gas station or diner, but it was just speculation. In truth, they had no idea where he was or what had happened to him.

By this time, it was being reported that he'd set the fraternity fire, and that he blamed the fraternity for his daughter's rape and death. At Sonia's insistence, I remained tight lipped as to how it all fit together, but I did confirm to the press that his daughter had been one of my students.

Tom became a huge story. His picture was circulated far and wide, so it was hard to imagine he could escape capture forever. But, so far, the police had gotten nothing but thousands of false leads. Despite everything, I found myself rooting for him, although I was skeptical about the escape theory. I thought it more likely he'd gone out in the desert and used the gun.

∞

I'd been back for just over a month when something surprising happened. The police arrested two students for rape. Misha sent me a link to an article about it in the local newspaper. According to the article, one was associated with the fraternity whose house Tom had destroyed and the other was a member of a nearby student housing co-op. So far, there were just the two, but they were suspected of raping multiple girls. Although she wasn't mentioned, I knew immediately that London was one of them, because the story included a photograph of a basement where the rapes reportedly occurred. The picture, complete with bicycles hanging from the rafters, perfectly matched London's description. I later discovered that information in London's diary led them to find both the basement and two other girls who'd been raped on the same "scratchy" couch. One of them, it turned out, was a friend of London's roommate, Riley.

Immediately after I read the story, I called one of the police detectives I'd spoken to on several occasions and told her I'd seen the report in the paper.

"Yes," she said when I asked her about it. "We talked to London's roommate and a couple of fraternity members she pointed us to, and this time they were cooperative. The roommate referred us to one of the victims, and she eventually led us to the other. Both girls are saying more or less the same thing. They'd been drinking heavily and were afraid to go to the police. We've done DNA analysis on the couch. The cushions were missing; someone got rid of them before we did the search. But there was DNA on the frame, which was still there, and we found matches for both girls, and also for London. We have London's DNA from the earlier investigation that didn't go anywhere."

"Do you think there's any hope of getting convictions?" I asked.

"I don't know," she said. "I'm sure you know that rape cases are famously hard to prove, and juries don't like convicting these types of defendants."

"Young white college students."

"Exactly. And where there's a lot of drinking involved, it's that much harder. The girls are *always* blamed. But, we'll see. Maybe this time it'll be different. But I wouldn't get your hopes up about anything quite yet. Even if these guys are convicted, they may get a slap on the wrist. Judges don't like sending these kinds of kids to prison any more than juries do. And there's always a chance the girls will change their minds and decide not to cooperate. They know they'll be put through the wringer. At the very least, it'll be made out like they were asking for it."

"What about roofies? London was probably drugged. Maybe the other girls were, too."

"That'll be impossible to prove because, just like London, these girls never got tested. All we have for the moment is their statements and DNA on the couch. But, unfortunately, the DNA doesn't prove anything with respect to consent."

She sighed, and I could hear she was genuinely frustrated. "These days, no one wants to say anything that seems to be blaming the girls, and I'm not blaming them either, but the sad truth is some of them make them themselves extremely vulnerable by drinking so much. The boys, of course, should be held accountable. Rape is rape. But I wish, for their own sakes, these girls would be smarter. A lot of rapes on college campuses go unreported. We only ever see the tip of the iceberg."

CHAPTER FIFTY

BY THE END OF my sixth week back, I'd completed more than thirty chapters, and the writing was going more swiftly than I expected. It was rough starting out, but once I finally resigned myself to rewriting and gave up trying to re-create exactly what I'd written before, it was easier than I thought it would be—partly, I think, because I was finally back to writing on a computer. Writing in long-hand had been terrible. Now, with the benefit of a keyboard, and with everything still so fresh in my mind, words began to flow with surprising ease.

The only thing that hung me up was Steven. I was reluctant to recreate the sections where I used his behavior to explain my own. For example, the condom wrapper. Would any of what happened in Montana have occurred if I hadn't found that in his luggage? If I hadn't known for years that he'd been unfaithful? The answer was an unambiguous "*No.*" And yet writing about it the second time around—knowing how Steven was suffering because of the recording—was terrible. It was equally terrible leaving it out. I had to ask myself if I was willing to sacrifice myself, and what I considered to be at least *some* justification for my actions, for the benefit of Steven. It was no small question, especially adding Misha and Sam into the equation. I hated further tarnishing their image of their father. But what about their image of me? In the end, I decided to simply opt for the truth. I was tired of sacrificing myself for the purpose of not rocking the boat. I wanted, finally, to be honest. But I'll probably never be sure I did the right thing. If I were a better person, maybe I'd have done it differently.

It was also difficult writing about my kids. In the end, I chose to write sparingly about their reactions to my home-coming. And it's not because their behavior was poor. On the contrary, under the circumstances, they were shocking-ly loving and generous—both to me and to their father. But they were also hurt and confused and needed space to process all that had happened. They'd been through hell, and it wasn't magically over once I returned, so despite push-ing from my editor to "show and not tell," I refrained from showing very much. I wanted to give them the privacy they deserved. It was the least I could do. They'd lost something incalculable, and through it all, conducted themselves with astonishing maturity. I could only pray that, in time, we'd be able to come back together as some semblance of a family. As I reminded them often—and with London and Tom in mind—there is always hope for something better as long as we're alive to keep trying.

CB

After two and a half months, I was almost finished with a first draft of the new manuscript. Once I was done, it would be another few weeks of going back and forth with my editor before the book would be ready to go into the production phase. During all this time I continued to live with Carol, who was a saint. She not only housed and fed me, she also read and provided helpful comments as I wrote. Steven and I filed for divorce, and I told him he could have the house, including what would have been my share by California law, but only in return for an agreement on his part to relinquish any claim to the proceeds of my book. I wanted most of the money to go to Misha and Sam. He surprised me by consenting.

The kids were gradually getting better, although, increasingly, they were keeping their distance. I was glad they had each other, and I tried not to push for too much too fast. I just let them know I loved them and gave them as much space as they needed. As for me, I was in an emotional holding pattern, focused almost exclusively on writing. It was the only way I could initially stay afloat. I probably had some form of PTSD, because I felt like a soldier back from war. Everything had changed. No one looked at me the same way anymore. And I wasn't the same. My entire life had blown up, and I had more or less blown up, too. I had to figure out how to put myself back together, but it was hard when it felt like the whole world was gawking at me. Carol was great, and I had other friends who reached out and tried to shepherd me back to something resembling my previous existence, but there was a chasm between me and everyone else that was hard to bridge.

As crazy as it sounds, I almost missed Tom. He was the only person who had any real understanding of what I'd been through. I hoped that eventually things would improve and I would feel better, but, in the meantime, I fantasized about going someplace where no one knew me. It was cowardly, but now that I was back, I wanted to run away. I began looking into various possibilities for overseas volunteer work, but before I could make any concrete plans, I needed to finish the book. Unfortunately, I was struggling with the ending.

I was in the middle of that battle at the desk in Carol's guest room when she tapped on the door. "Come on in," I said, welcoming the diversion.

"Okay if I interrupt you?" she said, poking her head inside the room.

"Of course," I said. I saved my document and she walked in and sat down on the bed.

"How's it going?" she asked. "Any better?"

"Probably not," I said. "I've written some new stuff today, but it's still not right."

"What's the problem? You've been doing so well up till now."

"I don't know," I said. "Everything I've written today seems either contrived or irrelevant. My editor's been pushing me to write more about my homecoming and what it's like being back, but I don't really want to write about being back. I feel like now that I'm back, the book's over."

I closed my laptop and spun around in my chair. "I had another dream about London last night. I don't remember all the details—some of it didn't make much sense—but it was essentially another one where I beg her to give me another chance."

Carol frowned. "You need to be easier on yourself, Valerie. You didn't kill that girl, and you had no earthly way of knowing what was going on with her when she came to your door. You've gotta let that go. You really do."

"I don't know if I can," I said.

Carol leaned forward in sympathy. "Even conceding you might have done something differently, you could never have anticipated what happened. It was just a tragic accident. None of us has any way of predicting how any little thing we do might have some unfortunate effect down the line."

"It's just really hard knowing that if I'd given her two minutes of my precious time, she'd almost certainly be alive."

"It doesn't do any good to torture yourself," Carol said. "Finish the book and try to help make sure the same thing doesn't happen to other girls. Do interviews, talk about it to the press, turn the book into a movie. It's all you can do. And, believe me, her story's going to resonate with a lot of women." She paused and her expression turned somber. "Did I ever tell you I was raped?"

"No," I said, and I was shocked. "When was this?"

"It was when I was in college. It wasn't as horrendous as what London experienced, but it was bad, and it took me years to get over it. It took me almost as long to even understand I'd been raped. For a long time, I blamed my-self."

"Why did you blame yourself?"

"I put myself in a position I should have known better than to be in. But, *oh my God*, I was so naive. I didn't un-derstand, at that age, how driven some men are to have sex. I always pictured rapists as monsters in ski masks. No one, especially my mother, ever talked to me about sex or men very realistically. I was beyond naive."

A look of regret spread across her face, and she pushed her curly hair behind one ear. "It happened the semester I spent in Greece. I invited someone into my apartment not understanding that, as far as he was concerned, I was inviting him in for sex."

She paused—remembering. "I'd been at a party, and the person I came with, who was my ride, left me there with no way to get home. So I ended up getting a ride back with someone I'd been talking to who said he was an artist. He seemed like a nice guy, so I was happy when he offered to drive me home. I'd been telling him about a painting I was working on, and when we got to my place, he asked if he could come in and see it."

She rolled her eyes. "I was so stupid. I actually thought he wanted to see the painting, so I said *Sure.* It wasn't that late. It was maybe ten-thirty, and I expected my roommate to be there. Unfortunately, she wasn't, and almost the second he walked in the door, he was all over me.

"As soon as he made a move, I pushed him away, and I apologized for giving him the wrong impression and all that. But he just kept going even though I was telling him no. I was firm, but I also tried to keep things reasonably light, because I was afraid of making him mad. *You know what I mean?* I didn't want things to escalate. But he wasn't having it, and he did get mad. He ended up throwing me down on the couch and pinning me underneath him."

She crimped her lips in disgust, and I could see that even after decades, the memory was painful.

"When I started to really struggle to get him off of me, he raised a hand and, I'll never forget it, he said, *Don't you even think about it.*" She imitated his Greek accent. "It was like he'd become a completely different person."

Her brow creased with the memory. "I was really scared he was going to beat me up, or maybe even kill me. When I tried to talk, or maybe scream—I can't remember— he put his hand over my mouth and warned me to keep quiet.

"I was wearing kind of a flowy skirt, and the next thing I knew, he pulled off my underwear and raped me. I didn't scream, and I even stopped struggling at that point. I just closed my eyes and waited for it to be over. I doubt it was more than two or three minutes, but it felt like forever. Then, as soon as he finished, he was up and out the door."

She shook her head, and I thought she might cry, but she didn't, although there was a tremble in her lips when she went on.

"Just like London, I didn't tell anyone," she said. "Not even my roommate when she got home. It never even occurred to me to go to the police. *I was in a foreign country.* And also, in my mind—because I didn't fight very hard—I didn't think of it as rape. I thought of it as me giving in and letting him do it. But I hated myself afterwards, and it was a really long time before I let anyone else touch me. I felt so dirty."

She shifted her eyes to the floor and her expression was grim. "I actually ran into him again later that summer, and he said something, kind of laughing it off, like, *I'm sorry if I was too forward when we met before. I'd had a lot to drink."* Again, she imitated his accent.

She scoffed in disgust. "It took me literally years to get over it. I still feel sick when I think about it."

"I'm so sorry," I said. "What a horrible experience."

"It *was* a horrible experience. But not a very uncommon one, I'm afraid. Maybe telling London's story will help spark some awareness."

"That's the hope," I said.

"Anyway," Carol said, standing to leave, "that's my little story and two cents about your book. As far as your ending is concerned, I know you'll figure it out."

"I have to one way or another," I said.

She stepped to the door and turned around before leaving. "It's my night to cook. How does chicken marsala sound?"

"Sounds great," I said. "And thank you for telling me all that."

She nodded and smiled, then disappeared into the hallway as I turned around and opened my laptop.

Two hours later, Carol and I had a beautiful dinner, and I had a mostly finished first draft.

ᙣ

I spent the better part of the next month going back and forth with my editor until we eventually had a final version and official release date. During that time, I also researched the Peace Corps and various NGOs that work in the Third World. I didn't want to be in the country when the book came out. My publisher wasn't happy and Sonia was livid, but I held my ground, promising I'd do interviews remotely by phone or video. I needed to go someplace where no one knew me, where I could gain some perspective and heal.

For some reason I couldn't get Tom's smiling children out of my head, so I started looking at programs in Africa. I wanted to find those children, those smiles. Eventually I found an organization doing work in Kenya that looked perfect, so I made plans to fly to Nairobi as soon as I turned in my final draft. I wasn't sure what I'd find there, but what I hoped to find was some peace.

As it turned out, neither of my kids wanted to read the book, although I sent them drafts on several occasions. They hadn't read any of my books, which I'd always thought was odd, but I assumed they'd want to read this one. It seemed I was wrong. When I asked Misha why they weren't interested, she simply shrugged and said, "We're just not." I understood. There are some things you don't want to read about your mother—or your father. I'm hoping one day they might change their minds, but it's probably just as well. I've told them everything they need to know.

They've told me all I need to know, too: They love me, and they're okay. They also appear to forgive me, and that's worth a thousand bestsellers and all the money in the world. That's worth everything.

CHAPTER FIFTY-ONE
Epilogue

AS THIS BOOK IS heading towards a second paperback edition, several developments are worth noting. To start, just as we were receiving the first-edition manuscript proofs, my backpack was found in an empty locker at the hanger where the helicopter that rescued me is serviced. By that time, it was too late to swap in any of the original text, so in the interest of avoiding frustration, I resisted the temptation to compare the two drafts. I did, however, discover that Tom had scrawled a note at the top of one of my yellow pads. He'd obviously written it in a hurry before driving me to the motel. It read simply, *"I'm sorry for everything. You're a hell of a woman."*

It may seem ridiculous, but seeing those words meant a lot to me.

When the book was finally done and in pre-release for reviewers, I did leave the country. With the blessing of both my kids and the university, I signed up to spend a year volunteering for a non-profit that digs wells and provides solar cooking alternatives to villages in Kenya. I was originally assigned to a small crew doing mostly labor, but once it was discovered that I was an English teacher, I was recruited to teach English to both children and adults in a lush part of Kenya known for growing coffee. For the better part of a year, I lived in small red-earth hut and communed with lovely people to whom I was simply *"VahLAH-ree."* I found the smiling children I was looking for, and so much more. It was like a palate cleanse for my spirit.

Towards the end of my stay, Misha and Sam flew to Kenya and treated me to a three-week tour of the country that included "glamping" in game parks, tours of ancient towns on the east coast, and three days on a small island in the Indian Ocean called Lamu. It was the trip of a lifetime, and the experience brought us back together in a way that I feared might never happen.

While I was in Kenya, there were crazy rumors that I was secretly meeting with Tom, but they were absurd. They started when someone took a picture of me talking to a British tourist in an outdoor market. I was surprised that anyone in Kenya would recognize me, and even more surprised when the photo generated international news. But as Sonia likes to remind me, all publicity is good publicity, and the bogus story caused a noticeable spike in book sales. It also brought me to the attention of a professor at Falmouth University in Cornwall. The result was an offer to join their faculty as an assistant professor and teach Creative Writing. I accepted, and look forward to a fresh start in the UK.

As for the real Tom, no one knows at this point if he's alive or dead. I try not to think about him, but when I do, I'm inclined to think of him with sympathy. I think of London often. I haven't yet forgiven myself for the way I spoke to her outside my office. It's an agony I live with every day. Maybe, in time, the pain will lessen and I'll stop seeing her in my dreams. I hope so.

The investigation into her rape and the rapes of the other girls (now there are four) is ongoing. At the time of this writing, three young men have been arrested. In a strange twist of fate, it's believed that the student who died in the fire may also have been involved in the attacks. Trial dates have not yet been set, but they should be announced soon. I know I need to brace myself for poor results, but you never know. The case is getting a lot of publicity. Maybe it will help.

Since the story broke, other mostly female rape victims have begun coming forward on campuses all over the country. Universities are also starting to mount campaigns against what is being described as "a dangerous rise in student binge drinking." I dearly hope these trends continue.

One last thing. Although I've speculated that Tom may no longer be alive, I was heartened by a review that appeared on Amazon the first week the book was out. I can't say for certain that he wrote it, but I like to think it was Tom. The reviewer wrote simply, *"Thank you."*

ACKNOWLEDGEMENTS

I like feedback as I write, so I benefit greatly from relatives and friends who graciously agree to read drafts and offer encouragement and guidance as I slowly find my way to the resolution of a story. For this book, my most faithful readers, the ones who sometimes received pages daily, were Beth Moose, Katy Culver, and Sue Grether. You three—thank you so much for all your kind words of encouragement. I love and appreciate you more than I can say. Other A-listers who provided sustaining enthusiasm and support were Carolyn Hammel, David Silva, Tracy Laughlin, and Ruth Mary (Rutti) Lovitt. (Rutti: This book might not exist if not for your endorsement of the idea when we had dinner together in the Gallatin Valley. So thank you for that, and for being such a loving friend and ardent supporter.)

Others who deserve special thanks for their advice along the way include Martha Casey, Richard Turner, Diane Takashima, Nancy Klann Moren, Kay Marshall, Ara Gregorian, Pam Schneider, Ona Russell, Raul Ramos-Sanchez, and Rosie de Guzman. A huge thank you, also, to Baron Birtcher, Dennis Palumbo, and Michelle Kuo for reading this book and generously providing quotes for the cover. Praise from such amazing writers means the world to me. I need to add a super-sized thank you to my husband, Peter Dingus, for his continuous encouragement and especially his patience when I was glued to my computer for so many months. Finally, to my kids, their wives, and everyone else who's encouraged me as a writer, thank you for seeing value in my stories. I hope you like this one.

ABOUT THE AUTHOR

Anne Moose was raised in Sacramento, California and has a BA in Social/Cultural Anthropology from UC Berkeley. She's had a forty-plus-year career as a writer, editor, and small publisher, starting with the publication of *Berkeley USA* in 1981. *When You Read This I'll Be Gone* is her third novel. She has two grown sons and lives with her husband, Peter Dingus, in Mission Viejo, California.